The Ruined Map

FICTION BY KOBO ABE

Novels

The Ark Sakura

Secret Rendezvous

The Box Man

Inter Ice Age 4

The Ruined Map

The Face of Another

The Woman in the Dunes

Short Story Collection

Beyond the Curve

Translated from the Japanese by
E. DALE SAUNDERS

THE RUINED MAP

by

KOBO ABE

KODANSHA INTERNATIONAL
New York • Tokyo • London

Kodansha America, Inc.
114 Fifth Avenue, New York, New York 10011, U.S.A.

Kodansha International Ltd.
17-14 Otowa 1-chome, Bunkyo-ku, Tokyo 112, Japan

Published in 1993 by Kodansha America, Inc.
by arrangement with Alfred A. Knopf, Inc.

Printed in the United States of America

93   94   95   96   6   5   4   3   2   1

Library of Congress Cataloging-in-Publication Data

Abe Kōbō, 1924–
[Moetsukita chizu. English]
The ruined map / by Kobo Abe ; translated from the Japanese by
E. Dale Saunders.
p.   cm.
Translation of: Moetsukita chizu.
ISBN 4-7700-1635-2
I. Title.
PL845.B4M613   1993
895.6'35—dc20   92-16918
CIP

*The cover was printed by
Phoenix Color Corporation,
Long Island City, New York.*

*Printed and bound by
Arcata Graphics,
Fairfield, Pennsylvania.*

NOTE

The ornaments and maps are by ROBERT STEELE WALLACE

The Ruined Map

THE CITY—a bounded infinity. A labyrinth where you are never lost. Your private map where every block bears exactly the same number.

Even if you lose your way, you cannot go wrong.

APPLICATION FOR INVESTIGATION

Particulars of request: Ascertain the movements and whereabouts
of the missing person.

Name: Nemuro Hiroshi.

Sex: Male.

Age: 34.

Profession: Section head for sales and expansion, Dainen Enterprises.

Comments: The missing man is the applicant's husband. No
communication whatever since his disappearance six months
ago. Everything necessary for the investigation will be made
available.

*I hereby make official application for investigation and enclose
herewith the requisite fee. Furthermore, I swear to observe the
strictest secrecy concerning all information, to make no dis-
closures, to make no abuse of any knowledge obtained.*

2 February 1967

T——— Detective Agency
Chief of Section for the   *Signature of applicant*
Investigation of Persons   Nemuro Haru

[5]

I PRESSED down the clutch and slipped the gear into low. The incline was a little too much for the light, twenty-horsepower car.

The surface of the street was not asphalt but a rough-textured concrete with narrow grooves about five inches apart, apparently to prevent slipping. But they did not look as though they would be much help to pedestrians. The purposely rough concrete surface was covered with dust and tire shavings, and on rainy days, even if one wore rubber-soled shoes, it would surely make for difficult walking. No doubt the pavement was made in this way for cars. If so, the grooves every five inches would be very effective. When the drainage of the street was obstructed by melting snow and sleet, they looked as though they would be useful in channeling the water into the gutters. Yet there were few cars, despite the trouble taken to build such a road. Since there were no sidewalks, four or five women carrying shopping baskets had spread out over the width of the street and were walking along completely absorbed in their chattering. I sounded the horn softly and passed through them. Then, instinctively, I jammed on the emergency brake. A young boy, perched on one roller skate and imitating a horn, sailed around the curve and came sliding down toward me.

On the left was a sharp rise with a high protective wall of stone blocks piled on top of each other. On the right was an almost perpendicular cliff, set off from the street by a minimally low guardrail and a ditch. I saw the drawn, pale face of the boy: he came sliding and tumbling down, as if he were holding the guardrail under his arm. My heart leapt thumping to my throat. I started to open the window with the thought of scolding the boy, but I flinched at the reproachful looks which the women cast at me. It would be easier to let him go on by, I supposed. It would be ridiculous if by agitating the women I found myself in the position of having to take responsibility for the boy's bruises. Nothing would jeopardize my situation more than their trumping up some story against me. I had to be without blemish for the present, at least around here.

I stepped on the accelerator. The car barely moved, and there was the smell of burning rubber. Suddenly the curve was there. The colors of the women, clustered around the boy who had missed death with neither loss of blood nor broken bones, flew to the side of my rear-view mirror, and clear sky appeared like the surface of a Braun tube after the picture has disappeared. The stretch of road was flat, and a small bus station lay in a wide space carved out of the hillside. There were benches with roofs to ward off the rain, a public telephone, and even a drinking fountain beside a brick enclosure that perhaps was a flower bed in summer. Only a short distance beyond the station the road rose sharply again. Immediately ahead stood a large signboard with a yellow background like a traffic sign:

UNAUTHORIZED VEHICLES FORBIDDEN
WITHIN THESE PRECINCTS.

Despite the firm style of the letters, which appeared to have been the work of a professional sign painter, I ignored the threat and drove rapidly up the remainder of the slope. Suddenly the scenery changed, and a straight, white line of road stretched to a sky daubed with white. It was some thirty feet wide. Between it and the footpaths on either side lay a belt of withered lawn, contained by a knee-high fence. The perspective was strangely exaggerated, perhaps because the grass had withered unevenly, and I was struck with an optical illusion. It was as if I were looking at some patterned infinity: the four-storied buildings, identical in height, each floor with six doors, were lined up in rows of six to the right and left. Only the fronts of the buildings, facing the road, were painted white, and the color stood out against the darkish green of the sides, emphasizing even more the geometric character of the view. With the roadway as an axis, the housing development extended in two great wings, somewhat greater in width than in depth. Perhaps it was for the lighting, but as the buildings were laid out in staggered lines, on both sides one's view met only white walls supporting a milk-white dome of sky.

An unattended child swathed in blankets in a red baby carriage was crying shrilly. A young boy on a bicycle made of some light alloy, which had a glittering transmission, gave a deliberate, boisterous laugh as he sped by, his cheeks rosy with the cold. It was all ordinary enough at first glance, but when one focused on the distant landscape, people seemed like fanciful reflections. Of course, if one were used to living here, I should imagine the viewpoint would be quite the opposite. The view became fainter and fainter, transparent almost to the point of extinction, and only my face emerged like a picture printed from a negative. I had had enough of distinguishing myself. For this human filing cabinet with its endless filing-card apartments was merely the glass frame, each encasing its own family portraits.

12 East 3. East stands for the right side of the street, 3 for the third building from the front, facing the street, 12 for the second-floor apartment facing the landing at the left end. In the spaces between the blocks of lawn stood No Entry and No Parking signs, but cars were parked in front of the buildings. My luggage consisted of one small case containing a set of miniature equipment. The case was a foot and a half long, a foot wide, and something less than eight inches thick. The surface was flat and hard and served at times as a desk. In the end of the handle were hidden a mike and a switch with which one could start the tape recorder from the outside; other than that, it was a quite ordinary case. It was made of a nappy artificial leather that gave the feeling of being rather worn. Showy metal fittings had been added to the four corners. Anyway, it looked like nothing more than a traveling salesman's bag. Its appearance was useful for my purposes, but an inconvenience too.

Suddenly the wind, like an icy dust, struck my face. I shifted the briefcase to my leeward hand and, crossing the sidewalk, directed my footsteps into a dark rectangle surrounded by nothing but the narrow eaves of the buildings. The sound of my shoes, like the clanking of an empty can, leapt up along the stairs. Eight mailboxes arranged in two horizontal rows. Written in white paint underneath number 12, the name Nemuro inscribed in a small hand on a piece of paper attached with Scotch tape. Walking slowly up the stairs, I wondered if I should not prepare myself so that, as soon as I knew what my client wanted, I could play the required role at once. It was our business to be well aware that there is no set type.

A WHITE steel door bordered by a dark green frame. A white buzzer with a cracked plastic cover. The corner of the cloth over the postcard-sized window placed in the middle of the door at face height was raised at an angle. I heard the sound of a chain being removed; the knob turned and the door, which appeared to weigh all of a ton, was opened. There was the faint smell of burning oil. The kerosene stove had probably just been lit in preparation for my visit. The door opened in two movements, first twenty degrees and then sixty. The opener withdrew a step, clasping her hands together before her. It was a woman, younger than I had expected, though I could not make her out clearly since she was against the light. She was short, with a long neck, and she gave the feeling of swaying. Had it been a little darker I could have mistaken her for a child.

I drew out my card and modestly presented myself in the manner of a bank employee. Of course, I had never seen an actual bank employee under such circumstances in order to know just how he would present himself, but, anyway, I adopted that completely self-confident courtesy possible only of one who has not the slightest qualm. I was not merely play-acting to put the girl at ease. I had come on orders; there was no question of my having come to force a sale. But it would be best to keep my distance. If I did not, I would be looked down on professionally. There is no need to act out a snake for someone who's afraid of them.

The woman spoke in a husky whisper. It was not due to strain, for this was apparently her natural voice. It was as if she were sucking on some piece of candy—perhaps it was because her tongue was short—but it put me at ease. The curtain rose, in this dimly lit vestibule, on my somber functions.

Directly to the left as one entered was a narrow kitchenette and dining room combined. Then came the living room, cut off by a heavy curtain. The next room on the right, looking from the vestibule, seemed to be a bedroom.

The first noticeable thing on entering the living room was a cylindrical kerosene stove with its flickering circle of blue flame. Then, in the middle of the room was a round table, with a vinyl throw, printed with a lacy design, that reached all the way to the floor. Bookcases occupied half of the left wall and the rest was taken up by a window. On the facing wall was a Picasso lithograph, perhaps clipped out of some magazine, depicting a girl looking up and to the left. The fact that it had been framed indicated it had a definite importance for the owner. Next to it was a cutaway sketch of an engine, Formula I, three times the size of the Picasso. There was a line drawn to one part of the engine and an annotation in red written with a ballpoint pen. A triangular telephone shelf fitted into the window corner. In the opposite corner, against the wall of the next room, stood a stereo amplifier, clearly a do-it-yourself assembly. The speakers were installed in the wall about three yards above it, at right angles. Thus they mutually canceled out the sound, and the stereo effect was probably nil. A chair was placed with its back to the amplifier. Offering the fact that she lived alone as an apology, the girl parted the curtain and went into the kitchen, doubtless to prepare some tea. As she passed, the faint breeze created by her movement dissipated the smell of kerosene, and in its place lingered a fragrance of cosmetics.

With the girl's disappearance beyond the curtain even my impression of her suddenly became faint and indistinct. I was annoyed. Once again I slowly breathed in, and after ascertaining that there was neither the smell of tobacco nor that of a man, I lit a cigarette. I turned up the hem of the floor-length table throw and made sure there was nothing suspicious there. Yet, it was a strange business. The window was beginning to grow dark in the early winter evening, but it was not yet time to turn on the lights. If I concentrated I could just make out the black pen cap that had rolled under the telephone shelf. I had really seen her clearly. She had advanced a chair for me on the other side of the table and we had faced each other scarcely six feet apart. I was quite unable to understand why my impression had suddenly blurred. It was already four and a half years since I had been in the business. Though I was not particularly aware of it, I had the habit of grasping the distinguishing features of things seen and filing them away. I formed portraits with them, and when I needed to I could draw them out and at once restore them to their original state. For example, the child on the roller skate a little while ago . . . His overcoat was a dark blue woolen material with a wide, reversible collar. The muffler was of gray woolen yarn, the shoes white duck. The corners of his eyes turned down, his hair was stiff and thin, the hairline almost straight, the space between his mouth and his nose was red and inflamed. Fortunately the gradient was abrupt, and as my brakes had functioned well it turned out all right, but if the slope had been only half of what it was and the horsepower of my car twice as much, no matter how I might have cut the wheels it would have been too late. The boy would have tried to avoid the car, twisting his body to the left, but in so doing would have exposed his right flank and been forced under the wheels of the car from the other side. It would have been even better for him to have broken his leg. He would have had no ground resistance because of the roller skate, and the part of his body that was struck by the car wheels would have become a fulcrum. He would have been swung far out and flung full against the guard railing. If he hadn't had his skull broken, his collar bone would have snapped. His eyes would twitch and frothy vermilion blood, brilliantly clear, would well out of his mouth and ears. It was quite obvious I would not be here now if that had happened.

A tinkling noise came from beyond the curtain. It was not a chinaware sound but rather that of glass. It would certainly not be a cold drink at this time of year. Or I wondered if she were planning to serve something alcoholic. No, surely not. What was going to begin now was an unbearably tragic scene. If she were just preparing a cup of tea, she was certainly taking her time. A woman's quiet way. The monotonous sound of water continuously flowing from the faucet. If she had felt some consolation in getting me to listen to her complaints, in continuing to talk, paying no attention to the curtain, jabbering on, begrudging even a moment, I would have played the unpleasant role I usually did, needling her by interrupting with talk of expenses, fully realizing she was sick, but she did not.

A woman I could not recall . . . a woman whose face vanished with a ripple of the curtain as if by sleight of hand. Was her face so impersonal? I wondered. Yet I could describe in detail over a hundred items of her clothing. Through them I could recall the contours of her body. She was on the slender side and had a subtle, well-balanced build. Her skin was fine-textured, but not too light in color; and instinctively one felt she had a down of hair on her back. Her spine was deeply arched and straight. It was obvious that for her years she was more mature, more womanly, than I had thought her when I had first seen her against the light. Yet her somehow childish body harmonized with the breasts that were neither too big nor too small, and she seemed quite suited to the latest style of dancing, with its violent body contortions. Since I could imagine this much, I might push my imagination a step further and propose a more fitting head for the body.

From imagination alone, it was a most striking face, large, sharply outlined, with a mobile expression. I tried in vain to sketch it, but I could not. There were spots on it, like pale, indistinct smudges on a wall—perhaps freckles. But the face aside, I could recall the appearance of the hair. It was rather fine, black and long. Softly masking the left half of her clear forehead it looked as if it would be difficult to comb. There was a metallic gleam to it. I had come thus far, without knowing how. Possibly she was consciously avoiding having her expression read. Or had she exhibited in the short time I had been here five or six quite different expressions at the same time? She may have taken some dislike to me. If she had, this affair was more than I had anticipated, insidious, wheels within wheels. It would soon be three minutes since she had gone into the kitchen. Suddenly fretful, I lit a second cigarette. Rising from my seat, I walked around the table and stood by the window.

Individually, the panes of glass were small, but the aluminum frame left the view unobstructed. Across the flagstone walkway, about ten yards wide, rose the north wall of East 2. There was only an emergency stairway along the smooth, dark, windowless surface. Immediately down to the left ran the main road I mentioned before, which permitted an unimpeded view for some distance. When I brought my face close to the glass I could see my own parked car. When I crowded as closely as possible up to the bookcases at the left edge of the window, the vista stretched to a point just before the slope beyond the road; this joined the corner line of the next building at about a thirty-degree angle, and thus the view of the walkway was delimited by the far end of East 2.

At a point about the middle of my car, on an angle with my line of vision, the street light suddenly and eerily went out. Perhaps an automatic cutoff switch, functioning with hypersensitivity, had gone out of order somewhere. But, perhaps, too, it was time for the light to go out. The number of passers-by had increased amazingly from what it had been—not only women coming back from their shopping, but men returning home from work. Perhaps a bus had pulled in. Looking down on them as I was, I realized very well that man was a walking animal.

No, rather than walking, I had the feeling he was fighting gravitation, diligently lugging around his heavy bag of skin packed with viscera. Some were returning, going back to the place they had left . . . leaving in order to return. They go out to obtain walling material to make the thick walls of their houses thicker, stronger than ever to return to.

But sometimes, though rarely, some men go out never to return.

"WELL THEN, what about clues? Tell me in detail whatever occurs to you."

"I can't. There's absolutely nothing at all."

"Just anything that comes to you. Even if you don't have proof or anything to back it up."

"Well, all right . . . There are the matches, for one thing."

"What did you say?"

"A matchbox. A half-used box of matches from some coffee house. It was in his raincoat pocket along with a sports paper."

"I see." Suddenly her expression changed. Looking again at her face, which quite confused me, I found it rather unpleasant. Her face—the shallow smile quite suited it, as if the disappearance of her husband were a kind of satisfaction —was strangely composed, in perfect balance. Or could it be that after a half year of sorrow and despair the mainspring that controlled her will had been completely broken, and she had sunk to the depths of distraction at having been abandoned? Perhaps she had been a beautiful woman. Her features seemed to have slipped out of their proper place; it was as if I was looking at her through an unfocused lens.

"If you think the matchbox might be some sort of clue . . ."

"No, not particularly. It's just that it was in the raincoat pocket, and I thought..."

"Now if I could just get you to sign this application, we'll get on with the investigation. But as I've explained to you, the deposit which you pay covers the investigation expenses for a week. In case we cannot locate your husband within one week we take no remuneration, of course; but there is no question of returning the thirty thousand yen on deposit, you understand. In case the investigation continues, that will mean another thirty thousand. And besides that, we are obliged to charge for the actual expenses connected with the investigation."

"Is this the place I sign?"

"But I can't carry on much of an investigation with the vague information you have given. It's all right, I suppose, since it's our business to get it, but don't you feel as if you were throwing thirty thousand yen out the window?"

"Oh, what a mess this is!"

"There must be something, something more concrete, like who you want me to tail, where you want me to look."

"If only there was," she sighed, turning her head slightly to the side. She raised the glass of beer to her mouth, drinking alone, for I had refused, since I was driving. "But I can't believe this whole thing happened. He had all kinds of opportunities, nobody could understand . . . nobody."

"Opportunities?"

"Business ones, I mean."

"You've done some investigation yourself, haven't you? It's already been half a year."

"Yes, my younger brother has."

"Ah. He was the one on the telephone, wasn't he? He

talked as if he represented you. If that's the case, it would be simpler if I addressed myself directly to him, I think."

"But . . . well . . . I don't know exactly where he is."

"Come now. It's a vicious circle, a man looking for someone who's disappeared and who has himself disappeared."

"My brother isn't lost, you know. He always telephones me once every three days. He does. As long as he phones, there's still hope. I have such terrible thoughts. I can't stand not knowing my husband's motives."

"But it doesn't seem all that terrible, does it, really?"

"It's strange. Maybe I've just got into the habit of being patient."

"Since you've entrusted things to your brother, haven't you done anything yourself?"

"I've waited. Every day, every single day."

"You've just been waiting . . . ?"

"My brother was against my doing anything, and then I was afraid to leave the house empty, too."

"Why?"

"Well, it would have been awkward if by any chance my husband had taken it into his head to come home while I was away. We would have missed each other altogether."

"I'd like to know your brother's reason for not wanting you to do anything."

"Ah, yes, I suppose . . ." Her expression became more and more distant, more and more vague; the dark spots under her eyes, like a veil enfolding her dream, suited her well. "I suppose my brother had a mind of his own. But it was too much for him after all. I couldn't wait any longer either. Well, finally my brother gave up and we decided to go to you."

"Mrs. Nemuro, are you something of a drinker?"

The bottle of beer she was absently pouring into her glass immobilized in mid-air; she was stunned.

"Once in a while," she said, nodding her head distractedly, "since my husband's been away. When I'm just waiting here alone, I dream with my eyes wide open. It's a strange dream. I seem to be following him. And then he pops out right behind me and starts tickling me like this. I know it's a dream, yet I laugh and laugh with the tickling . . . it makes me feel very funny. A strange dream."

"It is indeed. I think it would be well if I met your brother."

"I'll tell him the next time he calls. But . . . I wonder . . . if he'll be very anxious to meet *you*."

"Why do you say that?"

"How shall I say? I just feel it. I'm afraid I don't express myself very well."

"Is it all right then? I've got to have information. I'm sure you understand, don't you? I don't intend to go prying into your brother's affairs at all. I'd just like to get him to give me the information he has. Isn't it a waste of time to start in all over again on what your brother's already done? As far as I'm concerned, I don't have anything more to say here."

"I'll tell you everything I know. But what?"

"Well . . . any clues."

"Oh, but there aren't any, no matter what you say."

"All right then, let it go." I too was ready to give up. "Now, let's begin by your explaining things as they happened."

"Well, it's all terribly simple.Too simple, really . . . surprisingly so. Let me see," she said, rising lightly from her seat and running to the window corner where she beckoned to me with a finger. "Over there. Can you see it? About ten paces in front of that street light. There, near the sidewalk on the lawn. See that small manhole? Right there, he vanished into thin air. Why? Why in a place like that? There was no need for it, absolutely none at all."

THE DARK street . . . too dark . . . The street, which until a short while ago had been too white, linked as it had been with the milky sky, was now a street in the depths of a gorge, sunk at the bottom of a sky stained with street lights. I stepped off ten paces from the light, groping for the manhole cover with the tip of my shoe—the place where the husband had, so she said, vanished.

Women out for their evening shopping and of course the red baby carriage and the boy with his bicycle were wiped away with a paintbrush of darkness, workers who had gone directly home were already settling down in their respective filing-cabinet homes while their friends, thinking it too early to return, tarried along the way . . . the abandoned gorges of unfinished time. I stood motionless in the very place where he had vanished.

The wind blew, threading its way between the dwellings. Freezing blasts of air, striking the sharp corners of the buildings, howled in a bass that the ear could barely catch. Even so, the moaning of this great pipe organ penetrated to the very quick of me. My whole body became gooseflesh, my blood congealed, my heart was transformed into a red, heart-shaped ice bag. A trampled asphalt walkway. The broken, abandoned rubber ball visible as a white speck on the lawn. The cracked corpse of the street, illuminated by the street lights that gilded even my dust-speckled shoes. One could scarcely hope to arrive at any place worth mentioning along such a street.

Yes, of course, it was a half year ago, August to be exact, and the summer heat was at its worst. The asphalt was as sticky as gum and swarms of insects clustered around the street lights. The grass was a green pond rippled by the wind, into which the castaway ball had sunk to the bottom. One had to stamp one's feet, not because of the cold but because of the swarms of mosquitoes that welled up from the man-hole. Supposing the husband had paused at such a place . . . No, that was wrong. It was still morning when he had passed here for the last time. Moreover, early morning; the street lights had blinked off and the insects had sunk into the depths of the grass. It was the time when the gorges stripped themselves of their darkness and again became the hillside town, so white, so close to the sky. Perhaps it was a marvelous morning of blue sky, a day with a strong southwesterly breeze. The first beat of the city's heart is a signal; within a five-minute period hundreds of filing cabinets are unlocked at one click and swarms of different but indistinguishable workers, like a wall of water released from the floodgates of a dam, suddenly throng the streets . . . a time of living.

[21]

"Yes, it's true. They're like a legion of rats cast under a magic spell. You know, like in the fairy tale." The woman spread her arms wide, perhaps intending to show the width of the street. Her eyes blurred, no doubt from having drunk the beer alone, and looking from one to the other of her outstretched arms, she murmured as if in surprise, "How dark!" Suddenly she stood up, switched on the light in the room, and then went into the kitchen. She continued speaking in the same tone through the curtain. "It's not only the sidewalks; even the streets are packed. And they're all rushing for fear they'll miss their bus . . . little by little they swarm together in the middle of the street."

"But a bus can't keep its schedule in such a crowd, can it?"

"Of course not," she said, holding in her hand another bottle of beer, as she came back into the room. "They rush all the more because it's unreliable, I suppose."

Placing the bottle on the table, she casually turned toward the window. With the light on, it was already evening outside. The Picasso print was reflected in the panes. As if threatened by something, she roughly pulled the curtains that covered half the wall, and their lemon-yellow color transformed the room. Lemon-yellow it was, but it was not very fresh. A rather withered and shop-worn lemon. The masterless room, which had been like a cast-off cicada skin, suddenly came alive again, thanks to the color. One could say that it was not the lost man that had been missing but simply the lemon color. Suddenly a stuffed cat appeared above the bookcases. Below the cutaway view, Formula I, was a small sconce and on it a lace-net glove. A room well suited to lemon-yellow. A woman well suited to lemon-yellow. Her room. A room for her, adjusted to her life. I tilted my head. My sixth cigarette. And she with her second bottle of beer. Something was suspicious.

A place about ten paces from the street light in the direction of the hill. Where there was a small manhole on the border of the lawn. There he was, absorbed in his thoughts, walking slowly along the edge of the sidewalk, skirting the crowd of workers, hurrying down the street as if pursued. Someone in the neighborhood had observed him. Even if it was true that this was the last sight of him, what could it possibly mean?

"Wouldn't it be more intelligent to assume that rather than running in the direction of the bus, which was unreliable, he had quietly gone down the hill with the intention of taking the subway from the very first? That very morning he must have had an appointment in S—— station, for if he were going directly to work the bus would have been more convenient."

"But he didn't keep the appointment."

"It is significant that his not keeping the appointment was deliberate and willful."

"You're wrong there. I'll put it another way. How shall I say..."

"Did you say he'd been going back and forth to work by car until three days before he disappeared?"

"Yes. He put it in the garage with something or other wrong with it."

"And what about the car now?"

"Yes, I wonder what's happened to it," she said, her eyes wide in what one could only suppose to be surprised innocence. "My brother would surely know."

"Your brother again? But unfortunately your brother isn't available."

"Oh, my brother's the one who had the idea of helping you like this. It's true. Please believe me. My brother's like that." Then suddenly her voice became more intense. "It's true. My husband didn't break his word. He didn't, really. I've proof. It just occurred to me I have. That morning, he left once and then came back again right away. That's important, I think. It was only a minute after he had gone downstairs. He forgot the paper clip. It occurred to him that he should clip separately some of the documents he was supposed to hand over at S—— station."

"I've heard that already."

"Oh dear. I suppose you have." The girl smiled tightly with her lips, showing her teeth, but she could not conceal the anxiety in her eyes. "I'm always talking to myself. I'm sorry. It's a habit. No one objects no matter how many times I say things to myself, you see. It's stupid . . . the paper clip . . . I always thought so. But I wondered if the fact that he came back for it wasn't proof he really intended to keep the appointment. Since I'm asked by everyone, I've got in the habit of repeating only that."

"Everyone?"

"The ones I talk to when I talk to myself. But the clip business is so trivial. It's all right for attaching papers, I suppose. But I realize my only real hope depends on that little clip."

I WALKED slowly ahead, halted, turned on my heel, and walked back again over the rough asphalt sidewalk. With normal strides, it was thirty-two paces from the corner of building number three. When I looked up, the row of street lights, artificial eyes that had forgotten how to blink, seemed to be waiting for a festival procession that would never come. The pale, rectangular lights reflected in the windows had long since abandoned such festivals. The wind slapped at my sides like a wet rag. Raising the collar of my coat, I began walking again.

If I believed her literally—or the words she spoke to herself —within these thirty some paces an unreasonable and unforeseen event had lain in wait for him. And as a result of it he had not only disregarded the appointment at S— station, but had boldly and irreversibly stepped across a chasm, turning his back on the world.

"ALL RIGHT. Purely in terms of imagination, the following is conceivable. For example—don't take it amiss—a blackmailer who knew some weakness of your husband's. For example, an old mistress, a child he may have had by her—these things happen—some youthful error still outstanding that could crop up like an unexpected ghost. Furthermore, it's August, the month when they say dead souls come back to earth, just the right season for ghosts. And women aren't the only ones who come back as spirits. A sometime accomplice in embezzlement, now ruined by dissipation, is a fine candidate too . . . a vindictive second offender just out of prison. Don't you know of some habitual blackmailer who may have been arrested through secret information given by your husband? Of course, the trap might also have been set by some perfect stranger. We've had our hands full with forgery cases lately. Apparently, forceful methods are in fashion . . . like secretly taking out insurance on a man in one's own name and then killing him by running him over in a car. Of course, unless the body is discovered and the identity confirmed, it isn't worth a yen. But I should imagine that's not your husband's case. Perhaps, since there's still no word from the police, we should consider the case as accidental death or the same as accidental death. If it's murder, he's probably incased in cement at the bottom of the ocean somewhere. But if that's true, it complicates matters. It would mean that he was involved with a pretty dangerous gang. A smuggling organization, maybe, or a counterfeiting ring."

The girl had stopped drinking halfway through her second glass. One by one the bubbles collapsed, the beer turning to dregs before my eyes. I didn't stir. Was she deep in thought, was she angry, or was it absent-mindedness? Her lower lip protruded slightly, a lip like that of a still-nursing child. Because of that—at the angle at which her head was bent, the nostrils were barely visible—her nose had a certain impertinence.

"No, what would probably be more difficult to handle than such an organization would be a nobody. A worthless cigarette butt tossed away in the street. The fated accident, as it were. This happens to be a true story: a certain head of a branch bank, who was reputed to be especially conservative among his naturally conservative fellow bank employees, had arrived at the age of retirement. On the day he left work, he happened to go to see a nude show and was instantly infatuated with one of the girls. She was just one of the chorus line, nothing much in particular. She had the habit of constantly gnawing at her fingernails. Even while she was performing on the stage she was liable to keep on biting at them —perhaps she didn't care. Anyway, she made a rather poor showing. However, the fact that she bit her nails seemed to please him privately. After going back to the place for three days, he wrote a fan letter. On the fourth day, things seemed to be going pretty well, and he thought he would take her out to dinner or something. Then, suddenly on the fifth day things took an unexpected turn—a sensational double suicide in the girl's room. It was done with something like a safety-razor blade. The harder they are the easier they break, you know."

Not the slightest change was visible in the girl's expression. The bubbles in her glass were rapidly fading away. Seen from the side, the surface of the foam made one think of the top of a jungle in an aerial photograph. What was she seeing? I wondered. Suddenly there was a swelling, like freshly painted enamel, along her lower eyelid. A tear perhaps? I was disconcerted. I hadn't really meant it that way.

"But, let me say . . . about the paper clip . . . perhaps, as you claim, it is proof he was really thinking about the documents. But whether he intended to deliver them to S—— station or not, as he had in fact promised, is another question, I think. Of course, it also depends on the contents of the documents."

"He said no one knew what the contents were."

Her answer had come back effortlessly, like a ball rebounding with its own momentum, but the tone of her voice did not differ in the slightest from before she had fallen silent.

"But was it company business?"

"It certainly wasn't very important, I know."

"I need the truth, not a conjecture like that. Now, about the documents . . . tomorrow I'll go and investigate at the company. But I really don't understand. You yourself claim to have no clues. Yet the fact that not a single concrete item was left—no diary, calling cards, or address book—is incomprehensible, since he was a most orderly man. There's some contradiction here. You, his wife, have no clues, so you apparently want to believe that his disappearance was accidental. But aren't the facts rather the opposite? 'Flying birds leave no tracks' would seem to fit the case somewhat better, I should think."

"But there's the clip. And then he absolutely didn't touch the savings book."

"Clip, clip, clip . . . If I may say so, how can you positively claim it wasn't a feint in order to convince you? You can't, can you? And then, maybe he was trying to say goodbye to you for the last time."

"Certainly not. All the time I was looking for the clip he kept whistling in a funny way as he brushed his shoes."

"Funny?"

"It was some television commercial, I guess."

"Come, come, now. You're welcome to pull the wool over your own eyes, but it serves no purpose to hoodwink me."

"Well, then, maybe there was something. Maybe a book for addresses and phone numbers . . ."

For the first time she turned in confusion toward the corner of the room where the telephone was located, and just as she was on the verge of biting her thumbnail, she pressed her hand which she had doubled hastily into a fist against her lips. It was no use to hide it. Even though she fought against the habit, there was a white scar along the edge of the nail, on which the polish had been applied especially thick. She smiled apologetically.

"There was an address book, wasn't there?"

"Now that you speak of it, I guess there was. When you slid the button to the initial and pressed the cover it opened up. It was black enamel . . . about this big. If I remember right, it was always on that shelf."

"Did it disappear along with your husband?"

"No. If it was taken, then it was my brother who took it.

He couldn't just let me wait around and do nothing. He looked and looked, but there wasn't a single entry of any use. I wonder if he just didn't put it away and forget it. If a thing like that were where it would always catch my eye, even I would have had to do something. My brother was against my doing anything so dangerous."

"Dangerous?"

"He says a single map for life is all you need. It's a saying of his. The world is a forest, a woods, full of wild beasts and poisonous insects. You should go only through places where everyone goes, places that are considered absolutely safe, he says."

"It's rather like saying one should disinfect the soap before washing one's hands."

"Yes. It is. Really, my brother's that kind of person. Even when he comes home he spends forever washing his hands, gargling, and things like that."

"Well, would you please try getting him on the phone for me now."

Suddenly a gray shadow masked the girl's expression. No, a curtain rose. Perhaps it was the real color of her skin that was coming out. For the first time she focused her eyes. As she gently felt along the edge of the table with the aligned fingertips of both hands, she stood up soundlessly and passed round in back of the narrow chair, making a shallow billow in the lemon-yellow curtains. She was a girl that black suited. A slender waist that defied gravity. Taking up the receiver, she dialed without consulting an address book, and, using the same finger she had used for dialing, she pinched a pleat in the curtain. A slender finger that seemed quite without articulations. She was apparently in the habit of pinching anything—perhaps some newly formed propensity to avoid

biting her nails. The pinched curtain moved gently. I wondered if she weren't a little drunk. But black and yellow were
signs of "Danger, beware!"

"It's true," she murmured in a low, rasping voice, as if she
were beginning to talk to someone in front of her. "I'm
always too inclined to let things take care of themselves by
talking to myself. Of course, the best thing is to hear directly
from the person in question. Even I couldn't believe it at
once . . . just after that casual whistling . . . he said he rather
had the feeling my brother was surprised. Hmm . . . strange,
isn't it . . . no one answers . . . could he be out? I wonder."

"Where are you phoning to?"

"To someone who lives in the back of the house."

"A last eyewitness? Oh, let it go. Surely, he's already sick of
your telephone calls. Anyway, that's not the telephoning I'm
asking for."

Surprised, she replaced the receiver on its hook as if she
were holding a caterpillar.

"Well, then, where should I call?"

"To your brother, of course."

"That's impossible. Because . . ."

"As for me, I need maps, ten or twenty of them. What in
heaven's name do you expect me to do with an old matchbox and a photograph like this? I'm different from you; it's
my business to go around snooping in dangerous places. It's
written right here in the request application I showed you.
I don't think it's at all unreasonable of me to ask you to
provide any and all evidence you can."

"My brother knows there's nothing of any use. He's done
some investigating on his own."

"He's got a lot of confidence. For god's sake, why did you
hire me then?"

"Because I couldn't stand waiting any longer."

Of course, it was hard to wait. Even so, I would keep on waiting. Slowly I walked along, paused, turned around, and walked back again. At intervals, a bus pulled up and stopped. Then came the straggling sounds of footsteps . . . invisible figures. It was not only the figures I did not see, I also could not distinguish a single trace of anything resembling a fault, a fissure, a magic circle, a secret subway entrance. There was only the black and empty perspective I had grown weary of waiting for. That, and the biting wind of a February night.

To say nothing of seven thirty of an early morning, that most cheerless of all hours . . . an hour like distilled water when nothing strange ever happens. What in heaven's name could be the worst imaginable mishap in the life of a section head for a fuel wholesaler? They had tried to make a fool of me, or maybe I had chanced on a half-witted client. It made no difference which; in either case, invisible was invisible. There was no reason why one should be able to see, nor did I intend to look.

Something I wanted to see was already visible. I would continue to concentrate on the single point I could see. That faint rectangle of light . . . the lemon-yellow window . . . the window of the room I had taken leave of only a moment ago. The lemon-yellow curtains mocked me derisively—I who was frozen in the dark, who, for her sake, resolutely held in check the invasion of darkness. Yet, one way or another, I was the one who would betray her. I would wait. I would keep on waiting until then.

The sound of footsteps, as if someone were walking only on heels, drew hurriedly near, and for the first time I diverted my eyes from the lemon-yellow window. The clippity-clop of high heels of someone late . . . a woman's timid footsteps.

Even the darkness could not hide the white coat, fur-trimmed at the collar and cuffs, and a paper sack carried under her arm. She pretended to take no notice of me, but she could not fool me; the upper half of her body facing me was still, armor-like. How would it be if, suddenly, I were to drag her over and throw her down on the grass? She would fall easily, without a sound, like a stone statue—and, of course, pretend to lose consciousness. Since the white coat would be too conspicuous, perhaps I should sprinkle some dry grass over her . . . a motionless girl buried under dead grass. Under the grass, she would quickly slip out of her clothes—naked. Only her arms and legs, projecting from the grass, would be uncovered. The wind would blow, carrying away the grass around her face . . . and then the face would suddenly change into that of the woman on the other side of the lemon-yellow curtains. A still stronger wind would arise and scatter the remaining grass. But instead of the naked body that I expected, only a black hole would appear. The white-coated silhouette of the girl turned directly under the street light, swelling out before my eyes, and then vanishing into the darkness. Her arms and legs disappeared too, and only the hole, like a bottomless well, was left.

She seemed to be wearing frozen fish bladders for shoes. But I would wait another half hour. If my expectations were justified—and I could only assume they were—the silhouette of the girl leaning over beyond the curtains would surely appear. This was a different situation from the one of the girl under the grass. The choice was not mine but hers.

I had verified this before: when she had tried telephoning, there was only one posture she could take, since the chair was in her way. By the window, facing sideways, the very top of her head seemed cut off against the light. The curtain material was rather heavy, but the weave was coarse and it was practically certain that a shadow would show through. If only I could catch her telephoning I would not have waited in vain, frozen as I was. The person on the phone was decidedly a curious fellow, someone she called "brother." A strange one, who, she said, was kind, clever, self-sacrificing, and who, because of a profound philosophy of life, had no permanent address. He had acted on behalf of the applicant, yet at the crucial moment he was leaving negotiations in the hands of a woman in the early stages of alcoholism, drowning in her own monologues, rolling in laughter, tickled by a phantom husband, dreaming a nightmare with her eyes wide open. He was an irresponsible adviser who did not even show his face.

No, it made no difference. I had absolutely no intention of poking and prying into the right and wrong of my client's words. This was business, and so as long as I got my fee, I would work seriously even if I was dealing with a lie. But if I didn't more or less grasp the outlines of the plot, I couldn't play the role of dunce very well. Rather, the more stupid the character the more difficult the situation. And there was also the business of self-respect. A stupid impersonation was fine, but I couldn't stand being treated as stupid from the beginning. Since the fee was thirty thousand yen, I would go that far but no further.

Putting my briefcase at my feet, I rubbed my sides with both hands through my coat pockets, all the time keeping my eyes on the lemon-yellow curtains. A taxi, chugging up the hill, gears screaming to the breaking point, stripped away the darkness and plunged deep into the precincts of the housing project. I would wait at least until the taxi returned. But supposing her shadow didn't appear as I expected? Impossible—it must. The existence of this "brother" was most questionable. It is a lot easier and more natural to put a puzzle ring back together than to take it apart.

Somewhere, far away, the sound of a roughly closed iron door struck my ears like a sigh from the earth, reverberating back and forth through buried pipes. The feeble howling of a dog rent the air. I wanted to urinate. Involuntarily, my body began to tremble. I had apparently come to the end of my endurance. I thought that the snow had begun to sparkle, but it was manifestly an illusion from having strained my eyes too much in the darkness. Even when I shut my eyes, the snow kept falling behind my closed lids. But what was harder to believe than the snow was . . .

The taxi came back with the For Hire light on. What was so difficult to believe? Filled with unbelievable things, I no longer knew what I was trying to be suspicious of. My mental faculties seemed to be numb. The lemon-yellow curtains showed no change. A glass bead in the mouth when I wanted a piece of candy. Well, I was lucky I hadn't munched on it. I shuddered as I finished urinating, picked up my briefcase, and returned to the car. The engine sputtered and groaned. If things had gone as I had anticipated the sound of the motor would have announced my triumph to her, but now it was simply irksome and depressing. Well, if she maintained what she said to be the truth, there was nothing to do but begin with that truth.

A photograph and a worn-out matchbox with advertising. There were too many blank spaces on the map. Therefore, I had no obligation to force myself to fill them in. I was no guardian of the law.

REPORT

12 February: 9:40 A.M.—I investigated the origin of the matchbox. About twenty minutes by foot from the client's house, I faced in the direction of S—— station on the main road, and looking to the right at the subway station at the bottom of the hill below the housing project, I saw on the left an open-air parking lot. Immediately diagonally in front, I could see a sign bearing the word "Camellia," just like the name on the matchbox. A very ordinary coffee house: capacity about eighteen seats. Besides the owner, there was one waitress . . . about twenty-two, more or less . . . fattish, with a round face and small eyes . . . traces of pimples on her forehead. She had a liking for showy things and wore patterned stockings, but she was an unattractive girl. She is doubtless outside the scope of this investigation. On the door there was a sign "Girl Wanted," and I imagined that someone must have quit recently. I inquired directly of the proprietor, but it was not that. They simply needed a new girl. They had no reaction to the picture of the missing man, no special comment; at least both agreed in testifying that he had not been a regular customer. (N.B. eighty yen for coffee.)

THIS MORNING I was hung over. So, though I usually drink two cups of coffee, I decided to let it go at one.

There was no intentional negligence in my report concerning the Camellia coffee house. The damaged condition of the matchbox, the worn label, the close yet inconvenient location of the coffee house itself—all coincided very well with the proprietor's statement that Nemuro had not been a regular customer. What more could I add?

The tired old walls with traces of former shelving had been left just as they were. Fastened on one wall was a color print of a coffee plantation, maybe in South America. Dust had gathered on the turned-up corners. The person who put it up would certainly not remember that there ever had been such a picture. And yet, in it everyone was wearing wide-brimmed straw hats—if you stood in front of it the sun seemed to be shining brilliantly. But from over here, where the bleak dregs of the February day lay stagnant on the other side of the meshed curtain, there was only the red flame of the kerosene stove, smoking away under a faded rubber tree. Furthermore, I was the only customer the whole time I was there. The sour-looking girl stayed bent over a weekly magazine beside the counter, and the proprietor, too, with a puffy face, as if he had a head cold, went around sluggishly wiping off the tables. Every time he finished a table, he would raise his eyes and look over those he had done and heave a long, reproachful sigh. If I must add something else, I suppose it would be the remark: Dead End. Anything more would be as ridiculous as searching the print of the coffee plantation with a magnifying glass. Not only Nemuro but also anyone else walking into this place would at once be struck with the thought of how fortunate he was to have a home to go back to. Under any circumstances there were no untruths in my report.

Using as a pretext the fact that the proprietor had reached the table next to mine, I closed my briefcase and left my seat. The shop extended along the street and was long and narrow. In order to make way for me, the proprietor had to wait for me to pass, standing sideways between the tables. With every step a black oil oozed up between the floorboards. I gave a two-hundred yen note to the girl, who raised a reluctant face from her magazine, and waited for the change. Well, I would give up visiting the other woman. I had told myself so many times that I had convinced myself not to go. But what about the brother? I thought it made little difference if I just wanted to inquire a bit into his past. Apparently, in the present instance, the advantages and disadvantages for the girl and her brother coincided, and even if there were no reason at all for me to include this in the report, the fraud, if there was one, would be unmasked by the facts and circumstances. In any case they would probably have a falling-out. She was the one who was the official client all the way, and I had no need to trouble myself about him.

A public telephone, the dial holes soiled with use, was located next to the cash register. I dialed the office and asked to be connected with the data section. I requested that they go round at once to the precinct office where the girl was originally registered, some place downtown, if I remembered rightly, and look up the brother in the family dossier. Then I deliberately mentioned the girl's present name as well as her maiden one, wanting to be overheard. Neither the proprietor nor the waitress showed any reaction. It was natural that they should not, I suppose. Even if my worst conjecture proved true for the moment, it did not necessarily mean that they contacted each other by using a real name.

Caught in a fit of coughing, the proprietor was clearing my table. When I went out into the street, listening to the girl's voice behind my back with its trace of Kantō dialect, the sky, a dirty white, was nonetheless dazzlingly bright. Immediately in front of the shop large buses squeezed by each other, cramped by the narrowness of the street. In a moment, when the flow of traffic slowed, I crossed the street and headed toward the parking lot. Three signs hung in a line on the barbed wire that enclosed it.

PARKING—ONE HOUR 70 YEN

SPECIAL MONTHLY RATES

Underneath appeared a telephone number in red letters. A hotel sign was also suspended with a yard-long hand, on which appeared the words

RIGHT HERE

Then, acting as a kind of awning for the guard house at the entrance:

HANAWA PRIVATE TAXI—OFFICE

I paid my seventy yen to the wizened guard, who was seated with his legs wrapped around a brazier. I thrust the stamped receipt into my wallet, thinking that I must not forget to add this to my report. When I looked back, the curtain, which had seemed to be mesh when I was inside, was blocking the window of the Camellia coffee house like black paint, reflecting in all its gaudy coloring the front of the drugstore on the opposite corner. A cat as fat as a pig appeared on the eaves of the second story and composedly began to walk along the edge, but after five or six steps it suddenly vanished. Just at the point where the eaves left off, the chimney of a public bath rose up, trailing smoke as transparent as gossamer. My immediate reflex was to seize my camera, but it was not that important. The probability of coming back here was so slight, what particular evidence could it be?

My car was the third one in the left-hand row. It was hidden by the car in front, and I did not locate it at once. When I finally spied its pig-nosed snout, a man approached rapidly from the direction of the guard house, crunching over the gravel.

Was he going to ask for more money?

His face was covered in smiles as he boldly looked me over, slowly, from head to foot. He had an unpleasant glint about his eyes. He was on the slim side, and his black coat hung straight down from his wide shoulders, breaking sharply at the pocket, perhaps because of something in it. His somewhat too long sideburns gave him a rather rowdy appearance, which in turn gave the lie to his fixed smile. He had a peculiar way of walking, as if purposely wanting to attract attention with his swagger. Maybe the aggressive impression he made was due to his eyes, which were too close together.

"Say! You from the detective agency?"

It was a voice I remembered hearing. There was no stammering, but the timbre was heavy, as if too much saliva had accumulated in his mouth. So that was it: the voice on the telephone that had placed the request on behalf of the woman. My interrogator continued to smile, but I could not answer at once. I was confused, and more than anything I experienced a deep feeling of defeat.

Frankly, I had given up hope of meeting the man. Perhaps it was because last night's vigil had proved fruitless and had simply numbed me. I was beginning to have the feeling that it was more difficult to believe that the man existed at all than that he was the actual brother. She could have easily hired a man to make the telephone call in her behalf. On the other hand, suppose it had actually been the brother, the situation would be no better at all. The fact would remain that he was a man who could not be seen—any more than the one who had disappeared. Moreover, having to pretend at such a childish game suggested something very shady. He was playing a game, fully counting on being suspected of complicity. I realized this with a feeling bordering on resignation.

Apparently, without my realizing it, things were getting to a point where I myself was being drawn into what could be a crime.

And, yes, there was also the matchbox. I felt that the matchbox itself, independent of the Camellia coffee house, was suspicious. The box had already been opened, and it contained matchsticks with two different kinds of tips. White-tipped sticks and black-tipped sticks.

If I thought about this too much, I had the perilous presentiment that I could not help but tread willy-nilly among the blank spaces on the map. I had no intention of rashly letting my opponent in on these misgivings. That much I knew. The money that had been paid was completely for the benefit and protection of my client, and the pursuit of facts was in all events secondary.

I gave up. How could I be anything but confused with the appearance of such a fellow as this, just as I had drunk my hangover away with coffee?

I was at a loss for a reply, and the fellow followed up his advantage, motioning with his head in the direction of the coffee house.

"Any results? What a coincidence, meeting you here. I imagine we've a lot in common to talk about."

"A coincidence?" I shot back, my voice unconsciously taking on a challenging tone.

"Well, it was happenstance, I should imagine." He looked over his shoulder back to where I had parked my car. "I certainly couldn't have trailed you here. If I had, our roles would have been reversed."

"How did you know me?"

My companion's glance dropped an instant to my briefcase with seeming interest.

"You knew me too, didn't you? It's the same thing."

It was that strange voice of his that had let me recognize him. And also the too perfect combination of time and place. I wondered if there were not, in this self-styled "brother,"

characteristics closely resembling those of the sister. The slim
neck in proportion to the wide shoulders. But that could be
the result of padding or the cut of the clothes. And then his
muffled voice, as if produced through woolen vocal cords.
The swarthy skin that suggested shrewdness. One could not
claim there was *no* resemblance; any human being could
more or less resemble any other, for that matter. The face,
stiff with a sizing of hostility, was quite out of keeping with
the smile. Piercing eyes that never slept, never dreamt. And
too, the extravagance of his formal way of speaking, to which
he was not accustomed, fitted in poorly with the atmosphere
he created. But that did not alter the fact that he was associ-
ated with the applicant, and I had no intention of opposing
him. What a great mistake it is to suppose that with thirty
thousand yen one can engage people's likes and dislikes.

"I expected to meet you, of course, last night. Looking for
two people is simply beyond me."

The man peered again into my face, flipping the metal
fitting of the windshield wiper of my car with the tips of his
black gloves.

"You tend to a heavy beard, don't you? I envy you that.
I can grow only a pretty sad excuse for a mustache. Maybe it's
a hormone deficiency, I don't know."

"Anyway, she's at her wit's end—I mean your sister—she
persists in saying she doesn't have a notion or even a clue.
When we start talking about the basic facts, she says it's her
brother who knows. But where is this brother? She doesn't
know. And then she just drinks her beer alone. It's as if
she didn't want the riddle of her husband's disappearance
solved."

"Hmm. You seem to have a good head. Yes, indeed, you're
pretty quick to catch on."

My companion undid the two top buttons of his coat, his smile lingering at the corners of his lips. He slipped his white muffler to the side and turned out the underside of his jacket lapel. There was a thick badge about the size of a thumbnail. It was in the form of an equilateral triangle with the corners rounded and was made of blue cloisonné bordered in silver. In the middle, likewise in silver, stood an S in relief. It was a modified form of letter composed of straight lines, and according to how one looked at it, might just as well be representing lightning. Or maybe originally it had not been an S, but lightning all along.

Unfortunately it was a badge I had never set eyes on before, but I could grasp at once that it was something intended to suggest a special threat. I could understand indeed, but I deliberately said nothing.

"I think you understand," he said, quickly flipping the collar of his coat closed. "I don't want you to have any funny prejudice about me. My sister's husband's a fine fellow, the real thing. On that score, I want you to understand perfectly that you can't call him—how shall I put it?—you can't say he's a tramp."

"Well then, all the more reason you should be open and tell me anything that might provide a clue."

"To say I'm hiding something isn't nice." He burst out with a single, abrupt laugh and, after a pause, added: "My sister's been saying some pretty tall things, I'm afraid."

"Unless a disappearance is deliberately planned, it's impossible to vanish without leaving a single trace of one's life."

"Actually, maybe it was deliberate . . ." Suddenly he lowered his voice and bent his head, kicking the car tire with the tip of his shoe. "On that score, my views are somewhat different from my sister's. Because she's a girl. She can't stand being thrown out like an old rag. Maybe she wants some other reason. She's a girl. If she could, she'd accept an absolutely unexplainable fairy story. But how will you be able to prove something unexplainable? It's a big order. I know how she feels."

"There's such a thing as amnesia, you know."

The man gave the tire another kick and, as if making some estimate, walked slowly along the side of the car toward the board fence of the parking lot. "Yes, I realized that. I even consulted a doctor. According to him . . ."

"Let's go back to the Camellia over there and have a cup of coffee or something."

"Why?"

"What do you mean 'Why'? Because it's getting pretty chilly."

"Yes, I suppose so," he replied, slipping through the space between the car and the fence, and then even more slowly approaching me. "Sorry. I seem to be excitable. Do you have anything left to do over there?"

"No. It was a complete miss."

"You know, the doctor claimed there were two types of amnesia," he said, thrusting his joined hands at me suddenly, pawing at my chest as if he were kneading an invisible piece of clay. "One is where you only forget about the past; present events—how shall I say . . . ?"

"You don't lose your discernment."

Perhaps it was imagination, but I sensed his strong bad breath and stepped back involuntarily, whereupon my companion bent forward slightly and peered into the car.

"Right . . . discernment . . . and then he said there was another kind . . . where even discernment is lost. In the end you get to be a moron, batty. With the first kind you change completely into another person and apparently can live in a different world, but you usually get back your memory in about two or three months. The problem is the kind where you really go insane. But then you're soon picked up by the police. Right? And they check the list of missing persons and you're identified in no time. Besides, Nemuro's not like us; he always carries his driver's license and what not."

"If that's so, you for one accept the explanation that his disappearance was deliberate, don't you?"

"I haven't made up my mind. He's not a child, and it's a little childish to leave the way he did with no reason."

"If the disappearance was scrupulously prepared, then I suppose he left no clues. However, so far as I can judge from what your sister told me last evening, that's still uncertain. Undoubtedly, the address book is in your possession, isn't it?"

I had intended to take him by surprise, but he showed no sign of perturbation.

"Oh, if that's the type of thing you're after, there are other things: the diary and the calling cards from his desk at the office." Innocently he looked up at the sky, and on either side of his Adam's apple his well-developed muscles tensed like the neck of a barbecued bird. "But more than half a year's gone by since he disappeared. I haven't been just an idle spectator for all that time. I looked into every one of them. I suppose you think I'm a bungler . . . anyway, I spent a lot of time and money. Of course, I'll show you what I've got any time you need it. But to tell the truth, I don't want you to waste time on such things. I say that because my own investigation was a big flop. I'd like you to start from the beginning."

"With only a matchbox and a photograph to go on, it's like trying to find a house that has no number."

"I wouldn't say that." He slowly took off his gloves and firmly rubbed the corner of his right eye with his middle finger—perhaps a piece of dust. "I realized very well that the coffee house was a wild goose chase. But the matchbox is interesting. While I was imagining the scene of your investigating the place, it suddenly occurred to me. My brother-in-law's real objective was not the coffee house, but very probably the parking lot. And then I smelled a rat, a sour tomato. My brother-in-law's pretty clever with his fingers. He got a first-class mechanic's license for fixing cars. He takes advantage of that. When he's lucky enough to discover some old rattletrap, he buys it for practically nothing. While he's fixing it up, he rides around in it, and then sells it for a good price, I guess. Perhaps there's some hope. Surprisingly enough, he uses this place for his transactions."

"That's the kind of information I was looking for." Immediately I recalled that there was indeed a manual on the repair of automobiles among the terribly indiscriminate yet practical collection of books that stood together on the shelf by the lemon-yellow curtains. Furthermore, I recognized my own negligence, and now took into account the cutaway sketch of the "Formula I" engine, on which there were entries in red ink, next to the Picasso. "You know, it's a very distinct peculiarity, his having a first-class mechanic's license. It's not at all like a scar from an appendectomy or a mole. I'm hard put because you people don't give me that kind of information."

"You're right. That's bad." He laughed, sticking out his thin lips. The finger which he suddenly extended grazed my side. "I'll wager my sister's mistaken you, a detective, for some tidbit to have along with her beer."

"So what results did you get with your investigations?"

"Not a thing." Turning in the direction of the attendant's shack, he stuck out the little whitish tip of his tongue and spat. The spittle described a high arc and landed on the roof of a neighboring car. "The old fellow's been penned in here all by himself for about a half year, I guess. But when you get into a conversation with him, he's surprisingly alert for his age, a shrewd old guy. He sees things pretty well with that eye of his. It's amusing to see things as a third person. You're suddenly aware of things that would never have occurred to you otherwise."

A line of dust flowed from the alley at the back—perhaps the direction of the wind had changed—whirling up the sand, surging and undulating among the cars. I could hear the continuous sound of some music box . . . no, it was the piping tune of a garbage-collector's cart. Abruptly, the brother, his expression hardening, adjusted his muffler and said exasperatedly: "I don't like that . . ."

"You mean the trash man?"

"It's stupid—refuse and music, like that. If it's all right with you, let's go back to the coffee house and take a little breather."

This time the invitation came from my companion in his restless voice, and I began to feel able to assess my own position, however vaguely.

"Among the things you have in your possessions, I would especially like to see the diary as soon as possible."

"The diary? All right. But it's nothing like a diary, you know. You're only going to be disappointed." He took a step forward, as if pressing me. "By the way, to change the subject, what do you think of my sister . . . as a woman? I'd like to hear your frank opinion."

We were between two cars, with barely enough room for

one person. If I did not move, we could only collide. Since I did nothing, my companion brought himself to a stop in the unnatural posture of taking a step forward.

"I really want you to tell me. Not as a professional detective, but seeing her as a man. I've been harping on a lot of things, but when I met you today that's what I wanted to ask you most of all."

"But we met by accident, didn't we?"

An iron box, like an armored car with no loopholes, loudly spewing its saccharine tune, passed in front of the wire fence.

"Yes, sure it was by accident," he said with his frozen laugh, twitching his cheeks. "You've got a good head on your shoulders. It looks as if I can rest assured about leaving matters in your hands."

"The diary . . . when can I have the diary?"

There was an instant of sharp hostility in the glance he shot back at me. I withdrew a step, opening up the way. When he realized that I had no intention of accompanying him, he let the tenseness ebb from his shoulders as if he were suddenly giving up; his eyes lost their focus and already he appeared to have abandoned all interest.

"Any time's all right . . . tomorrow . . . sure, I'll leave it at my sister's place for you . . . by noon."

The sister . . . as a woman . . . I had not put it into words yet, but I was transfixed by something like a pointed tool— was it the sharp pin sticking out from the opening in the lemon-yellow curtains? I was nailed to an invisible wall like an insect specimen . . . a bit of paper pinned to the edge of the curtain. Yet what in heaven's name was this? Once again I had forgotten her face. Even though my retreating companion was leaning forward, his broad shoulders were still stiff . . . like a wall. The only thing missing was the black hole in a picture painted on a wooden panel.

Same day: 11:05 A.M.—Visited Dainen Commercial Enterprises. Requested interview with the man in charge of sales in order to check further on the details concerning the contents of the documents, which Nemuro had promised to hand over personally to a subordinate at S—— station on the morning in question.

". . . MM, YES, a half year's already gone by since then," mused the director. On the table stood a china ashtray, like a miniature hibachi, bearing the name Dainen Commercial Enterprises in gaudy gold script, perhaps a leftover from those ordered for last year's traditional midsummer gift. The devices for holding cigarettes that graced the four corners were very elaborate: four brightly colored Kutani-ware cats, with their paws raised, were attached by their backs. They were faintly grinning a saccharine smile. The company president was a man from the country who had probably made his money in real estate. But the enterprise itself seemed to have made a good start for now. His office was located on the third floor of an old, run-down building. At least half of it was a loft room with a sloping ceiling. Only the reception area, partitioned off by decorative plywood, had furniture, tables and chairs of stainless-steel piping, and it was clear at a glance that they had cost money. Three walls, except for the one with windows, were covered with large, hand-made maps, dividing among them the suburbs into three sections: north, northwest, and west. The complicated diagrams, which were broken up into divisions by the use of red, blue, and green, gave a feeling of rawness quite like human anatomical charts, some places being like tangled skeins of thread, others like frayed nets. Moreover, cream-colored, triangular flags were pinned on them: Government Belt Line and Outer Belt Parkway. The building was located in a dilapidated section of town. The first floor contained a bicycle shop, and the second a mahjong parlor. Despite such surroundings, the president gave the impression of being a tough man to be reckoned with, if only because of his strength of character in doing business in a place like this. —"A half year ago. I think it must have been at the worst of the summer heat," mused the executive director, the immediate superior of the missing husband. He stroked his bald head, covered with drops of perspiration like specks of isinglass—perhaps the heating was too high—rocking against the black-leather chair back, as he squirmed with pleasure. "Well, I understood that. Because nothing provokes curiosity so much as someone else's misfortune once you know you're not responsible for it. Nothing is more natural proof of innocence than wanting to hear about another's misfortune." I went along with his mood and put my question to him casually. —"Since then, isn't there something new, some clue that suddenly occurs to you for the first time?" —"No, no, I've nothing at all." He waved his plump hand exaggeratedly. "Yes, frankly, I can say now that right after his disappearance I began to be suspicious of everything. I've had my hand bitten by a pet dog, so that for the time being I am quite prepared for anything." —"But you weren't hurt." —"No, I don't bear a single scratch." —"Then actually there was no harm done, but was there a possibility of being hurt?" —"Of course, I can't claim there was no harm at all. Because Nemuro had taken on a rather large market. He was most conversant with the situation, and if he intended to take advantage of his position . . ." —"Well, do you mean to imply that there was some suspicious remark or behavior in the past?" —"No, I don't think so. What's that siren? A fire? No, probably an ambulance or a blood bank. Anyway, Nemuro—how shall I put it?—is really a hard worker, a serious type, straightforward, you know. A golden tongue is capital in this kind of cutthroat business. He's a clever fellow with a lot of grit and stamina along with his gift of gab. And he is absolutely honest. You don't get that every day; you can use his wallet as a safe deposit box." —"Is he rather timid by disposition?" —"Timid? Well, I wouldn't exactly say timid." —"Put it very simply in a word." —"Well, in a word, he's steady, a plodder, really a bulldog type that never lets go. And there's an obstinate side to him too. Once he says something he never goes back on it; then he's like an angry toad." —"What did he do when he made an enemy of someone?" —"Enemy? Well . . . this is a sharp dealer's business; it's not surprising you make enemies. But you're not cut out for the work if you worry about that." —"Suppos-

ing there was someone Nemuro caught up in some crime?"
—"I see what you mean. Did he disappear or was he liquidated? Such a view is possible, frankly speaking. In your type
of work you don't hesitate to pry into the underside of
people's lives, and I don't doubt that you come up with some
interesting experiences." —"Hmm, some, thanks to you."
—"I know you do. Anyone has to take a pee or a crap."
—"But to change the subject, wasn't there some indication
that Mr. Nemuro was perhaps dissatisfied with the work
here?" —"Quite impossible! Listen, just about a month before Nemuro vanished he was promoted from chief sales
clerk to section head." —"Yes, I've heard that." —"My business, as you see, is not very good now, but it's a little annoying to have it judged on appearance alone, you know. It's the
nature of the work that when some new area develops, especially in the suburbs, the sale of propane gas naturally goes
up at the same time. But as soon as it gets to a certain point
city gas comes in, and when that happens that's the end
for us. We give the clarion call to advance toward new,
promising, and as yet undeveloped markets. We run around
to the central and local authorities collecting reports, entic-
ing small businessmen to come in, and so forth. Well, thanks
to the amazing growth of the city—it's going full blast now
—the sown seed matures fast. But in that sense it's the
quicker to dry up too. If the clerks sit at their desks doing
nothing we'll be a definite loser in this constant war of nerves
that goes on. It's better for the office to be quiet. The proof
is that we're sixth in this business. Even the bankers have
confidence in us." —"I realize that. Well now, the problem
is the documents we're looking for, the ones Mr. Nemuro
supposedly handed over that morning to some young em-

ployee at S—— station." —"Ah, Tashiro, I suppose. Tashiro must be here. I'll call him in and ask him." Without giving me a moment to interrupt, the director at once sprang up and, as he pushed with his hand, kicked open the ill-fitting veneer door. Through the opening facing the dusty office, which was partitioned off irregularly by a single-paneled screen, he bellowed: "Tashiro! Tashiro! On the double!" With his palms, he wiped away the perspiration that had sprung out on his head and then rubbed them on the seat of his trousers. How far, indeed, could one trust that falsely smiling face that looked back at me? —"He's here. A promising young man. Well, don't hesitate to ask him anything you want."

The promising young clerk at length put in a trembling appearance. Perhaps it was in contrast to the director, but he had an unpleasantly bad complexion, and behind his thick glasses his eyes were shifty; along with his baggy trousers he wore rubbers—on inspection, an unprepossessing, under-sized young man. The fact that he showed no particular sign of emotion at the director's introduction was due perhaps not so much to calmness as to the expression on his face, which was one of constant perplexity. He seated himself next to me on the sofa at the end nearest the entrance and answered me in a surprisingly unfaltering way, although in a high, nasal voice. He incessantly pushed up his glasses.

—"No, I don't know why. Only because he thought it would be a waste of time to return once he had left the office, I think. He specified S—— station, but then I supposed it was a matter that needed urgent attention." —"You had no idea of the contents?" —"No, none at all." —"But you knew the recipient's address, didn't you?" —"No, that too I was to have had handed over to me, along with a map, at the time I received the documents." —"Didn't you have a general idea, judging from the situation before and after and from your work at that time?" —"No, even at the time, everybody asked the same thing. I tried to guess, but . . ."

—"What about you, sir?" I said, suddenly changing my attack to the director. "You were in a position of controlling the whole affair. You have more of an idea than Tashiro, I imagine, don't you?" —"No, no, not at all," he said, lighting a cigarette and waving away the first smoke that went into his eyes. Then, in his normal voice, he continued: "I'm convinced that the knack of dealing with subordinates is never to interfere without good reason in their individual schemes. As for a report, I'm satisfied with the conclusion; and if the conclusion's first-rate, that's even better, I always say. Don't I, Tashiro?"

—"But, in any case," I went on, gazing in the neighborhood of the beckoning cat on the ashtray, "you've got to admit that the documents were a matter that apparently required great secrecy." The director was first to react: "Why?" —"Because, it's true, isn't it? If they had been unimportant papers they could have been sent through the mails." Instantly the younger man agreed. —"I said so, didn't I. Certainly, time was a question. Even if it had been out in the country, special delivery would have got there the next day." —"Hmm, but the telephone would have been even faster. I don't think it's *only* a question of time." —"But, it must have been a case of handing over something with a personal signature on it, something you couldn't get over by word of mouth on the telephone, or on the other hand, a case of having something signed."

A pretty shrewd character, Tashiro. Turning my body

ninety degrees, I looked straight at him. But his eyes remained fixed ahead. His half-sitting, half-standing posture did not change; only his chair creaked.
—"Indeed, it's quite possibly as you say. If that is so, try and draw a map of the rendezvous spot that morning while we're on the subject—a simple one will do." The young clerk gave a short nod of assent and bowed only to the director, whereupon he left the room quietly with a light step made more silent by his soundless rubbers. The indentation left by his weight at the end of the sofa slowly rose. The dirty sky was still more tarnished by the grimy windows . . . a reddish-brown light that cast no shadow. Suddenly, aiming at a beckoning cat on the ashtray, the director thrust out his cigarette and crushed it on the face as he began to chuckle.
—"Too bad, wasn't it, and you a professional detective. I thought you would get something out of him. I had great expectations. He's a clever fellow, I suppose, though he doesn't look it." —"Well then, you, as director, are concerned about something, aren't you?" —"I have no reason to be. I merely take a little pride in the company's men. But, all right, I feel better thanks to you. There's a weight off my chest. Of course, I have no clue, but on occasion I do have a prick of conscience. Even so, Nemuro's wife went to the trouble of engaging you and that's proof she herself knows nothing of her husband's whereabouts. Fine. Fine. No, I sympathize with everybody directly involved. A sad affair. But if Nemuro happens to have some understanding with his wife, he might be trying to hide his whereabouts from me alone. Such doubts do linger on in a corner of my mind."
—"Is there any concrete basis for them?" —"My god, if I'm to be caught up on each little remark, I'll end up by being tongue-tied. An unintentional mistake isn't all that strange.

It's a trait of mine to worry. Appearances are deceiving in my case." Then he heaved a long sigh and clasped the short, fat fingers of both hands in his portly lap. "Can you really go so far as to toss your family aside and completely vanish? I don't understand Nemuro. He didn't seem to have that kind of courage at all." —"Courage, you say?" —"Well, yes. Even though I can understand how relieved a man might feel in doing what he did, I couldn't have done it myself. I could never do a thing like that. I'm going to stay right here till I die unless I'm forced out. A man eats and defecates. It's a handicap to move away from the place where you get your food. And it's always a lot better to defecate in the same place too."

SOMEONE WAS following me. Paying no heed, I continued to walk.

Leaving Dainen Enterprises, I went about two blocks south, down the main street, turned right, and climbed the abrupt incline. I came to a railroad crossing with no gate. The street which lay alongside the tracks on the other side was, in this neighborhood, the only place where parking was possible. A line of cars stretched almost solid from there to the next main street. Most of the parked cars were small-sized trucks, since the whole area was crowded with small factories. Every time a train came by, it would raise a metallic dust, and here even the road appeared rusty-red.

My car was parked at the end of the street. When I turned and looked over my shoulder, the figure of the man shadowing me had vanished. There was nothing to get excited about. He would, I suspected, soon reappear. I got in the car and shoved the seat back as far as it would go, inserted a carbon between two sheets of paper on top of my briefcase, which I propped on my knees, and lit a cigarette. Putting records in order in places like this was a habit in which we had had to acquire some skill. The same was true for information and shadowing techniques. Yet, after the few lines of stereotyped opening, the following sentences simply didn't come. "No results," I wrote—an incredibly wretched expression that only corroborated my alibi. Fortunately I did have the sheet with the map of the meeting place at S—— station, which I had had young Tashiro draw up, a sketch like a plumber's draft for some water conduit. That was something to pad out the report with. Nothing is so devastating at such times as one's own incompetence. Well, maybe I was really incompetent. Had I ever once been competent? I wondered. Once in a long while, when my words flowed, when I was able to draw out my "No results" over thirty lines, I had the illusion of competency. Since I took a rather aggressive attitude toward my abilities, there was no need to be particularly competent. I would manage some way to forget about my inefficiency.

Tearing off a length of Scotch tape, I attached the piece of paper with the map to the left-hand corner of my report sheet.

A long freight train crowned with snow—it had come through the mountains—beating and bending the rails, taking an endless time, began to pass by. Once again the figure of my follower appeared in the corner of the rear-view mirror.

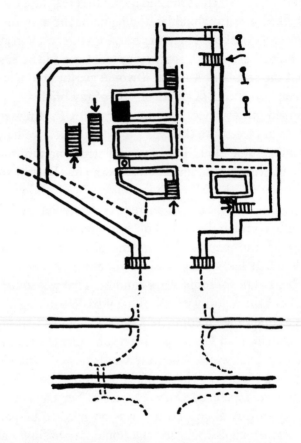

It was, as I expected, young Tashiro. He vanished into a
dead angle of the mirror and was transformed at once into
a real person standing at my window. Opening the opposite
door, I signaled to him with my finger to go round to the
other side. The window groaned as if it would break under
the pressure set up by the train, and the report sheets on
my knees fluttered violently. He pitched, almost collapsing, into the car, and I was struck with the pungent

odor, like that of an old icebox, coming from his overcoat. For the several minutes—actually a score of seconds—until the train had passed completely by, the pupils of my companion's eyes became smaller and smaller behind his glasses, and his head sank deeper and deeper into his coat collar. His rigid body trembled in unison with the train, vibrating quite as if he were a thin iron plate. What tale had he come to bear? I wondered. If he was carrying tales, good enough, but perhaps he had come to throw a little sand in my eyes, as he had done a short while ago. The promising young clerk, and for that matter the missing husband too, were, in the words of the director, pretty rare types.

At length the train passed by. After it had gone, a sound like the buzzing of insects lingered in my ears.

"Depressing weather, isn't it?"

With these words the rigidity suddenly left his knees, like a film that begins to roll; and he shifted his body, turning slightly in my direction. When I flipped my cigarette out the side vent, he in turn took out one and lit it, pushing up his glasses, which kept slipping down.

"I'm sorry. I . . . to tell the truth . . . I told a lie back there. I'm sorry. There was really no need to."

"You did it out of deference to the director, I suppose."

"Well . . . no, I don't think so. Because it was something the director knew all about. But why did he act as if he didn't know anything at all about it and why didn't he correct me? I feel awful. It goes against my conscience . . . because I've become an accomplice in betraying Mr. Nemuro, who's the head of my section."

"Don't worry about it. If in the long run it's to Mr. Nemuro's advantage, it's all right."

"No, it's not to his advantage. I knew from the start that

it wasn't. Otherwise, I wouldn't be telling a lie. I realized that telling it was probably useless."

"Just let me decide whether it was useless or not."

"It's about the destination of those documents."

"Did you know?"

"The section manager ... here," he began, extracting from his breast pocket a calling card, which he brandished with a histrionic gesture. "I actually do recall hearing him make a telephone call about delivering some documents or other. Possibly about two days before he disappeared."

"Oh, yes. A ward councilman. But it's a ward you don't often hear about."

"It's a newly formed one under joint management. But you won't get anything by going there. We haven't been sitting around with our arms folded."

That was a line I seemed to have heard before. Yes, it had come from the brother back in the parking lot. Suddenly I was overcome with an uncontrollable anger.

"Look, come on now. While you're at it why not have the courage to come clean?"

"What do you mean?"

"Just what I'm asking—you know that much."

I turned on the radio, catching out of the corner of my eye my companion's expression, which was stiff, as if pasted on. Someone accompanied by a guitar was singing in a sweet, childlike voice:

That's all!
That's all!
Just seeing you in my dreams,
That's all!

Young Tashiro heaved his shoulders in a great sigh, wiping

away the mist on the window with the flat of his hand. Actually, he wanted to say something. A wall of rainy sky loomed immediately beyond the tracks. The car seat was cramped, with no place really to stretch out in, no matter how one shifted around. The thumping of my companion's heart seemed audible in my own body. Perversely, I waited in silence.

"All right, I'll tell you," he said, stretching out an arm and shifting his seat. Looking into the distance, he continued: "So please turn off the radio."

"Yes, you had better tell me. I never do anything that might have an adverse effect on someone giving information to me. That's my business."

Two trains passed each other going in opposite directions, and the car was whipped as if by a steel lash as they sped by. The radio emitted a startled shriek as I hastily turned it off, making me think involuntarily of a dentist's drill. I had lost a molar about a month before. If I sucked hard, I could still taste blood.

"Yes, I'll tell you. Maybe I can't claim to be entirely honest, but I didn't intend to be uncooperative. I didn't, really . . . because I was one of those who stood to lose by the section manager's disappearance. It's frightening when I think about it, like at night, alone. I get the shudders . . . vanishing like that into nothing. But it's hard for me to speak up. I don't like hurting others' reputations with things like this."

"Complete secrecy is an obligation I have to observe in my work."

"Actually, he had a side to him people didn't know. He had one slightly strange quirk. He was all wrapped up in pictures—photographs—of nudes."

"You mean he collected them?"

"No, he takes them. He always seemed to be going to a studio. But I imagine I'm the only one who knows that. It so happens I introduced him to a friend who rents a darkroom."

"Did there seem to be some particular model?"

"Well, I can't go so far as to say a particular one." At length his voice loosened up, and even his expression became relaxed and comfortable, like an old shoe. "Apparently there was one girl he liked a lot."

"Do you know her name or anything?"

"I know where the studio is. And I've got the pictures too. Shall I show them to you next time? They're amateurish, but the amateurishness itself gives them a lot of feeling, you know. If he had passed out such pictures to his customers, they'd have loved it."

"We might as well go on over to your place after this."

"I can't. I used lunch as an excuse to get away and come over here. It's really quite impossible—the section manager eloping with that girl. He wouldn't ever do that. I really don't think he liked people. When I was invited for a drink —once in a long while—it was impossible. It didn't bother him at all not to say a word for ten or twenty minutes."

Suddenly someone was slapping at the window on my side with a wet sponge. I wiped the window with my hand and looked out. A young boy about ten, dressed in a skimpy uniform, with a large bald spot on the left side of his head, was looking sheepishly up at me as if he would burst out crying at any moment. I half lowered the window. "I'm sorry, mister," he said in confusion, preparing to take to his heels and pointing under the car. "My ball fell in that hole."

"You're a lot of trouble. Do I have to move the car?"

"If you don't mind me squeezing under, then you don't have to."

"All right. Go on."

A fine, almost invisible drizzle was changing the russet surface of the ground into the color of crude oil. Certainly the elbows and knees of the boy would be soaked to the same hue. At length he came crawling out, holding the ball in one hand. "How many miles do you get to a gallon, mister?" "Sixty." "Oh, yeah!" he muttered derisively, sliding down the slope on the opposite side of the tracks. I burst into laughter in spite of myself, drawing my young companion into my hilarity. Without knowing why, I was relieved. It might be well to spend more time with young Tashiro and get to be friends.

While I was closing the window, I started the motor and turned on the heater. The cold two-cylinder engine set up a racket like a bad percussion instrument.

"Say. Are you a drinker?"

"Well, maybe I can take a couple of highballs . . ."

"All right. Shall we plan on tomorrow night . . . with Mr. Nemuro's nudes? Let's get in touch by phone tomorrow about time and place."

THE CHIEF, sprawling flaccidly over his chair, his back to an enormous progress chart in which the investigators' names formed a vertical column cut by horizontal lines for dates and days, gave one the feeling of a wrinkled balloon bulging with water. If it had not been for the movement of his fingers clasped on his stomach one could only suppose he was napping. A profusion of deep wrinkles were etched like embedded strings in the slackened flesh of his chin, and traces of pimples stood side by side like the warts on a prickly pear.

Without stirring, the chief half opened a wary eye and gave a sarcastic chuckle. In a rasping voice, rather like a dog with a cold, he snapped: "You've gotten damn serious about this."

"Why shouldn't I be serious?"

"Well then. Do you have a little hope?"

"I don't, no."

"I thought so. It's better not to get too deeply involved in this kind of case."

"She's just letting her steam off."

"If that's all it is, it doesn't do us any good."

"Anyway, it's only for this week. Putting out thirty thousand yen a week doesn't last very long with the average family."

"But she's a real beauty, apparently . . . that client of yours."

"Unfortunately the so-called brother's always hanging around . . . a pretty ominous fellow."

"Oh yes, the brother. I wonder if some sort of word hasn't come in from the data section we contacted a while back."

"I saw it. There was something fishy, so I had his record investigated."

"Well?"

"I tentatively established that there is a brother with such a name. But no picture of him was attached to the papers, and I still can't prove entirely that it's not some double."

After I had blurted it out, I was sorry. But it was too late.

The balloon at once leaned forward, his chair creaking, and with penetrating eyes he scanned my face in silence.

"A double . . . hmm . . . If she's having a double take the brother's name, that's really something. Does it mean that your client's a slippery one too?"

"Ah. It's possible, I suppose, for a variety of reasons."

"Whatever made you suspect that?"

"Rather than motives, it's a weakness of motives . . . or a vagueness of them . . ."

"The motives are obvious," he interrupted suddenly in a sharp voice. "Doesn't the disappearance of the client's husband constitute a motive?"

"Yes, indeed it does."

"Listen. I think you understand. In our work, you don't invade the privacy of the client. You don't stick your nose in business you can't write in your report. If you can't observe the rules you had better wash your hands right now . . . and change your profession to priest or extortioner."

I had come close to starting in on the business of the matchbox. The single piece of evidence I could verify with my eyes, touch with my hands. A single lens by which I could substantiate, bring to a point of focus, the numberless hypotheses. Among the infinite projections, which produced something resembling actuality, only those that were photographed on the matchbox were my unique, three-dimensional color picture. If only I could get just two or three words of testimony from her . . . if only I could . . . But what would be the use? I would mock myself and flagellate myself for doing such a thing. I knew before I heard it what the chief's answer would be: the investigation of the brother's record was precisely the invasion of privacy he was talking about. The point was probably well taken.

THIS MORNING, in the parking lot in front of the Camellia coffee house, he—my client's brother—had actually been ingeniously evasive with me. He had cleverly urged me to take care, for I had been close to overlooking the No Entrance sign.

Certainly, only the area where I was licensed was the hunting ground indicated by my client. Since one motive the client had placed out of bounds for the investigation, as was clearly set forth in the application, was the one connected with his—her husband's—disappearance, I would pursue him in all events, successful or not, and there was no need to question why I should be doing so. In the meantime, even though my client might begrudge me information or force conflicting information on me, I must not worry about it.

You knew that all the time. You were not about to be enlightened by the chief. Supposing that the client was using us to cover up her own crime, even so it was our business to keep the line clear and we had no right to refuse her.

For example, the brother's clever explanation about our much too accidental encounter in the parking lot saved me from giving up my role as investigator and at the same time, from another angle, strengthened my suspicions. If the husband was so conversant with car repair and equipment, then there was the possibility of his having something to do with a ring of car thieves. That was brought to my mind by a newspaper article I had recently read about the arrest of a gang of crooks that had been operating on a large scale. No, it had to be something a lot more run-of-the-mill. He was working on the scratches on a car in some hit-and-run case, for instance; or he was changing license plates; or he had been compelled by someone to do so; or he himself was the hit-and-run driver.

Fortunately, thanks to the excellence of his techniques, the incident had become labyrinthine, and contrary to his expectations had resulted in his being cornered himself. In the end, it would get too hot for him and he would go into hiding somewhere. However, supposing the wife, who was the client, knew all about these events and was covering up his escape ... Then I had no role to play here.

But if I did nothing at all, I would be sorry later. Whatever happened I could not give up—there was some hope, albeit slight. I had been numbed to the bone like a frozen fish by that frigid wind, but the faint light of the lemon-yellow window had transfixed me. I could not help but feel I was being beckoned in, that she wanted me to ignore the fence and come in. There was no basis for such a thought. Yet my heart throbbed. I had a nagging suspicion that my client's fence was not necessarily one and the same as that of her self-styled brother. No, I was not happy with things. Somehow I had a terrible feeling of alienation from the brother. So I would be as watchful as a hunting dog, hiding myself in the breach in the fence ready to jump through at any time.

The breach in the fence was the matchbox ...

There were no untruths in the report I had composed con-

cerning the Camellia coffee house. Not only were there no
untruths; there was a definite line of thought. I had not been
able to make a single discovery linking the husband with the
Camellia. Providing I took into consideration only the ex-
terior of the matchbox. Once I looked inside, there was that
bothersome fact which I could not make jibe with the plot
no matter how I might plead and entreat: the different kinds
of tips—nine white tips mixed with twenty-six black tips.
For, yes, the tips of the matchsticks which I had received
this morning at the Camellia were white, and so the twenty-
six black ones must obviously have been added later. Could
there be anyone today who went around filling coffee house
matchboxes? No matter how prices soar, matches and water
are still free wherever you go.

But I had passed over that in my report. I had not broken
down the protective fence. I wanted very much to, but I
hadn't got up enough determination . . . yet.

It was sometime last night that I had noticed the different
kinds of matches. After I had been rejected by the lemon-
yellow window and at last got in my car, the heater simply
drove my cold numbness inward; and my frustration became
a ceaseless trembling, which I could not control, so great,
indeed, that I had misgivings about being able to drive.
Impatient with the increasingly congested traffic, I decided
to leave my car in the lot in front of S—— station.

I went past a movie theater and turned down an alleyway.
Dark depressions, ripped asphalt, uneven walls crowded
against expectant faces. But the commotion was illusory, and
what I saw was in reality only a man, squatting in the shadow
of a telephone pole plastered with advertisements. Hastily I
finished urinating and with a blank expressionless face
pushed open the left-hand side of the great double doors

leading into a brightly lit saké cafeteria on the next corner. I
was surprised at how late it was. I had an unpleasant feeling
of quiet, for there was less than half of the usual number of
customers. At the cashier's box by the entrance I changed
four hundred-yen coins into ten-yen pieces. Against the back
wall, side by side, stood white rectangular boxes bordered in
vermilion—eight in all—which, had brand names not been
painted on them, would have looked for all the world like
pumps in a gas station. Slipping between the long, narrow
tables, which were arranged in five parallel rows, I at once
placed myself in front of the machine on the far right, which
happened to be free. A characteristic pungent smell. The city
stench of foul water backing up when, after ten in the evening, the flushing of sewage suddenly slackened. I inserted a
ten-yen coin into the brass-framed opening beneath the red
arrow on the right of the machine. With every succeeding
coin a piano wire resounded, and at the eighth a red bulb
flashed on. I shoved the paper cup provided for the purpose
into place and when I pulled on the stainless-steel lever, precisely 4.0 ounces of a slightly overheated amber liquid spurted
out. I cradled the cup in my two hands lest the warmth
escape, downing in a swallow about a third of the drink. Then
I drank the rest in five or so gulps as I shifted to the machine
bearing my preferred brand name.

There was already a customer standing at my machine.
Under his faded dark-blue work clothes he wore a gaudy
muffler, into which was knitted a design. He wore no overcoat. He was well built and thick-set. Black oil had collected
underneath the nails of the hand holding the paper cup;
perhaps he was a boilerman from a nearby building. Most of
the eight-o'clock customers were white-collar workers, but
after that hour, the type abruptly changed. As the fellow

made place for me, he looked over his shoulder and re-
marked: "Hey! If we pissed in dribbles like that, we'd be
diabetics." He put the tip of his tongue between his gaping
front teeth. He seemed to be drunk already, and as he swayed,
his center of gravity shifted back and forth between his heels
and his toes, but unfortunately there were no chairs in the
place. Noisily sipping at his paper cup, he kept steadily observing my hands. "Hey, you like this saké too. What about
that!" Then lowering his voice: "Come on, lend me ten yen.
I'm a regular customer here. I'm not trying to get away with
anything. If you think I'm lying I'll sign an I.O.U. Just ten
yen. You can't be crooked here."

The advantage of the place was that no one usually talked
to you very much. I began to feel the effects of the saké.
Good-naturedly, I took out a ten-yen piece and gave it to
him. Snatching the coin, he thrust it into his ear and without
a word of thanks went off toward the window where they
sold specially boiled vegetables, there being no automatic
machine for that.

On the tables, side by side, stood smaller vending machines, which carried over thirty kinds of peanuts, salted
beans, pine seeds, dried shellfish, and even fortune slips. Besides these, there was a contrivance like a toy robot whose
arms and legs had been severed that sold boiled bean curd;
it was the only one in the whole country. There was usually
a humming like that of a vacuum cleaner as the queue of
customers was being served, but this evening, because the
machine was all sold out, it was hushed and motionless. First,
ten yen for pine seeds. I caught them in the palm of my hand
and popped them into my mouth in a single gesture—there
were only twenty or so. As I finished half of my second cup

of saké, my nose suddenly began to run. Then I bought boiled whale bits that came in a three-cornered bag. I began to feel the effect of my drinking this night in the region of my forehead, and it seemed gradually to be descending, making a noise quite like that of a cat on a tin roof. When I had drunk my third cup and returned to my place, I felt somehow weightless.

A fortune machine happened to be at the place I went back to. Perhaps it was because the easing of my tension was too sudden or again it might have been that there was no need to protect my paper cup by extending my elbows as I always had to in the rush hours—anyway, I gave myself up to the whirlpool of my tipsiness that was revolving faster and faster. Suddenly I noticed that the top of the table was a synthetic contact paper printed to represent knotted wood; furthermore, I saw that the whole surface was in reality pockmarked by cigarette burns. Among the pockmarks a number seemed to be moving, and I discovered that they contained cockroaches. I was overcome by an impulse to stop time right there and limit the world to what I saw before me.

There were aluminum ashtrays here and there on the tables big enough to be bothersome. Between the tables were unsightly wastebaskets covered with galvanized iron. Cigarettes had been rubbed out on the table tops, and paper cups, plastic saucers, and chopsticks, deliberately thrown wide of the wastebaskets, littered the whole floor. When the cafeteria was jammed you almost took no notice. The open-hearted, easy-going quality of the place came perhaps from the peculiar sensation underfoot when one trod heedlessly on the abundance of refuse. The only merit of the automatic vendors was faithfulness and obedience. The customers, in their solitude, could enjoy royal privilege in full measure. Thus they vented their anger as much as they could, not on the ashtrays, but on the much larger tables; not on the waste-baskets, but all over the much more spacious imitation-tile floor.

I wanted to talk with somebody I didn't know about flying saucers. But detachment was the highlight of the place. Since I did not dislike the convention I felt compelled to slip my ten-yen piece into the nearest fortune machine.

Good luck. The sign of auspicious clouds in the south. Your horse is a slow walker, but there is promise of an open gate. You may act positively about turning over a new leaf and about love. Take care of rainy weather and a wallet with holes. What you seek is at your feet. There will be spring rains and radiation. Stay under an umbrella.

The drawback of a paper cup is that it leaks no matter how careful you are. Perhaps that was why the match simply would not obey me when I tried to light my cigarette. In the end I was exasperated. I had the idea of putting two match-sticks together when suddenly I became aware of the difference of the two heads. As I kept turning the screw of my tipsiness, somewhere a part of me awakened and forged a link. It occurred to me that this matchbox which had casually come into my possession, was in fact an important piece of evidence given me by my client. I wrapped it in a hand-kerchief and thrust it into an inside pocket.

But before I put it away, the significance of the two kinds of matchsticks had been branded deeply on my mind.

White heads

and

Black heads.

My thoughts penetrated like gamma rays through the various events and conditions, and suddenly I was headed straight for the solution. I could easily deduce simply from the damage to the matchbox and the label that he was not a regular customer, constantly coming to the Camellia. Had he been, he could have procured new matches at any time. However, it was also difficult to deny that he was not merely a casual customer, inasmuch as there were the sticks with two kinds of heads. That he was carrying the matchsticks around and even replenishing them was the same as his being a regular customer, even if he actually wasn't. Otherwise, it was evident that there was an even greater tie-in. I emptied half of my third drink, lit an edge of the fortune slip—with other matches, of course—and pursued the cockroaches, who fled helter-skelter, but my thoughts continued in their straight line. A matchbox from a coffee house he rarely frequented. What conceivable interest could that have? The label design? Ridiculous! Well, then, the telephone number? Yes, conceivably the telephone number. Perhaps in the Camellia there was some doelike girl with a sign on her—"Caretaker Wanted"—that would put a middle-aged man into ecstasies. She would keep his interest alive by pretending to nibble at the bait he cast over the telephone.

At that same moment, my reasoning took such a sharp curve that the cart was almost upset. Don't laugh. If such a girl really did exist, the very nosy brother would not have overlooked her. He would have got wind of that long ago, and the objective from the beginning would have been to follow her. Perhaps such a girl didn't exist (and actually she didn't). If I could believe my client's words that the match-box had come from the husband's raincoat . . . No, the hypothesis was packed with ramifications. Let's stop that. There was the business of the old newspaper being in the pocket with the matchbox, and also it might be well to look again into two or three of her explanations after I had cleared away the bothersome trimmings.

A voice spoke to me from the other side of the table: "Hey. Having them for a snack?" It was the fellow who had pan-handled the ten-yen piece a little while ago. "I bet they're poison. But they've got a lot of oil, so they're probably good for you." When he said this, I noticed I had already wasted over ten matchsticks chasing the cockroaches around and had gathered into a mound over twenty-four that I had killed. "Ah ha. They must be really good, they live on spilt saké. It's true. Shall we give it a try?" Thinking he was joking, I remained silent, whereupon my companion suddenly stretched out his hand and before my eyes picked up several cock-roaches, which he popped into his mouth. I tried to stop him, but he was too fast. A young man, apparently an employee, shoved me aside and swept the remaining dead cockroaches to the floor. "Stop it! It's disgusting," he said sharply, without raising his eyes, and passed on. The man who had swallowed the cockroaches, groping with his tongue between his missing front teeth, intently searched for something, his gaze restless. "Boy! This is salty," he muttered, "dry as paper . . . toasted seaweed . . . really cheap, no mistake about that."

Obviously, if there was anything significant on the matchbox, it must be the telephone number on the label. Contrary to what one might expect, my client or her brother were probably the ones who really needed the number, not the husband. Perhaps it would be more appropriate to put "needed" into the present and say "the ones who need." It was probably a feint. They were most assuredly pretending that there was some relation between Nemuro and the Camellia for fear of having me get wind of the actual purpose of the telephone number. By decoying me, they were establishing the number's irrelevance and thus directing my attention away from the Camellia. Was that not their real goal?

As the time drew near for closing the place, a middle-aged woman, her hair done up in a bun, was beginning at the back of the shop to gather up the refuse on the floor. There were only some fifteen or sixteen weary customers left; they seemed to have nowhere to go. All right, there was absolutely no reason to think I was carrying logic to nonsensical extremes. At first blush, the client seemed to be cast in the role of an unfortunate victim, abandoned by her husband. But the truth of the matter was quite the opposite: she, or her brother, could be said to be aggressors among aggressors . . . and supposing they were murderers . . . I did not come to that conclusion particularly, but what if, in some situation, I were to give up my position as investigator? Or, having had the presentiment, supposing I could forecast that between her and her brother there were differences in motive for requesting the investigation and that exposing the brother's weak point would not necessarily mean hurting her? Naturally, they were quarry for the hunt and it would not do to shun the chase. I did not want them to take me too lightly. Indeed, even if they were indicted, it would probably not mean much money for me. But along with blackmail, there was nothing like murder for a quick buck. So, do me a favor and don't get me too stirred up.

THE CHIEF was returning to his usual self. He murmured like a water-filled balloon.

"Well, now. I understand he's gone back to the hospital again."

There was no need for further explanation between us. *He* was the one—the very lowest among the numerous investigators—who happened to be obsessed by the strange dream that he would not advance. He had taken an umbrella and jumped off the roof of the building and at once plunged down—lower than the lowest of us all.

On a particular case, the fellow had got himself into the predicament of causing a client to commit suicide. His makeup was such that he took pride in betraying a client by selling information back to the person under investigation. He would say that in a dispute both sides stood to lose. But he knew the rules. He was a shrewd fellow. No actual betrayal of a client had ever come to light, nor had he ever incurred a client's displeasure. Of course, he was able to do such things because clients are definitely not merely victims. By the very fact of having sustained an injustice a man had to pursue a case. And if he considered the situation carefully, he would realize that he embodied at the same time a goodly proportion of aggressive elements. In extreme cases, the client could be completely the aggressor. There are cases, for example, where the contents of a report really made for the purpose of a character investigation have actually been used as materials for extortion.

However, the client he forced into suicide was, strangely enough, a hundred-per cent victim. The client did not know who her father was and had been raised by women. She had become a lonely young girl with great determination to succeed. She was running a small beauty parlor at the corner of a building. One day a shabby old man, whom she at once recognized as an alcoholic, appeared and testily proclaimed himself to be her father. Since, thanks to him, she had experienced a lot of hardship in growing up, she did not believe him at once. But as she listened to his story, all kinds of details came out which only her father could have known. The little scar, for instance, back of her dead mother's ear that was invisible since it was usually covered by hair . . . the coral hair ornament, a memento of her grandmother . . . the story about the high suspension bridge in her mother's village, that she herself had seen only in a photograph. And then when he guessed right about her blood type and even the birthmark on her shoulder, she gradually began to feel that the shape of the ears and nose of the man before her were somehow quite like her own.

That day, in view of everything, she handed him a thousand-yen note and got him to go away. But three days later, his breath smelling of alcohol, he put in another appearance, saying he just wanted to catch a glimpse of her—another thousand yen. It became an event that took place every three

days, then every other day, and finally daily. The girl gradually grew uneasy. If this were her real father she couldn't let
things go on as they were. So finally she came to our office,
and it so happened that *he* was put in charge of investigating
the identity of the self-styled father.

If he had thought only about satisfying her expectations,
without paying any attention to the truth, as was his wont,
perhaps the tragedy could have been avoided. But for some
reason he was suddenly tempted by his old devil. Quite un-
like himself, he volunteered to play the role of angel. But
unluckily his real nature surfaced at once.

The girl, however, was not satisfied with his report and
suggested another investigation. At that time he should have
done at once what she really wanted done. It would still have
been better to get money by threatening blackmail—he was
so good at that—and return to being lowest man as usual. But
apparently he was too assiduous in his role as angel. Like a
kindergarten teacher who tries to correct a child's unbalanced
diet, he decided to push things through with no concessions.
I cannot recall now whether it was a question of the real
father or a false one—if you ask someone, they'll tell you right
away, though it makes no great difference which—but anyway, the girl, who knew she had no alternative but to accept
the results, committed suicide. When he learned what she
had done, he came down with a serious mental disorder.
Then, about a half year later, he was put in the care of a
mental clinic and at the end of last year was at last dis-
charged. Anyway, that's the way I heard it.

Wearily, the chief repeated: "He's back in the hospital, I
hear. Anyway, take your eyes off him an instant and they say
he stops breathing to the point of fainting. Strange, isn't it?
Can you imagine someone being able to do that? He's really
lost his senses, I'd say."

Same day: 2:05 P.M.—Left the office. Headed in the direction of F—— City. I went to try to establish contact with Mr. M, the councilman there who on the day of the disappearance had an appointment to deliver some documents to T. Since the source of information relative to Mr. M is for the time being strictly confidential, please note well. (I took the Koshu Turnpike.)

Same day: 4:20 P.M.—Filled up the tank at a gas station (three gallons; receipt appended). To be on the safe side, questioned attendant about the streets. The whole west side, separated by the street, is the third ward of F—— City. In F—— Village which appears on my map (published in a previous year) there is no such division into wards, and the relative position of the streets appears to be quite different. When I inquired I found that they had decided to build near here an interchange for the turnpike at present under construction, that there was a lively buying and selling of land and subdividing into house lots, that the municipal cooperative movement was bearing fruit and was being extended to the present F—— City. So the place was crawling with heavy trucks filled with dirt.

The old F—— Village, where Mr. M's house is located, corresponds to the present first ward and is an area farther to the west screened by a lowish hill with scrub trees on the right of the highway. F.Y.I. I include below an abridged map of F—— City.

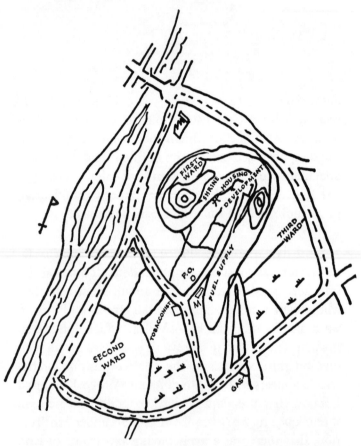

Same day: 4:28 P.M.—Right turn at the second bus stop after the gas station. I stopped the car at the first ward post office and inquired at the corner tobacconist's. Mr. M's house was the one to the right of the post office, visible diagonally in front of me. Long fence of building blocks. Garden with many trees. Ordinary residential house in a shopping neighborhood. Beside the gate, you can see a simple garage consisting of only a roof.

LEAVING MY car in front of the tobacconist's, I decided first to take a look at the post office. A set of painted folding doors with brass handles was flanked by a small flower bed, where nothing was planted now, and a pillar letterbox. The floor was concrete; to the right was a small bench and to the left a public telephone booth. Between the two front windows, side by side, was written: Money Orders, Postal Savings, Postal Life Insurance. Dirty cotton curtains were hung over the windows and there was a sign in the shape of an obelisk: Closed Today. Only the window inscribed Stamps—Parcels—Telephone was open. An oldish man, doubtless the chief, who was cleaning or repairing the rubber stamps, looked up at me. There was the pungent odor of a kerosene stove functioning inefficiently. A ten-ton truck sped by, making the earth vibrate; it suddenly slowed down (perhaps because my car was in the way) and changed gears. As I casually requested ten five-yen stamps, I asked if it were true that at Mr. M's place they had bought a car. I was posing as a salesman . . . an old trick in a case like this.

"A car?" The man slowly shifted his gaze from me to the next window place hidden behind the curtain. "Never heard that ..."

"There's no reason for him to have bought a car," answered the muffled voice of a middle-aged woman unexpectedly from behind the curtain. As in most small post offices, a married couple was in charge here. "A man who goes around boasting about the number of alarm clocks he has is certainly not going to keep silent about buying a car, is he?"

"Oh. I'm relieved to hear it. Because a rather plausible rumor has come to my attention according to which Mr. M is driving around in a red car."

"Impossible. The car next door is light blue," said the man.

"Ordinary light blue. He's really not a bad fellow, you know," added the wife.

"Be that as it may, what about you yourselves? If you had a car you could enjoy life twice as much, that's for sure. It's a lot more advantageous than life insurance."

"At our stage in life we're too old to start driving. That'll be fifty yen."

I drew out a hundred-yen note and asked for small change. "But Mr. M's business is apparently thriving, isn't it?"

"Apparently it is. He used to be only a charcoal dealer," the wife retorted dryly.

"With the increase in houses, he's changed from a black-charcoal seller to a propane dealer who takes a bath every day. It's the times," the clerk declared, drawing up his thin upper lip, as he pushed toward me the stack of five ten-yen pieces.

A propane dealer! In spite of me, my heart thumped. So could the fuel shop opposite M's house be his? Could it be that the small three-wheeled trucks driving back and forth with their tanks of gas, raising clouds of dust and rattling like tin horses, were in fact part of M's business? If M was not merely a councilman but the head of a fuel concern, the plot was much better. There was no longer the slightest mystery about the missing man's behavior that morning. Dainen Enterprises were tied up with M.

"But it's so unfair," said the man's wife in a cheerful tone, quite at odds with the substance of her remark. "I wonder just how long it's going to go on." I turned and looked over my shoulder through the glass in the door. Under the deep zinc eaves peculiar to fuel stores, two young men were unloading tanks, which they placed side by side at the edge of the road and then carried into the storehouse. Its interior was already dark, and I could not see in very well. Evening came more quickly than elsewhere to this valley town screened to the east and west by hills. Uttering a persistent series of little coughs, the wife got up. Then the lights in the post office were turned on. I lit a cigarette, and the few seconds of silence acted, as I thought they would, as a primer to their gossiping tongues.

"Here now. See how the housing project in the second ward is getting finished. They've already promised publicly to lay city gas in the town. The place is developing all the time . . . a real suburb. It's expanding—and the propane dealers' purses are expanding right along with it. But sooner or later city gas is going to come in, and when it does they've had it. Shops'll spread, telephones'll increase, shop clerks'll be at a premium. Already there are ten three-wheeled trucks, if you include those belonging to the branch stores."

"Nine."

"Anyway, they've had it. The balloon'll burst."

"For a while he came to ask us to sign petitions against

city gas. He said propane gas was sanitary, that you couldn't commit suicide with it."

"Stupid! At our age who's going to commit suicide with gas? Whatever method you choose, convenience is the main thing. These days, who's going to sympathize with the grievances of a charcoal dealer?"

FIRST WARD, F—— City. Former F—— Village's main street, which begins at the post office. A straight road on a gentle incline about four hundred yards long, ending at the stone steps leading up to the town hall. Mixed among the tile-roofed stores, the farmhouses stood out conspicuously with their lattice doors and high-pitched roofs—apparently the farmers had raised silkworms. In the spacious yards were small passenger cars, bought by the sale of mulberry fields. The same as everywhere else, the electrical appliance shops were unreasonably brilliant. There were even barrel makers, whose shops seemed on the verge of collapse. Generally the shops seemed affluent, still keeping some touch of the old days. However, the paucity of street lights suggested the fate of the old town, which was being left behind and forgotten. Although on the ridge of the low hill to the west the light was still bright enough so that one could distinguish each branch of the trees, the valley town was already completely in the shadow of night. I noted a deep ditch to the right as I slowly drove the car over the pocked asphalt road, which had long lain unrepaired.

An old, gnarled cypress just before the town hall had encroached over a third of the road and towered above me, at what was apparently the entrance to a shrine. There was quite a bit of free space, and a good many cars were parked there. A light-blue or a slightly dirty blue one? Among six, four were various shades of blue and thus provided no clue. The windows of the town hall, except for a part of the second floor, were still bright, probably people working overtime on accounts. I turned the car around and went slowly back over the way I had just come.

I was not well acquainted with the organization of a fuel supplier. But along with the spread of the residential areas toward the suburbs, the charcoal dealers were also extending their business in propane gas, and the more the population increased, the more they prospered. But just as inevitably as the great reptiles ultimately had to give way to the mammals, they too would be taken over by city gas. They were born of the city's growth and of that growth they would die—a paradoxical business. An appealing fate, where at their moment of greatest affluence they were sentenced to death. Uneasy moneymakers, sumptuously wined and dined, their tables were their gallows. Surely they must have deep anxieties.

Yet, no matter how they might suffer, they knew from the beginning what the results of the game would be. What alternative was there to city gas? What room for maneuver was left them? They were caught in the coils of events, and the disparity in strength was too great. What was the husband's goal in trying to send Tashiro on the mission that

morning? It would seem that he had not been forced to disappear. Perhaps I should believe the story of the sales manager when he insisted that there was no crime involved.
Perhaps Tashiro's parting taunt, that one way or another
my coming here would be fruitless, was not untrue. The
most a wholesaler like Dainen Enterprises could do for a
cornered retailer was to help him along to an easy death, or
perhaps to order the tombstone for him.

I stopped the car a little before the fuel supplier's.

Other than the outdoor floodlights suspended from the
edge of the eaves and projecting inward, I could see no
change in the scene. As before, the two men were tossing
down the tanks and carrying them into the storehouse. One
was a slim fellow about twenty, who looked as if he had
stomach trouble. The other was a man about thirty, who had
a weather-beaten, craggy look; a towel encircled his thick
neck. He worked sluggishly, as if he had no liking for it, and
he could hardly be blamed, since there were so many tanks.

"The boss here yet?"

"Boss?" the younger man shot back, with an expression as
if he were not used to hearing the word. He looked up at me
suspiciously, his hands resting on a tank. In color and shape
the tank was the image of a bomb, and in the middle of
one end there was a white trademark in the shape of a leaf.

Perhaps the expression I had used went against his grain.
Although originally a charcoal dealer, M was now a ward
councilman; maybe I should have called him the "proprietor." But my qualms were apparently groundless, for
with a slight motion of his chin he indicated the house beyond the road.

"He doesn't come to the store very often and he's not back
home yet ... the car's not there."

"I've just come from Dainen Enterprises."
It wasn't really an untruth. My starting point had been our office, but before that I had indeed passed by Dainen Enterprises. If I were questioned later I would get out of it by saying that the fellow had jumped to a hasty conclusion. The youth set down the tank, straightened up, and looked at the older man, who had just come back from inside the storehouse. There seemed to be some reaction. But just what was not obvious—the name Dainen Enterprises was apparently already familiar to them. The suspicious relationship between Dainen Enterprises and M, before the husband's disappearance, had resolved itself into a completely ordinary one after it; and thus my hopes of stumbling on a trace of the husband here had become more and more improbable.

But I did expect something, and I was not particularly disheartened at what I heard. If I could, I should have enjoyed getting in smaller doses the information I toiled to acquire. Being deceived and checkmated, being made to go miles out of my way and take all kinds of pains—I wanted at least to use this information to make my report plausible. My trip that had lasted a full two and a half hours had become just as obvious an act as casting a line in a pond.

Moreover, at the time when the possibilities were collapsing one after the other, the vexatious quiverings of huge, flesh-colored moth larvae nestling in my breast were growing in intensity, as if they were on the point of bursting forth from the cocoon and flying away. As soon as they were liberated, these gory moths would make a dash straight for that lemon-yellow window. The shadow of a man standing in their way as they passed with a rush through the glass and the curtains—the black-walled back of the self-styled brother, of course—aiming for the heart, they would sink their fangs into it. Hold on! Moths don't have fangs. So let them stop at the dentist's on the way and get themselves fitted with special custom-made teeth. Right. I would have to go right to the dentist's myself. When I put the tip of my tongue in the hole left by my molar, more and more I got the metallic taste of blood.

"When you say the Dainen, you mean the main office?"

Sucking up air into his nose, the younger man exhaled strongly on the tips of his oil-stained fingers peeping out from the torn work gloves. I wondered if he had swallowed the mucous he had inhaled. He inclined his head toward me as I nodded.

"Funny . . . his going out before noon. He said he was going to drop in at the Dainen main office."

"Who knows?" said the older man, tucking the ends of the towel round his neck into the collar of his overalls. He spoke in a thick dialect that was difficult to understand. "He's always got one excuse or another for going out. He can do it in his position . . . just drop out of sight like that."

I answered him at once with a smile and an air of complicity.

"He can afford a car, and the city's right around the corner."

"What do you mean?" The younger man made as if to cross his arms, his hands under his armpits, rocking his body as he spoke. "Once the working men's temporary flats were finished in the second ward, the city kind of began to come out here. Go around by the river on your way back and take a look, if you like. The hotels and restaurants are on the other side of the river. Even on this side they've got . . . oh, you know, the micro-something-or-other . . . the little buses they use for kindergarten kids. Every evening there's some ten of them hung with red lanterns. How about some noodles? Or a hot dog? Or some vegetable stew with a little cheap saké?"

"But don't be fooled. Filling up the belly's not the only use for a hot dog," added the older one, clearing his throat and spitting out a gob of phlegm. "The real thing for sale is right behind the counter. What do you think is on the other side of the partition in the bus? Back there they've got a fantastic gadget—a soft cushion with a hole."

"Why? Do you know why a cushion has to have a hole?" asked the younger laughingly, titillated, squatting on his heels as if to defecate. Thereupon his long dark shadow, darker than the dark surface of the ground, which was cast by the light under the eaves, suddenly grew shorter and slipped under the fellow's buttocks as if attached to him. "It's too cramped there . . . you can't lie down. So you call it a cushion, not a mattress."

"It's a cheap, money-eating hole."

Spitting out the words, the older man turned to go back to work, and the younger one casually followed after him. They slapped together their work gloves that, gummed with mud and oil, had become like old rubber.

"Well, that's the way it is, so you never know when he's going to come back, exactly. Another customer has been waiting an hour for him."

"Nervy guy. Making himself right at home . . . using the telephone any time he wants."

The two, as if by prearrangement, cast a hard look inside the building that was ostensibly the office—evidently not a very welcome customer, a bill-collector type or something like that. If I were going to get any information, it would be from these two. I put a cigarette in my mouth and offered the pack to the two men. "I have one or two things to ask you..."

"No fire!" the older one interrupted in a gruff voice. But the younger, unruffled, took one and when the flame of the lighter lengthened to almost an inch, applied it first to his own cigarette and then, with it still lit, brought it close to the tip of my nose.

"It doesn't make any difference. Tonight the wind's from the west."

"How can you say that? You have a license to deal with explosives and combustibles."

"I'm not the type to cling to life, I guess." I too, without a sign of perturbation, suddenly decided to take a light from the burning lighter, which he was holding out to me, thinking a cigarette was after all less dangerous than an open flame. "If things are going to catch fire they do in the first second. Anyway, it's all covered with insurance. The president himself would be just as happy to see it go."

The "president"? Ridiculous! Of course, with the outskirts of the city constantly expanding, in a single night town areas suddenly spring up from what had been fields. The large-scale development of presidents was nothing to be surprised at, particularly.

"Someone like you is called 'green.' "

"Sure enough, compared to your nose, mine is pretty green."

"So have the last word." With his fingers he blew his nose, which had become red either from the cold or from alcohol, whereupon a secretion that was neither tears nor eye gum oozed like honey from the corners of both eyes.

He jumped over a ditch and moved to the side of the road where the tanks were lined up. In a strangely soft and sympathetic tone he said: "The old guy here had his pocket picked at the bike races—twenty thousand yen from the money he made selling off his land . . . then he forgot thirty thousand yen in the baggage rack on the streetcar . . . and he turned Red for good."

"Don't talk nonsense," snapped the older man, as he too turned in the direction of the tanks in the same sluggish way, with an expressionlessness that was neither denial nor affirmation. "Well . . . if we don't put a little more muscle into it, the next load'll be here before we know it."

"I'd just like to ask . . ." I too jumped the ditch, starting after him. As I went toward the two men, I shifted my briefcase to under my arm and turned the switch on the tape recorder. "How long has it been since you two began working here?"

"It's a little over a year for me," said the younger one unconcernedly, setting to work. "Gramps, about three months maybe."

"It's exactly three months and ten days today. And it's not worth it."

"Then," I said, turning the mike chiefly toward the younger man, "I guess you know the firm's section head—Nemuro—head of sales. He must have showed up here a good many times."

"No, I haven't heard of him." Adroitly, he lifted the tank, which he had tipped to an angle, on to the board scarcely twelve inches wide that spanned the ditch beside the road. There he gave it a strong push, and taking advantage of the natural incline, steered it with his hands and his body as he rolled it along. "In any case, even when customers changed to Dainen from the old wholesaler we had nothing to do with it."

"When was that?" I said with unexpected emphasis, temporizing by pretending to be choked with cigarette smoke. Involuntarily my vocal cords tensed. "When was it that business shifted to here?"

"Must have been last summer . . . we got a day off at the time of the change-over and went swimming in the river. A kid was drowned."

He answered casually, and did not particularly seem to be holding anything back.

"July, was it? Or August?"

"Probably July, I guess."

Supposing it were July, that would be about the time the husband, as the new section head, was doing all he could to get the M Fuel Supplier to change its affiliations. Or perhaps he had been promoted section head because he had been successful in these maneuvers. One way or the other, his efforts had borne fruit, and now the place was going ahead doing business with Dainen Enterprises. If the situation were the opposite and the maneuvers had ended in failure, with no contract being signed, that might have had something to do with his disappearance. However, that wasn't the case. Again, I had wasted the battery of my tape recorder to no purpose.

Somewhere in the distance a metallic explosion sounded, reverberating on either side of the hill in long drawn-out echoes. Perhaps it was the backfire of some heavy-duty motor. I flipped the knob on my tape recorder and followed behind as the younger man expertly rolled the tank along.

"About the business . . . is there someone who's pretty well informed . . . about how matters stand?"

"Well, now," replied the younger man without interrupting his work, "there's an office girl inside but . . . well, she's new. Besides, she was teased by that ugly fellow and now she's on the verge of tears. You won't get much out of her."

"What ugly fellow?"

"Oh, some thug, I guess. Some deadhead with pull in the red-light district on the river."

We had arrived in front of the storehouse at the end of the roofed garage. With the help of the older one, who had followed along behind, in one movement he lifted the tank he had been rolling up to the top of the already three-tiered pile. Judging from the sound of steel striking steel, the tanks must have been heavy indeed.

"Want a peek inside the office?"

"It feels like it's going to be cool tonight, doesn't it."

The older man, manifesting no interest, humped his back and with a shuffling, dance-like gait went back toward the street.

"You go through here and it's to the left," said the younger one, sniffling, indicating with his chin the space between the storehouse and the building. Then he looked up at the viscous, black sky, and grasping the fingers of his worn gloves, followed after the older man.

Just as I had been told, the office was directly to the left as I emerged from the narrow alley. There was an ill-fitting sliding door of cypress in which the cracked glass window was mended with Scotch tape. It smelled like drain sludge dissolved with gasoline. Or else it was the stench of chemical fertilizer soaked in the urine of domestic animals. The sliding door screeched on the twisted rail. Hesitantly, I opened it enough of a crack to let me through, and instantly a blanket of hot, sticky air pressed against my face like a moist rag. It was obviously a fuel supplier's office.

Directly in front of me as I entered was a partition screen

that rose to the ceiling. A bus schedule, printed in two colors, was fastened to it with thumbtacks. I glanced to the left, along the partition; there were only a single old-fashioned office desk and what seemed to be a lookout platform. Above the desk rose the head of a girl in a page-boy bob, and under it two white, well-rounded knees were clamped tightly together.

"Good evening," I said in an unnecessarily cheerful voice, passing my hands over my arms and shoulders as if to rub in a little warmth and purposely not looking at the girl's face.

"Good evening."

For an instant I doubted my ears. What came to me sounded exactly like a man's voice. Yes, quite definitely, it was a man's voice. It had apparently not come from the girl at all, but from the other side of the partition wall. A disturbing voice. Probably the customer I had just heard about. As I advanced, there came into my field of vision, in the following order: steel shelves, white window curtains that made the vulgarity of the surroundings stand out even more, plastic artificial flowers of indeterminate variety, then a television set, a round table covered with a silvery vinyl, on it the familiar ashtray with the four beckoning cats, and then, in the background, a fellow with a receding chin I remembered having seen.

It was him!

Him . . . there was no mistake, it was him, the self-styled brother. He had taken off his coat, and his black necktie hung loose. He smirked at me insolently, his forehead beaded in sweat. In his shirtsleeves, his thin, crooked shoulders did not show to advantage as I had expected they would. What could he be doing, turning up in a place like this? A damned unamusing game. The key to catching a stray dog is to act as if you're completely absorbed in something else, and I intended to do just that for the time being. I would have the stray dog I was after, crawling to me with wagging tail from a completely unexpected place.

"AGAIN TODAY! The day's pretty full of coincidences. I'm amazed." He didn't appear to be in the slightest. "I'm absolutely flabbergasted. I thought you'd sniff this place out in due time, but, well, don't stand there . . . take a seat."

"But why didn't you say anything if you knew of the place?" Immediately I snapped on the tape recorder. "You know, it was written right there in the application for investigation: you were supposed to give me any and all information."

"But you surely don't expect me to report every single item, particularly those that have no informative value." Nonchalantly, he called the office girl: "Be so kind as to give our guest a cup of tea."

The girl silently rose from her seat. The wrinkled skirt, charged with static electricity, clung to the roundness of her buttocks.

"If you didn't think it was necessary, you should have informed me beforehand, including your reasons."

"Intolerably uncivil young lady," he said, ignoring my words, crossing his legs and shifting to the side. "Makes you feel funny. Everywhere I go, as you can see, I'm the villain. It's funny, if you're treated like a villain long enough you get used to it, and in the end you get to feel like one."

"What are you doing here, for heaven's sake?"

"Well, well. What indeed?"

"You're here just by accident, of course. Somehow, as you were walking along, you just happened to notice . . ."

"Chalk one up to you," he said, smiling cheerfully and snapping his fingers. "No, it's not a joke. Your suspicions are not unfounded. Actually, the various threads are all tangled up—in a very strange way."

"If that's what you think, you'd better explain."

"If I could, I wanted to pretend I didn't know, but . . . Well, when you looked at me in that dreadful way, I couldn't help myself. I'm prepared to tell you everything—the whole truth. Frankly speaking, I came here for a shakedown."

"A shakedown?"

"Yes, indeed. Not so, miss?"

The girl took the kettle from the kerosene stove in front of the shelves and poured the hot water into a large earthen teapot, her body rigid. She made no attempt to answer. But her very silence was a more eloquent response than anything she might have said. The brother continued in a calm tone.

"I notified them beforehand so they would have a check ready today. The boss took off and I have no idea where he is. This girl here sticks to her story that she doesn't know anything about anything. Listen, miss, such an obvious tack won't do you any good. You hold me up a day and I'll just increase the interest by that much. Right. You'd better tell the boss just that. I've plenty of time, and until further notice I'll be dropping in every day."

The girl, admirably expressionless, placed on the table two cheap teacups, which she had filled to overflowing with a weak brew, and returned to her seat in silence. Evidently she had more spirit than one would have thought.

"Cold chick. Don't get the wrong idea. A blackmailer's a scoundrel. All right, but the person who's being blackmailed here is just as bad."

There was something extraordinary about his casually announcing on our second meeting, without batting an eye, that he was engaged in blackmail. What a nerve. I didn't have to believe everything, but faced with this amazing situation I felt like a fly in a glue pot. I thought to myself that if I got the opportunity I was certainly going to show up this man for what he was. But I had never dreamt that my hope would materialize in this way. Somehow or other the fellow was an accomplice of my client. A privileged resident in forbidden territory. There was no need to let someone take him by the tail. Was he putting on a show? If that was the case, why? Or, could it be that he just liked to boast of his own wickedness? If so, he knew too little of his adversary.

"I'm sorry, but if things go on like this I can't continue," I said, although I realized it was to my disadvantage to become emotional. "In the first place, there seems to be some doubt as to just how serious the application for investigation is."

"Why do you say that?"

"Well, there are too many things kept secret. Even I didn't really expect much from a country fuel supplier's like this. It's pretty shabby if it's a crucial spot."

"But when a blackmailer and extortionist enters the picture . . ."

"Yes . . . and furthermore, if he's a relative of the missing man . . ."

With his eyes raised, he brought his lips close to the teacup and noisily sipped his tea. "Just as I thought, you're pretty clever. But even a monkey can fall out of a tree, as they say. This isn't monkey business. When it falls right on me it's too much. Where do you want me to start explaining? What about my purpose, for a starter? Why did I ever scheme up anything like blackmail?"

Suddenly he was interrupted by the blast of a horn. From the breathless wheeze of the engine, it must have been a rather antiquated three-wheeler. Apparently my car was in the way of the loading or unloading. Then came the sound of voices from the outside. —"Sorry, but would you move your car, sir." When I began to walk in the direction of the door, the brother stood up too and quickly slipped on his suit jacket. —"Well, I'll be leaving too for this evening." Wearing his jacket, he instantly became a black wall again. As he passed by, he suddenly reached out and tweaked the girl's nose. The girl sprang to her feet and the chair jumped with her, but even then she did not even try to cry out. "No, don't forget to give your boss the message." Taking up his overcoat from the corner by the screen where he had left it, he hung it over his arm. "I don't care how many days you take, but the interest goes up proportionately."

A breeze had sprung up. The sky rippled like a black blanket. I exchanged meaningless civilities with the men at the storehouse and then got in my car. The brother too stood waiting in the most natural way, his hand on the handle of the other door. I turned on the ignition. He had barely got in when I stepped hard on the accelerator, but as luck would have it the cold engine simply sputtered and I was helpless, paralyzed.

"No, you're quite wrong," the brother continued nonchalantly. "The main thing is the means, not the end. Why blackmail? I need money too. Right? Just the investigation expenses I pay you come to thirty thousand yen a week. I can't make do with just what my sister got when she quit her work. Thirty thousand yen a week. Let's see, that comes to one hundred and twenty thousand a month. I could never make ends meet with an honest job, could I."

"By the month? Are you planning on continuing the investigation that long?"

"Of course I am. I've been at wit's end for half a year now. I don't suppose that even you have the self-confidence to think you can clear things up in a week, do you? I can and will get the money. For a year if I need to. It'll be an endurance test."

He chuckled, and I was perplexed. Continuing the investigation—the very fact that I might not do so had already put my digestion out of kilter. The white heads and the black heads in the matchbox. The much too obviously happenstance meeting in the parking lot in front of the Camellia coffee house. The even more obvious encounter at M Fuel Supplier's. The blackmailer's confession. I could see things better if he remained a strange shadowy character. Though he had come rather into the light, he was still a strange character indeed. I wanted a smoke. Was it to go on forever? The rhythm of the motor was irregular. I pushed in the choke and turned on the heater. Could I have been mistaken? Supposing, on the client's side, she and her brother were seeking the truth, the facts in a precise sense of the

word, and not merely displaying a superficial harmony of
views. Well, I would see her again with that in mind. I had
to get the boundary lines of the map absolutely clear. But
only after first establishing whether—I remember her running the tips of her bloodless fingers along the corner of
the table, with the bookcases and the lemon-yellow curtains
in the background—whatever she was intently waiting for
was indeed one and the same thing the brother was looking for.

Perhaps he had read my thoughts, for he gave a little
chuckle and said in a self-deprecatory voice: "I can't forgive
him. I can't stand his self-centeredness. Even a thug, when
he wants out, pays for it. Unless he plays by the rules, how
can I forgive him? He said something about my sister's not
being a complete woman. He's some kind of queer. Let him
be, I don't care, but if he doesn't follow the rules . . . One
way or another, I've got to get him back and make him
smart for it. My sister's a mess, damn it. Do you understand?"

Unfortunately, I didn't. I automatically stepped on the
brake at an oncoming truck with its lights on high beam.
Why should he make him smart? Would finding the husband and bringing him back to her make him smart? I
wondered. Didn't he realize that such thinking would result
in hurting her? The road was swallowed up in the cloud of
dust left by the truck. They say the thief who pretends he's
been robbed is the cleverest thief.

"Well, no, you are the only one I can rely on. I'll take
the responsibility for the expenses. If it comes to that, I'll
ship off to Vietnam. I'd make roughly two hundred thousand
yen on one trip if I could get thirty men to sail with me. You
have a little more time now, don't you?"

"YOU'RE HIGH, I'm afraid," she said calmly, leaving the chain on the door. She could tell surely by just looking.

"I had something I wanted to ask you. It had to be tonight. Something I've got to know for the investigation tomorrow . . ."

Hesitantly, she removed the chain and, leaving me waiting in the vestibule, dodged away into the room, pushing up with one hand the wisps of hair at the nape of her neck and straightening with the other the collar of the coat she had slipped on over her nightgown. Involuntarily I found myself searching the vestibule floor for a man's shoes. At the same time I kept my ear tuned toward the other room. What was I suspicious about? I wondered. I was disappointed in myself. Was he or wasn't he there? A husband pretending to be missing, who in fact was quietly hiding away in his own house.

The idea was fantastic, but it was not altogether unfounded. Who would ever say the first thing this late in the evening, "You're high, I'm afraid"? She's the employer. Wouldn't it be natural for her to expect the latest report right off . . . the way any employer would?

No, that was not the truth. It was an evasion. One look at my apologetic attitude and she would have realized immediately that she could not expect very much in the way of news. First of all, if it was urgent news, good or bad, there was always the convenient little device of modern civilization called the telephone.

When she returned, she was wearing dark-blue slacks and a tan cardigan of a heavy-knit yarn; her hair was arranged in the usual way, but the freckles under her eyes were unpleasantly conspicuous and made her a completely different person, one with a hard, brittle air. I experienced a mood of warning, as it were. I began to talk falteringly in justification of my visit.

"Actually, I want to talk about the incident of the matchbox last night. I put it down in the report, but from the Camellia coffee house I got, to put it succinctly, exactly nothing. But, I find it a little bothersome, if I remember correctly, that you said something to the effect that the matchbox was found together with some old newspaper, wasn't it? Do you still have the paper? It would help if you did."

"I must have it, I suppose, but ..."

I restrained her from going off in search of it on the spot. The unpleasant paradox of having my explanation itself be a kind of justification caught in my throat. The first thing I wanted to know was the date line of the newspaper. Was there or wasn't there a relationship between the matchbox and the paper? Practically speaking, there would seem not to be, I thought. Yet I couldn't say for sure until I knew what the date was. I was a bit worried. What was the reason that the matchbox was so badly worn? That the vitally important Camellia coffee house had produced nothing at all was most significant. I could pose any number of hypotheses, but they were full of contradictions. Like a broken compass, they pointed now in one direction, now in another. But even broken, a compass was still a compass, wasn't it? If I could just get some sort of hint, I felt it would point somewhere pretty exactly for me.

"I'll go and look for it right away," she said, turning her joined hands at me and nodding in agreement at my words, which seemed to flow endlessly, and after a very slight pause, which I might have overlooked, had I for a moment been inattentive, she added: "Will you come in and wait?"

Again, in the lemon-yellow room, I seated myself in the same chair as the one I had occupied the evening before; I rubbed my hands together briskly. She had apparently just turned the stove off, and a little warmth still lingered along with the smell of kerosene. While there was no reason for it, I somehow had a feeling of indifference. I was indifferent to myself. When I thought about it, I had the impression that a chill had begun the instant I had sat down in the chair. A feeling as if, in sitting, I had pushed something aside—something like the shadow of a mist-shrouded tree, melancholic, unresistant, faint. I thought perhaps it was the husband. For the first time, however briefly, I felt the reality of him. At once he returned to the flat, depthless photograph that had submissively stood aside to let me sit, but in my heart there was a cold feeling of shame, slowly spreading, like a drop of ink suspended in water.

I had grown very suspicious. I would begin by reviewing again the same things I had seen on the preceding evening. First the ashtray on the table. Fortunately, it was clean and dry with no telltale traces that it had been recently used. I filled my lungs with air. There was indeed a faint smell of cosmetics mixed with the odor of kerosene. There was not the slightest smell of cigarette smoke. Beneath the table throw there was only a transparent gloom. Next, my eyes shifted from the curtains to the bookshelf and from there farther along to the telephone. Then a little piece of paper pinned to the corner of the curtain caught my eye and brought me back to the reality of his nonexistence. With my ears cocked for any sound in the next room, I walked softly round the table to investigate. Seven digits had been written on the slip with a ballpoint pen. Small but precise numerals characteristic of a woman. It was a telephone number I remembered seeing . . . the very one printed on the label of the Camellia matchbox. Yet why was I not surprised at the discovery? Rather than that, the chill within me deepened. Although I tried to reject the possibility that she knew something, hadn't I foreseen precisely that after all? Apparently she had not been purely a victim all along.

Suddenly I felt defiant and churlish. Well, why not? I said to myself. No one could drive me out of here now. The final trump card of the different matchsticks was mine and, furthermore, either way, my adversaries were a gang of black-mailers. But what terrific cold. —"You really must be drunk, I fear." —"It's probably because I'm sobering up." —"Well then, what do you want here?" Hmm, let me think, what was it then? Until a little while ago I had so much I couldn't handle it all, but . . . I stopped my car in the street down there and looked up at the lemon-yellow curtains, hesitating a while—should I get out or shouldn't I? I smiled to myself as if I were looking into a mirror when I turned off the motor. Stealthily mounting the concrete stairs . . . The inter-laced black and white rectangles of the landing were illumi-nated like an altar by an all-night light . . . But, no, I was empty-handed, as much so as if I had been fleeced by some highway robber.

—"You must be drunk, I fear." That was so wrong. On the contrary, I'd been sitting there about two hours with the heater on and the window wide open, my face exposed to the night air and its icy thorns. Then, the fault was with the saké, not with me. Nobody else but her esteemed and thoughtful confederate had stood me to it. If she wanted to blame it on someone's evil intent, then blame it on him.

What was that noise? It seemed to come from the vicinity of the kitchen just beyond the curtain. I could not help but hear the faint clinking of glass containers among the muffled noises . . . that peculiar, fricative sound of air and liquid. I did not realize that beer produced such a forlorn sobbing.

"You have nothing against a bottle of beer, I suppose?"

That had not been my reason for coming here especially. What had caused me to drop in at the microbus in the dry river bed was rather hunger. When I thought about it, I realized I had had only a bowl of noodles since morning. It did not mean there was a lack of eating places, for there were apparently some old-fashioned restaurants, of the kind seen but rarely now, near where you come out on the main street in the third ward. But my appetite was piqued by the possibility of getting somewhat closer to the real character of the self-styled brother in the microbuses.

"In the red-lantern stalls, you're pretty well known, I hear, aren't you?"

"You've got sharp ears. I expected as much."

There was not the slightest timidity in his arrogant laugh.

"When I took the examination for entering the company I wasn't very good. Why was it only in collecting information that I got top marks? You find it strange? We have to be examined. For instance, I took a turn around a department store with the examiner, and then I had to say how many girls were wearing red skirts or what the color was of the shoes the man who was making a purchase at the tie counter had on. But the test on collecting information was a little different. Certain situations were given and I was supposed to answer true or false in each instance: whom one should ask, what should be asked, and how it was to be done. I answered everything with a cross. The examiner questioned me, of course, on why I did that. So I told him. The technique of collecting information is hard, but it's even harder to stop up your ears."

The road between the cliff and the embankment of the pear orchard was as black as a tunnel, and I had the illusion of having forgotten to turn on my headlights. I felt the steering wheel wrenched by a sudden gust of wind. The rising ground and the pear orchard ended in a short, abrupt slope. The road formed a T with the bank. At once I could see a cluster of lanterns. But it was quite different from what I had imagined. The various cars were not in a single line, nor were they connected by strings of lights, and there was no music, no commotion as in a fair grounds. Red lanterns dangled saucily in the wind, and on the side of the broad, dry river bed several little buses, their gloomy, pale mouths open, were scattered here and there in a semicircle, irregularly spaced and facing in different directions.

But it was the view of the opposite side of the river, separated by the bank, that caught my attention. Until now it had not been visible, being concealed by the levee around the pear orchard, but a broad expanse of naked terrain clear of fields, houses, and woods was brilliantly illuminated from three sides, like a stage, by great projectors three feet in diameter. About a hundred yards to the left a field office and a number of mess buildings, like blocks of light, were brimming with animation; it was as bustling as a miniature city. Bulldozers and power shovels were biting into the front of the hill. Patterned stripes cut by the caterpillar trucks ran in and out among them. A dump road connected the highway with the work site. Suddenly the sound of a siren howled across the river bed, and the roar of motors and machinery that had reverberated through the black sky slipped into silence. Three trucks set out in the direction of the work site from the mess hall. Every truck, it appeared, had more than enough relief teams, and as I watched the ceaselessly lit area I realized that there were three reliefs working round the clock. "Now is the period of peak activity," he said, raising his voice. I drove the car into the dry river bed.

When we drew near the site, I could sense an even greater animation than I had from the river bank. They had placed boards for shelter from the rain over the folding doors in the back of the buses, and the rear alcove was turned into a counter where, standing up, one could consume boiled vegetables, saké, hot dogs, and noodles. Behind the counter was a gas range and, at the moment, what appeared to be a cook with a white apron was seated cross-legged on a rather thick cushion. As the counter rose only about four inches from the floor, one had to bend rather low to pick up the food. There were six miniature buses in all—I wondered if the fuel supply workers had lied to me or whether only tonight there were fewer than usual—and three of the six had a number of customers. In the center of the semicircle of buses, three girls and two men stood round a bonfire burning in a drum. The men wore low black boots and quilted jackets with wild vertical stripes and tawny waistbands—no doubt about what kind of crowd they were. The girls were swathed in heavy coats up to their ears, and the tops of their heads were all one could see. Their vulgar hairdos, teased by the blaze that spurted from the drum, were quite appropriate for a dirty mattress. A young man, carrying kerosene drums in both hands, clumped heavily over the stones from the direction of the river. Perhaps he had gone for water. It might be a good idea to disinfect the boiled vegetables here with a little saké. He went straight toward the bus at the right-hand edge of the semicircle. For some reason no customers were there nor were the lanterns burning.

Indeed, as the fuel supply workers had said, he seemed quite well known. In the livid light, the cook's yellow, conspicuously dropsical, unshaven face displayed a nonetheless friendly sloe-eyed smile as he wiped his hands on his apron.

"Pretty chilly."

"What about a cup of warm saké?" said the brother invitingly.

"I'll take noodles, since I'm driving."

I was not bluffing or being particularly obstinate. I had the tendency to arouse a policeman's antipathy more than was necessary. Perhaps it was because in some way our professions seemed to have too many points in common. For my own protection, I should try not to hurt feelings. If I could drink I would, of course. But if I did, I would have to leave my car here. If tomorrow, with the trouble of coming all the way out here again, I could still make the money seem right on the books, well, that would be another story. Supposing, for instance, that by coming again I was clever enough to put my hands on M and be able to get hold of some conclusive testimony . . .

He put the noodles, newly made, which were cleverly wrapped around his chopsticks, into the boiling kettle, carefully stirring them so they would not spread out. The characteristic smell of lard and flour stung my nostrils pleasantly.

"Say, if you're cold, I'll borrow a muffler for you." He turned to the unshaven cook and said: "Give him something."

I had refused before the cook began searching the shelf behind him, whereupon the brother said hurriedly: "Come on, give us a raw egg on the house." He stood up abruptly and walked off in the direction of the bonfire. The men there greeted him as they stood with their arms stiff by their sides, their legs apart, their shoulders back, only their heads bent. He simply nodded. Apparently, he was the leader. But the girls disinterestedly waved their hands. He was apparently more than a good customer. Well, the men at the fuel supplier's had described him as a tough. This self-styled brother met the description.

"You in the same gang as that guy?"

"No, only a friend."

The cook looked down at his hands; perhaps it was my imagination, but he seemed to be faintly smiling. With his empty hand he vigorously began to scratch his crotch. In an instant my appetite left me—but, well, his hand was on the outside and the crockery had apparently already been boiled. I would stand it this time.

If it were true that the brother was a thug, my intuition about him had been correct then. It was ridiculous of me to expect straight information from him. Of course, he had said he was going to use blackmail to get the money to pay for the expenses of the investigation. If the point of the investigation—or better, of its failure—was to give him an alibi for his wrongdoing, then it was a kind of vicious circle and he was not lying. There was no longer any room for me to do anything. As long as the investigation fee was not paid with a fake check or a rubber check—any money would do—it no longer had anything to do with me.

Standing round the bonfire, the brother and the men were talking casually together. The three girls remained aloof and indifferent. I had the feeling that somewhere, some place, I had witnessed precisely the same scene. The air holes pierced in the body of the drum shone green. A red pillar of flame spewed up into the black sky, scattering a fiery dust. The chill penetrated my body from my feet upward. I could not feel much of a wind, perhaps because we were cut off by the embankment, but directly above my head the sky resounded. It was like the static of a radio turned to full volume on no wave length of any station. A thousand shriveled fingers were strumming on the twigs and branches of the copse on the hill. I measured with my eye the position of the veneer partition with its tiny door beyond the unshaven cook. It seemed closer to the driver's seat than to the center of the bus. Indeed, if that were really true, there would seem to be enough room for a mattress. I flexed my toes in my shoes, trying to get the blood moving.

"Can you get it inside?"

"No, not here," said the cook, skillfully scooping up the boiled noodles in a metal net and shaking them firmly to drain the water. He glanced at me probingly out of the corner of his eye. "Better drop it. You can't call them women . . . coming to work in a place like this."

"Well then, isn't there any other kind of fun?"

"We just rent the room. It's that guy's regular pad. Unfortunately, I puke just seeing a female cat. I asked a doctor . . . said it was diabetes. I hate having a cat in heat hanging around: I want to club it to death. You can't club people to death. What a laugh. Well, anyway, I wish I *had* had diabetes when I was young. Once I let those bitches in here, I'd never get out of it. These eggs here are raw and over there they're hard-boiled. Besides, whether or not I let them use the place I have to pay squeeze money to the syndicate. So what's the difference?"

I broke an egg in a bowl and warmed my palms on the hot porcelain.

"You think it's interesting? Well, I wonder. I suppose I should thank my lucky stars if I can finish paying off the monthly installments by the time I shut this place down."

"Are you in business with your own car?"

"It hasn't been the paying work I expected.. There's a traffic law, you know. The Road Traffic Control Law, or something—anyway, even if you've got a car you can't park just anywhere you want to do your business."

"Pass the pepper."

"After all, there's a limit to places like this—a dry river

bed or the seashore—places where the traffic laws don't apply. Besides, I'm on the lookout for a spot that'd be good for business. If I don't give my contribution to the syndicate, I can't open up. That's the trick of it."

"You've only got to get in the good graces of some syndicate some place, don't you?"

"It's eat or be eaten. Nobody leaves me alone. But I'm not saying this because you seem to know that guy. He's not too hard on me. And he's not always plucking the goose. Like he promised from the first, we depend on each other. Well, when I finish my monthly payments and if the car lasts that long, I'm going to the seashore in the country this summer and try to get something."

The brother had said it was useless to look for traces of the husband here. The Dainen Enterprises' director and the young clerk Tashiro had stressed the same thing. And now . . . Having checked M Fuel Supplier with my own eyes and walked myself through F— Town, I too was inclined more and more to the same idea. It was the M Fuel Suppliers alone that connected F— Town with him. It was merely a commonplace, ordinary relationship of wholesaler and retailer. Yet, inasmuch as it was commonplace, the appearance of the brother on the scene posed something of a problem. Other than being the brother-in-law of the missing husband, he had no business connection with him. He was indeed connected through F— Town with the husband and that constituted a link; what in heaven's name could it mean? Was this just one more of his "happenstances" he was so fond of?

Of course, the thought occurred to me that the link between F— Town and the husband and the other link between F— Town and the brother were quite unrelated and independent, but then, the plot was too close to perfect. Since my client was the sister of the one and the wife of the other, both links possessed an inseparable point of contact. Maybe, by having joined the two links perfectly, I was producing more of a fiction. Even the director of Dainen Enterprises and young Tashiro had joined the accomplices by agreeing with what the brother had said, and it was conceivable that they might escape to some zone of safety out of my reach. If I wanted to follow the chief's advice, I should take the attitude that I was getting money to stop my ears, not to listen for something; to close my eyes, not to look around; to nap the day away, not to accomplish anything. Well...

For the second time the siren howled like a frightened calf. Finally the brother came back, biting his lower lip, grinding the pebbles under his feet, and making no attempt to hide his anger. The cook at once filled a steaming mug which the brother snatched up.

"Big joke. They told me there were only three girls. Are they up to something or what?"

"You know, nothing but colds just now," replied the cook, shaking his head vehemently left and right. Taking up a green kettle with an enamelware handle, he filled to the brim another mug he had set out.

"Colds? Come on!" he laughed nervously, turning slowly to look at me. "Bad people do bad things. I give up. I let them do business for a fixed fee—those old bags, nobody else would have anything to do with them. Why don't they really work hard and earn enough money and get out of the business? They're too old to be protected by pimps."

Suddenly the ground trembled and the darkness reverberated. Work had begun. The figures of several men came running down with short, dancing steps, outlined against the band of light that followed the horizon of the embankment. The relief gang was coming, probably after a quick bath or a swallow of saké.

"There are only three girls? What are you going to do?" This time, before taking the mug in his hands, he bent over and took several preliminary sips. The light that gathered in the bottom of the thick cup glistened. A ray shifted to his jaw, tracing a moon-shaped arc.

"Is this supposed to be your business?"

"Business?" he inquired, sniffing slightly and smiling bashfully. "Well, it's different from a robber or a highwayman, I guess. When you have a permanent building it's a bother, of course. But according to the law it's okay as long as you move around by car. Interesting, isn't it? The philosophy of the law here is a respect for human life in case of flood."

"Was it quite some time ago that you started here?"

"Right after the work began. About last July, I think."

Last July? Let's see. Yes, the month M Fuel Suppliers became connected with Dainen Enterprises. The points of contact between the two links had strengthened. But were there two links, really? On the contrary, wasn't there probably only one? In August the husband had vanished. I should make up my mind and ask about this; what in heaven's name can the basis for shaking the fuel suppliers down be? No, if it were simply a question of asking and getting an answer, he would have exposed the trick himself long ago. Then should I pull in the net of the investigation with him as the object? But if I deliberately closed the net and if I caught my client along with him, then what? I was going round and round in depressing circles.

"Come on, I'll have a drink too. It's okay if you park around here, isn't it? I can't stand this cold."

"Very commendable precaution," he said, looking up at me cunningly. "As far as this place is concerned, you can have confidence in me. You can park here, if you want. There's no ceiling, but I control this side of the embankment practically like my own house."

"Maybe so, but . . . ," the cook muttered inaudibly, sliding the mug in front of me.

"What do you mean by that?" Grimly the brother took him to task. "For Christ's sake, what are you griping about? Come on, speak up."

"I'm not griping," he replied indolently, swinging his body. "And don't say I am."

"Well, speak up then. What's the matter tonight?"

Like a bored monkey, the cook continued to swing his body.

"Hey! Look! Looks like the customers made a damn good start this evening. Maybe a little too good."

"A fine business."

"Really, haven't you heard anything?"

"What?"

"Well . . ." For the first time the cook seemed worried and raised his bloated face, looking directly at the brother. "I'm talking about the rowdiness around here tonight for some reason. Just when the construction chief is absent."

"Come on, let's have exactly what's on your mind."

"I don't know. It's just hearsay. There are no girls around and I'm relieved about that. But, what I don't like is that the girls aren't the only ones taking off. If what they say is true, they must be a bit short-handed, aren't they? Of the young boys in your gang only three showed up this evening, didn't they."

"So what's the rumor? I'm asking."

"Everybody knows. Well, since it's about you, I count on you taking the necessary precautions. Boy, it's really bad when *you* don't know what they're saying."

Our bus was the only one where customers had not gathered. In the space of several minutes, as we were absorbed in our saké, around each lantern four or five men—at the most seven or eight—welled up, as it were, out of the darkness and formed a human fence. But I did not sense a particularly uneasy atmosphere, perhaps because I did not know the usual pattern. Everyone of them, in the same hunched-over stance, merely pecked at his dish of boiled vegetables and gulped down his saké. If I were forced to find something worrisome, it would be, I suppose, the number of men wearing work helmets, although they were off duty. But even so, the helmets might be simply to keep out the cold. The five silhouettes, their stance unchanged, stood quietly around the bonfire. It looked as if no one was still bantering with the girls.

Suddenly, a sharp tensing appeared in the muscles of the brother's throat. He seemed to stretch his neck forward slightly, like a bird ready to strike, his hands still clasping the unfinished glass of saké. Abruptly he strode off in the direction of the bonfire. He walked on the balls of his feet, trying to keep from stumbling on the stones, and his back, swallowed by the larger darkness, was no longer like a wall.

"What's going to happen with those guys?"

"He's not a bad fellow," said the cook, beginning to shake his head in his usual fashion and taking another cigarette. "He's not bad, really, but he's not likable. And since he knows a thing or two, he's even worse. It was especially stupid for him to let the guys in the bunkhouse order food and drink on credit. He's been giving hush money to the head clerk in the office, you know. He gets him to take what they owe on credit out of their salaries."

"I see."

"It's no fun leaving home to work in a place like this. And when you can buy on credit, even though you know you're going to regret it later on, like it or not, the purse strings manage to loosen."

"But it's funny to go on a rampage because of that, isn't it?"

"Well, you see, payday's after tomorrow—the fifteenth. What about another sniff?"

"Well, okay . . . for cash . . ."

Placing his cigarette on a corner of the range, the cook chuckled, and when I looked, drawn toward a section of the frame of the chassis where he had glanced, I could see from where I sat the whole scene in the river bed mirrored in an oblong, curved reflector. The five shadows around the bonfire were all looking into the fire, motionless and quiet, like people in a picture. The cook continued speaking as if to himself.

"No, he's not a bad sort. Look, all these girls are rejects. The men living on a work site like this would fuck a hole in a tree, otherwise they'd take to their heels with soft pricks at the sight of them. The girl with the biggest clientele beats a mare's cunt. She can take on a hundred men, and right in the middle she snores away. The story goes she's put away a hundred thousand yen."

"Does he have some enemy?"

"Look," he lowered his voice abruptly, "I don't like the

way the customers are gathering a little before the corner over there . . . pretty strange. Don't you think it's funny? I don't like it . . . this rumble. The one on the embankment must be a lookout . . . there."

"Aren't you getting carried away?"

"I don't like the way those guys are pouring it down. One after the other the buses are emptying. They'll be coming over here soon."

"Somebody's pulling the strings from behind the scene, don't you think?"

"I . . . I don't know."

"Somebody local, with influence . . . a councilman, for instance."

"Do you have a badge? If you do, say behind your lapel, get rid of it quick."

Yet I couldn't take it all seriously. Even if something were brewing, it would doubtless be at most some unpleasant words or a demonstration. A demonstration would mean, in other words, that the brother had enemies. The most important thing now was to get some clue as to who the enemy was. There's a beginning and an end to every cycle. In any labyrinth, if there's an entrance there's got to be an exit. Well, do what you can and do your best to make a good showing.

It may have been the cold or the tension, but I felt no effects from the saké. Or was it that, since the glasses were so thick, I had not drunk so much as I calculated from the number of glasses piled up? I asked for still another; perhaps this was the fourth.

Finally, three workmen came swaying over to my bus, their arms linked together, and got in. The three were weaving because two of them were supporting on either side the already dead-drunk one in the middle, who was wearing a padded kimono. The big fellow on the left with a square jaw glanced sharply at my face and my chest, but said nothing. Was he, in fact, looking for a badge? Between shouts of "Saké! Saké!" the man in the padded kimono sobbed in a choked voice. —"You! I'm on the list of missing persons for investigation. Ha, ha. My wife's put in a request at the town hall for an all-out search." —"Never mind," said the smaller one, a friendly, balding man, patting his sobbing comrade on the back, "if you start worrying about that, there'll never be an end to it." —"Saké!" shouted the man in the padded kimono, still grumbling. "What's a missing person? I'll send a letter. If they knew I was working that'd be the end of the welfare checks. That's what I told my wife. Try and put up with it for two years and not say anything. Be patient, and just imagine your husband's dead. You can scratch along on welfare." The larger fellow spoke in a quiet voice that carried surprisingly: "Don't worry, it's not your wife's fault. It's the interference from the city government. Interference from the government wanting to cut off your welfare checks. The head of the gang came with the search papers and threatened her. Look at this. Shall I contact city hall, or will you write a letter yourself? Don't worry, we're witnesses that you're here. Look, you've got hands and feet; it's a big laugh, you being missing. You are right here, aren't you?" —"Right, I am. Ah ha!" —"You're right here," chimed the big fellow and the small one from either side. —"Saké, damn it! Still, do I have to write a letter? It's a plot in the government office. Never mind. I'm so sad. I can't play my favorite pinball any more. I'm missing. I get drunk all the time."

The cook raised his thumb in a kind of signal. When I

glanced in the wide-view mirror attached to the frame, the brother, standing in the darkness midway between the bonfire and the buses, was beckoning intently to me with his hand. I slipped out of the bus quietly so as not to be noticed by the three men. It was hard walking because of the irregular stones peculiar to the river bed. Or maybe I was drunker than I realized. The brother took hold of my arm as if inviting me into the darkness and suddenly began to walk away at an angle, breathing hard.

"Things look pretty funny. You'd better be taking off."

"Funny? In what way?"

"I don't know," he replied, glancing around restlessly. "I have the feeling they're plotting against me."

"I just saw a funny drunk. On the verge of blubbering. Says he's being investigated as a missing person."

"Such stupid morons, really."

"I hope the fuel supplier's boss is not in the plot."

Dropping my arm, he stopped an instant and peered at me. "Stop imagining such nonsense," he said. "I've been telling you. It's a waste of time to come snooping around here. Money comes and money goes, but thirty thousand yen is still quite a bit. I'm asking you . . . get out of here quick."

"But I'm drunk."

"Being drunk's nothing, if those guys really get rough. Don't be silly," he said. At that very instant a gang of men —seven or eight of them—who had slowly cut across near the bonfire, as if to move among the buses, suddenly changed direction and surrounded the fire. It was unclear who struck out first, but suddenly the dark silhouettes turned into a tangled mass. Two of the girls shrieked and began running toward us. But they were captured at once. More reinforcements came, and the girls, like sacks of potatoes, were hoisted on shoulders, several men to each one, and carried away into the darkness beyond the circle of buses. Their cracked voices, shouting abuses and calling for help, came wailing back. Instantly, outcries and sounds of things breaking exploded from the bus nearest the embankment, drowning out the girls' screams. There came the sound of breaking glass; and thrown rocks, clearing the bus, landed at my feet. Around the bonfire the situation had changed, and the three men had already shifted to counterattack. A screaming workman had been dragged in between them, something was swung over his head, and he was thrown violently down. He was kicked—possibly his arm was broken—and he fell writhing on the stones of the river bed. Several workmen knocked over the burning drum and, brandishing flaming pieces of wood, set upon the three men. But the reactions of the three youths were instantaneous and smooth. Apparently, they had got hold of some effective weapon, for they at once put their attackers to retreat. The workmen then began to use the fire to attack the buses. They began throwing the burning brands through the broken windows. They launched an attack against the three youths by throwing rocks. The three returned the fire, but victory went to the larger numbers. Little by little the young men gave ground; by that time all the buses had become objects of attack. The gas range had been dragged out. The gas tank had begun to send out flames. Pieces of crockery were smashed one after the other. But the destructive power of the mob could not be totally effective, for the force of the attacks was dispersed by the seductions of the saké and cheap whisky, which were now being swilled greedily, and, of course, by the two women who had been carried away down the river bed.

"I'm going to talk things over with the office people,"

yelled the brother, threading his way through the confusion and beginning to run. Just as he was crossing the semicircle of buses, he was overtaken by several workmen and thrown to the ground. Nevertheless, I made no move toward him. As I intently observed the black, agonizing, squirming mass, I did not regret nor did I feel particularly responsible for not extending a helping hand.

But, strangely enough, a bus came to his aid at the critical instant. The one situated at the deepest point in the circle —one that had been able to escape the destruction, relatively speaking, while everyone was concentrating on drinking, since the saké was flowing—suddenly started up its motor, and with the back doors wide open, spewing forth goods and workmen indiscriminately, kicking up a shower of pebbles, abruptly began to move.

Naturally, everyone's attention focused on the bus. They followed after it, throwing rocks, some of them trying to jump through the windows. The little bus, that seemed barely a single horsepower at the most, sounding like a metal saw, with its last ounce of power clambered up the embankment, shaking off its pursuers.

The driver's bold act had provided an opportunity for escape to the other buses as well. Waiting for the moment when the workmen had thinned out in pursuit of the escaping bus, the remaining buses started their motors together and went dashing helter-skelter full speed over the dry river bed.

Out of the corner of my eye I caught a glimpse of the brother creeping in the dry grasses below the embankment, his body stooped low to escape his pursuers. Then I too made a dash in the direction of my car, which had fortunately escaped attack until now. Suddenly I remembered something important I had forgotten. The husband's diary. I had asked for the diary, and he had said he would leave it at his sister's place tomorrow. I felt I should have once more confirmed the promise. But the brother's figure had already vanished. Doubtless he had succeeded in escaping. Then a rock suddenly came flying toward me. It struck my shoulder blade as I ran along as fast as I could, my head bent, but I felt no pain at all. Rather, it was as if my throat were strangled by my gasping breath. Obviously the effect of having drunk so much. Yet I felt surprisingly calm. Without much trouble I found the key and was able to start the motor in an instant. Now most of the workmen were gathering in a noisy band at the slope that formed the inclined plane of the embankment, the only road for cars that connected the river bed with the embankment. Just then the last two buses, which had been slow to get away, attempted to break through, charging along, their horns blaring, their headlights turned up. Somehow one got away. But the other, in its hurry, slipped its gear and suddenly halfway up the slope lost speed. Unresisting, it was turned on its side by the attacking workmen and then laid on its back at the foot of the slope. The inclined plane of the embankment was illuminated in bold relief by the headlights over an area of some twenty yards.

A white pole perpendicular in the dry grass was pregnant with meaning, but I did not know of what. Against the background of the embankment, the group, fused together in the dark, swarmed over the bus, its wheels spinning. If there was an agitator, he must surely be there among them. If only I could recognize his distinctive features, the opportunity of discovering the brother's enemy—provided he actually existed—would be most propitious. I could hear higher-pitched shouts and the sound of breaking glass. The motor

stopped and the lights went out, and there remained only
the glow of the burning embers that lay scattered here and
there in the area where the drum had been. Some men lay
motionless on the ground where they had fallen; some were
crawling around; others, like somnambulists, staggered and
reeled by the edge of the water—perhaps drunkenness, perhaps some injury. Anyway, with the bus overturned, the road
had been left unobstructed—a stroke of luck. My car, of
course, was not even half the size of a microbus. If I made
the slightest mistake in strategy, the fate I could expect
would be much the same.

With my headlights off, I deliberately made a wide cir-
cuit around the river bed. Three young men from the gang
came running toward me in search of help, but they were at
once overtaken by the attackers and roughly thrown to the
ground and dragged around. Or perhaps there were only two,
not three.

I let them pass without interference. I had greatly reduced
my speed, but even so, the car trembled violently, as if it
were undergoing some durability test, rattling as if it would
soon give up the ghost. If it went into a ditch or had its guts
torn out by some boulder, that would be the end for me.
Presently, I was headed straight into a clump of willows on
a slight rise. As I had anticipated, I encountered another
bunch of rampaging men. It was the gang that had made off
with the girls. I slowed down even more, watching for signs
of pursuers approaching. When I had sufficiently pulled
away I accelerated abruptly and with my foot clamped on the
gas I turned hard on the wheel and made for the foot of
the embankment. I was pursued by the threatening sound
of the motor; it was as if someone were knocking it to pieces
with a sledge hammer.

Somehow, it turned out well. Almost all the pursuers, unwilling to miss the ceremony in progress with the girls, had withdrawn there. Since my headlights were turned off, I did not know exactly what kind of ceremony they were enacting. My imagination went to work and I envisioned smooth hunks of meat suspended on hooks in a butcher's refrigeration room, skinned and carved up. There was no light, but in front of them stood a great candlestick and they were filled with a tense feeling of solemnity. Thanks to the girls, my car was ignored. When at last I arrived at the embankment, I turned on my lights. Suddenly my whole body stiffened, my shoulders and legs began to shake, and it appeared darker to me than when the lights had been off. I shifted into high, and although my foot had the accelerator to the floor, the car moved no faster than a hand cart; the back of my head tingled with an unspeakable fear. There was a smell of burning. The hand brake was not completely released. I turned on the heater and left the window open. For the first time, I felt with relief the weight of inebriation between my eyes.

THERE WAS still no sign of intoxication in her expression. With her shoulder she brushed aside the curtain that served to partition off the kitchen and entered the room with an affectedly light, girlish step, her weight borne forward, carrying over her arm a man's raincoat, on which she had placed a folded, used newspaper and on top of that her free hand.

Evidently she had made short work of putting on her make-up. The neat, velvety-soft color of her skin and even her freckles had restored her usual freshness, and her hair had been brushed. Perhaps the attempt to conceal her real face was because she had a woman's consciousness of being seen, or it might on the other hand be a manifestation of caution. But even so, the effectiveness was open to question. This woman became more transparent by using cosmetics, and she could easily be seen through. A distant dream village enshrouded in mist. Before I became what I am now, my breast was filled with yearning for it—a remote village that seemed lost among the trees, where I remember spending several days. But precisely because a picture frame was attached to it, it seemed a landscape, and because I was convinced it was a landscape, it became transparent. If the frame were removed, the mist would be quite ordinary. Insofar as it could not be touched with the hands, it was no different from a wall of concrete in its nontransparency. Don't be deceived. There was still no evidence that she was not an accomplice. Suddenly for no reason my ears were pierced by the weakened cries of the girls in the river bed, and the hunks of meat, cut into pieces, oozing a dark juice, appeared like small moons deep in the mist.

Crossing in front of the bookshelves, she laid the coat on a corner of the table, and slid the newspaper toward me. She seated herself on the same chair as last night, although it was now in a somewhat different position, and the line of demarcation between the bookshelves and the lemon-yellow curtains now fell to the level of her right ear, as fragile as china, ruined with rough handling. I suppose some men would feel protective toward it, while others might be carried away by the desire to break it into pieces. Which type was the husband? I wondered.

"This is the paper."

It was a sports sheet folded once horizontally and further into four vertical pleats. There was a conspicuous worn spot although not the size of a matchbox. Suddenly red letters leapt out at me: Sword of Wrath Trounces Cutthroat. It was an article on professional wrestling.

"June fourth, is it? He certainly carried it around long enough, didn't he." Turning the page, I saw next a forecast of professional baseball. Under it, in large letters, appeared an advertisement for a cold medicine. On the upper half of the third page was the photograph of an up-and-coming singer next to a gossip column relating how things were going with his sweetheart or something to that effect. Underneath, divided into small boxes, appeared classified ads at a thousand yen a line: jobs, hotel guide, financials, apartments, and sundry others. The sundries, with the exception of dogs for sale, all dealt with venereal clinics and operations for sterility and redundant foreskins. Then, on the last page, horse- and bicycle-racing forecasts. Movie listings appeared side by side with radio and television programs. Underneath, again three bands of job advertisements. Only one was for a missing person, but it seemed unrelated to this case.

"Was it this worn from the first? Or have you handled it a lot yourself?"

"Yes, I have, but . . . ," she said, lifting her innocent, untroubled eyes from my hands, which she had been staring at. "You know, it was worn before I got hold of it."

"When was the last time your husband used his raincoat? I suppose you don't remember, do you?"

"He almost always used to leave it in his car . . . either as a precaution or because he was lazy. He used to say he'd be ready for the rain. If the person my husband sold the car to hadn't gone to the trouble of bringing it back, I probably wouldn't have been able to remember that there ever was such a coat, I suppose."

"Car? He sold his car? When?"

Unconsciously my tone became insistent. One question followed on another, but she showed no signs of confusion as she slid the tips of her fingers along the edge of the table, as if in doubt. "It was the day before . . . or two days before. But it was about a week later that the coat was brought back. It had been forgotten in the trunk, he said."

"But last night you said something altogether different."

"Did I? Strange, isn't it."

"I definitely heard you say the car was in the repair shop, you remember."

"Well, I meant that that was what my husband said."

"Your brother must know the whereabouts of the car. Why was there any need to tell such a specious lie?"

Had I gone too far? I wondered. Had I cornered my client in an untenable position? Well, you reap what you sow. I had not set this trap for her. The fence by which she had been cornered was no more an obstruction for her than wet paper. She gave a weak, abashed smile.

"It looks as if I have the bad habit of saying things on the spur of the moment. I wonder if I don't tend to be arbitrary. I've spent half the day since this morning searching the house . . . from the bottom of the book boxes to the sideboard. I've been going in circles, it's like a game of hide-and-seek. I have the feeling my husband's become an insect. I'll try putting honey on paper and slipping it under the bed." Her lips compressed and her breathing was agitated. Thinking she was on the verge of tears, I was the more upset of the two of us.

"You realize it's to neither of our advantage to hold back information. It's not only that you'll have brought me on a fool's errand, but also that it's a waste of your money. Now then, tell me, what sort of a man was the fellow he got to buy the car?"

"Very nice, really," she said, looking at me frankly, as if suddenly regaining consciousness. "It's not true that I hold back information. You know, if he's somebody connected with my husband's disappearance, either he'll tell us something or he won't appear at all. If I say nothing, the buyer's the kind of person nobody'd pay any attention to."

"What does he do?"

"He said he was a taxi driver."

"And what was the price of the car?"

"I guess about a hundred thousand yen."

"Was the payment taken care of?"

"Yes. He even showed me the receipt."

"I wonder if he was going to use that money to leave home on."

"He couldn't have done that. That's inconceivable." Suddenly her smooth, waxlike expression became severe and rough, as if sprinkled with sand, and lines of small white wrinkles formed around her nipplelike lips. Unconcernedly she picked at her tooth with her thumbnail. "Don't say such things. You've no proof."

"But proof is a part of fact, you know. What am I supposed to do . . . since you don't seem to have much taste for facts?"

"Well, I can't believe he'd do that. I suppose it's a fact that he did disappear, but the question is what was he escaping from, isn't it. It wasn't only from me. I think it wasn't from me at all, in fact. It must have been from something else, something quite different."

I was suddenly dejected. I placed my briefcase on my lap and opened the flap. "Be that as it may, shall I show you my report? As you say yourself, only worthless facts."

Predictably she shifted in her seat, and with a tense expression, at first hurriedly and then more slowly, began to read with the intent watchfulness of someone crossing a stream on a single log.

"Of course, the facts are like clams: the more you tease them the more tightly they keep their mouths shut, and there's no way to pry them open. If you try to force them out they die, and you've lost the shadow as well as the substance. The only thing to do is wait until they open by themselves. The same with this newspaper. Perhaps the key is hidden, and looking back later, you'll say: 'Ah, so that was it!' As things stand now, the newspaper's no help. Why was it together with the matchbox? There would seem to be a reason for that too. Generally facts are not where you expect them."

She raised her face from the report. She had until now assumed any number of different expressions, but this time it was a new one that I had never seen before. The rims of her eyes reddened and her frightened, entreating breathing was labored, as if, inhaling, she would forget to let her breath out. Her first words were inaudible; then after a moment, she said: "There is a relationship. Please don't misunderstand me."

"Bicycle racing or horse racing? Is that it?"

"No. The telephone number."

"What about the telephone number?"

"I really didn't mean to conceal it or anything like that."

"What number?"

"The same one as on the matchbox. Now where is it . . . ?" Her finger ran irregularly, restlessly, like an ant with a broken neck, over the Help Wanted columns on the fourth page. The finger of a doll, unarticulated, slender, pliant—even though she lied—a fabricated finger without the slightest flaw.

"You mean Help Wanted—Female Clerk?"

"No, not that. Drivers . . . Here it is."

Her finger had at length stopped. Driver Wanted. Best salary. No age limit. Bring statement for interview or send same. May live in or out.

The telephone number at the lower left of the page was indeed the same as that of the Camellia coffee house.

"I didn't lie, really," she said, shaking her head back and forth, as if desperately supplicating. "I have no idea why I didn't say something. Yes, you may be right, maybe I am afraid of facts."

"You don't have to justify yourself, I'm not a prosecutor or a judge. I'm merely your employee, hired for money. Furthermore, I give preference to the protection and the interests of my clients over facts. If there is some terrible fact, tell me, please. It's my responsibility to protect you from it. For heaven's sake, can it be that bad?"

"No, it's not. It's already been settled, anyway," she said, lowering her eyes. Abruptly she arose. "Can't I bring you a beer or something?"

"All right . . . just to keep you company."

At this point it served no purpose to concern myself with her health. She needed beer. I needed the one who needed the beer. I was fed up with unnecessary setbacks. She darted into the kitchen beyond the curtain like a dog unleashed.

"Yes, I might as well call the issue settled. I went myself to the coffee house and inquired. I was told that the owner was acting as an intermediary and had been asked by an acquaintance to hunt for a driver for a private car. Of course, they said that one had been decided on long ago. It wasn't unreasonable. After all, the advertisement had appeared over a month before."

When she came back with the beer, flakes of white froth clung to the corners of her lips.

"I wonder if he wasn't acting as a middleman all along."

"It so happens that an acquaintance of his from home wanted a driver who knew Tokyo, so he acted as middleman to find one. If it hadn't been some special case like that, the friend could have inserted the advertisement himself, I suppose."

"Yes, it does make sense."

Pouring the beer with the utmost care into two glasses, she smiled as if seeking my agreement and returned to her seat.

"Well, that's settled."

"What about that telephone number pinned to the edge of the curtain?"

"The number . . ."

"Why do you have it there?"

"Well, I . . ." In one draught she downed a third of her

glass. "There's no particular reason. I really don't know why I have it. I wonder why you're so concerned about it."

"You're the one who's concerned, I'm afraid. When I touched on the business of the classified ads in the paper, you were unusually upset."

"That's true, I suppose. I wonder why." She held her glass in two hands as if she was going to lift it, and her eyes looked as if she had recalled something out of a distant past. "Really, I wonder why. It seems that my story always goes wrong somewhere. But even facts are not all that dependable. It's all the same to me wherever he is, whatever he's doing now. The fact is he's not here. That alone is a fact. What I want is the explanation for it. Why did he go away? The problem is to explain that. That's the question."

"But there can be no explanation without some factual corroboration."

"Just a simple explanation's enough."

"Your husband's the only one who can provide that, isn't he. The most I can do is locate him."

"You're awfully modest, aren't you."

"Modest?"

"Why did you choose such a profession? I wonder."

"Is there really any point in answering that?"

"I'm fascinated. Just what is it when someone chooses something?"

"It's not very important. Usually as soon as a missing person's been discovered, he calmly goes back to his former haunts, as if he has suddenly recovered from some demonic possession. Motives or explanations are not so important as people assume."

"Have you ever dealt with any other case like this?"

"Of course, but generally you have some clue from the beginning . . . a specific girlfriend—almost all have girlfriends. These are cases that can be settled after three or four days of observing and collecting information. It takes money, and unless the subject of the investigation is already fairly clear no one would bring it to our office."

"Is that right?"

"Was your husband a sensitive person?"

"He was rather nonchalant about things, I should say. Even about his clothes."

"Was he compulsive?"

"Whatever, he was an extremely cautious person."

"Don't be inconsistent. The significance is entirely different, depending on whether a given disappearance is deliberate or accidental."

"Anyway, it's a fact that he was enthusiastic about everything . . . amazingly so."

"What was he so enthusiastic about, then?"

"About everything. He was like a child."

"About cars . . . or cameras?"

"Yes. And he had a mechanic's license for fixing automobiles."

"Was he enthusiastic about gambling too?"

"He was fond of licenses. He had a kind of license mania, I guess. He even carried two driver's licenses—one for second-class trucks. And besides that, he was a radio operator, and electric welder, and a handler of explosives."

"Was there any relationship between the qualification for handling explosives and working for Dainen Enterprises?"

"Yes, I think there was."

"A very practical type, wasn't he?"

For the first time I understood the meaning of the library, which had eluded me before. Electricity, communications, machinery, law statistics, philology—all mixed together; and yet they were not particularly highly specialized works, but primers, or questions for national licensing examinations. Somehow it had been hard to coordinate my impressions about the variety of titles, but her expression "license mania" had clarified the whole thing.

"He also had a movie projectionist's license and a secondary teacher's license . . ."

"A strange character."

"I suppose he just had to be tops in everything."

"What was the latest license he was concentrating on?"

"When he disappeared . . . oh, yes . . . he said something about wanting to pass radio operator second grade. Whenever he had a free moment he was always tapping out something with his finger."

"Second-grade radio operator?"

"If he got second grade, he said, he could ship on one of the big merchantmen. If he did that he claimed he'd get three times as much salary as he was getting. He was always counting his chickens before they hatched."

"I don't mean to be impertinent, but about what was he getting with Dainen Enterprises?"

"A little over fifty thousand a month."

"Well, even a taxi driver would make that much, I should imagine."

"But since his strong point was mechanics, he worked as a commission agent with second-hand cars."

"I know. I already heard that from your brother."

"My brother? Have you met?"

"Curiously enough, we seem to see each other wherever we go. Actually, just before I came here, we had a friendly little drink together."

"That's very curious."

"He's a pleasant fellow. At the rate we're going, we seem to be meeting ten times a day. Oh, yes, before I forget it, he promised to bring your husband's diary over here for me tomorrow."

"A diary?"

"It's apparently of no value at all."

I observed her, trying to catch the slightest change in her expression when the subject of her brother came up. Her lips were slightly open, her brow knit. Was she confused, perplexed; or had misgivings about her brother suddenly come to her? But she just smiled mischievously, biting her lower lip.

"My brother's always taking people by surprise like that. That's the way he's always been."

"If I can read the diary, perhaps I can get some general idea of what sort of dreams your husband had."

"Dreams?"

"For instance, did he dream of the sea, or something like that?"

"My husband is a very matter-of-fact man. When he became section head he was very happy because he had somehow stopped sliding down the slope of life."

"But he did leave you, didn't he."

"It wasn't because of his dreams. He used to say licenses were the anchor of human life."

"Using so many anchors for such a small boat certainly puts him in the category of dreamers, doesn't it? If he didn't use them he'd float away."

She slowly returned the glass, which she had raised to her lips, to the table and fell into silence as if her thoughts were someplace else. Like a withering flower photographed at high speed, her two eyes hollowed as I watched her, her nose constricted, and even the color of her soft skin lost its vitality like an old chamois skin. I was beginning to feel a deep remorse for what I had said. Those to whom murder is legal are only executioners and soldiers on the battlefield; doctors have no right to practice euthanasia no matter how much they are badgered by the patient.

The clock on the wall told me it was one in the morning.

REPORT

13 February: 10:20 A.M.—Went to the library and checked a photo copy of the newspaper. Rainy days before 4 August, the day the man under investigation disappeared, were 28 and 29 July. But rain on the 28th had been forecast as cloudiness the day before, and since late in the afternoon there was a shower, he used his raincoat on the 29th for the last time...

My hand stopped writing and I closed my eyes with an unbearable feeling of weakness. It wasn't only my eyes; I wanted to shut off my nerves, my senses, my whole being. The reading room of the library was almost full, but it was almost as hushed as if no one were there. There was only now and then a sound of sniffling, of the turning of a page, of the shuffling of a foot. My nostrils caught the smell of the cheap wax with which the floor had been buffed.

Behind my closed eyes, all turned lemon-yellow. I could imagine the contours of her ear, bright with lemon-yellow, luminous with the light reflected from the lemon-yellow curtains. Lemon-yellow fragrance. Lemon-yellow . . . Ridiculous. Why not say banana-yellow or squash-yellow freckles? Yes, this was not a battlefield or an execution. I had no right to harm her by even so much as a hypodermic puncture. All that I could do was go on writing my reports. The client is always right. Even if he tells a lie, for instance, if he says it's the truth the truth it is. But facts were no longer necessary; it was even unreasonable to demand only motives and omit the facts. If I went on ferreting out facts, I could expect nothing but my client's despair. I keep circling at a distance round senseless facts, trying to explain the unexplainable.

Suddenly the student seated to my left, a girl, pushed her body against the desk beyond the partition between us, and leaning inward, slashed at a photograph with a razor blade. I too leaned forward again behind the partition and in embarrassment continued writing my report.

. . . it may be concluded. However, there is no evidence he used his raincoat that day. There is simply a strong possibility he did not, since in the week from the 29th until his disappearance the weather turned relatively clear and the temperature was quite high. We must consider that the said newspaper and matchbox (or the telephone number on it) had already been used before then. These facts demonstrate that we cannot deny that the disappearance of the man under investigation was certainly not unexpected and that there is a possibility he had laid plans and made preparations in advance.

THE GIRL next to me finished cutting up the picture. Tearing about an inch from the last page of my report pad, I quickly wrote a note: "I saw you. I'll say nothing if you come along with me. If okay, crumble this paper into a ball and return."

I folded the note in two and slipped it gently under the girl's elbow. Startled, she shrank back and looked at me, but I began to clear the top of my desk, oblivious of her. She opened the paper and began to read in a flustered way; at once her stubby nose and plump cheeks were dappled with red. She ceased all movement, she seemed even to have suspended her breathing. I patiently awaited her answer, savoring the moment like a piquant spice.

At last, she shot me a tentative glance. Her shoulders relaxed and she heaved a sigh. Rolling the paper into a ball, she flipped it back to me with the tip of her fingernail. Her aim was bad and it fell to the floor. As I leaned over to pick it up I looked up at her. I had the impression that below her thick-set ankles the flat-soled black shoes, cracked and worn, were somehow not capable of supporting her weight. Only the depression at the back of her knees created a shadow that was somehow feminine and clean. Adolescence drawing to a close, a time out of kilter, like catching a cold in the nose. She was apparently aware of my look, and the tendons in her legs tensed.

I picked up the paper ball and put it in my pocket, folded the photocopy of the newspaper, placed my pad and fountain pen in my briefcase, and stood up as if nothing at all had occurred. Without so much as a glance back, I headed across the overly waxed floor in the direction of the loan desk at a speed befitting a library. Having returned the newspaper, I looked only once in the girl's direction, but she had not yet left her seat, and only her eyes peeped over the edge of the partition as she spied on me. I raised my hand slightly as a sign, and, seating myself on a little bench in the smoking area between the reading room and the exit, I lit a cigarette. I had barely taken four puffs when the girl appeared in front of the loan desk, walking stiffly. Nervously she was watching for me outside and did not seem to see where I was. She quickly returned her books and picked up her coat at the cloakroom, and just as she was hurrying toward the door she recognized me, the rhythm of her step faltering as if she had stumbled. Immediately I arose from my seat and went to the door. The girl followed with slightly shorter steps, making no attempt to flee.

When I brought the car round from the parking lot, the girl was standing in the middle of the steps, buried in her coat collar up to her nose. I drew up to her and opened the window on my side; she shifted her briefcase and with an agitated step came directly toward me. Her nose was bloodless, as if squeezed between two glass slides. Her discontented expression had assumed a weird glow, perhaps because of the rush of blood or the cold. Only the green scarf that appeared above her coat collar was strangely gaudy and made one feel the inner pressure which propelled her. I half opened the door.

"Let me give you a lift. Which way are you going?"

"You mean *where* am I going?" Her voice was challenging and unexpectedly contained. "There's no use my deciding that."

Involuntarily I gave a forced smile, and she too contorted her features in a mirror image.

"Does that mean you're ready for anything?"

"You're a despicable person."

Suddenly I slammed the door in the girl's face. I put my foot on the gas; the tires churned up the gravel and the front end of the light car sprang up like a boat cresting a wave. The girl, abandoned, was dumbfounded, standing there as expressionless as a frozen fish.

I WAS standing around. Just standing around, outside of time, in front of the telephone at the corner of the counter in the Camellia coffee house.

"Is he dead?"

"It looks as if they tortured him slowly to death." The strangely excited voice of the chief came ringing from the diaphragm of the receiver. "Is anything wrong? Don't tell me you don't have an alibi."

"How could I?"

"Well, anyway, get in touch with the client right away. She's already called here three times since this morning."

"Where did you get this information?"

"The client, of course." Suddenly his tone changed. "Oh, do we get information any place else?"

"I was just asking. All right. I'll get in touch with her immediately."

"May I remind you once again that every one of us has to take the responsibility for his own complications."

"Yes, I understand. I'll show up at the office around noon."

I stood motionless. He was dead! I replaced the receiver and stood motionless.

By this time the police were in an uproar no doubt. I wondered if, in the investigation, my existence might possibly come to their attention. Supposing it did, then the extending ramifications of the inquiry would reach to the M Fuel Suppliers. The man in the light car. The man who claimed he came from Dainen Enterprises. The inquiry would shift to Dainen Enterprises. And there again the man in the light car would come up. So whether I liked it or not my presence would come out. But it didn't necessarily follow that this would mean trouble for me right away. First, I had no motive. And then, if they wanted a suspect there were lots of others. But if I could, I wanted to avoid getting involved.

Perhaps I needn't worry. There was no reason for the police to entertain the wild fancy that, behind the dramatic events, M Fuel Supplier's was involved. At this point, I was sorry I had not been able to establish clearly what he intended to use as blackmail.

And there was something else, something that was basically changed by his death: the funds for paying the investigation expenses were cut off. Perhaps my work ran counter to the fundamental wishes of my client—which would mean that the curtain would fall all too soon, doubtless within the week.

Yet, wherever did this feeling of being balked in my expectations come from? I wondered. I returned to my seat, and as I stirred my lukewarm coffee, I began to be invaded by the gloomy and sentimental feeling that I had only myself to thank. Perhaps it was a feeling of sadness for the dead man. No, that couldn't be. Beyond the black-mesh curtain lay, today too, the open-air parking lot, bleak as a head cold. If I remember right, yesterday about this time he had called to me from the second pillar there, his oily smell spreading like a gelatinous sap, especially from his stiffened shoulders. It had begun then, a prickliness like hives, created by my awareness of him and even now not in the least quenched.

If there was anything at all strange, it was perhaps a variation of my impression of his pride which became arrogance. Definitely my client had paid her money to retain me; she was my employer. But she usually made eyes like a begging dog or else flashed her servile smile as if she somehow felt guilty. At such times, in order to make her feel at ease, I would smile servilely along with her, thinking that people were like that. I would show her I was willing to handle her dirty wash. Since within our hearts we secretly want everything in existence to be dirty, we always recover our self-respect and discover light and hope in life. But her brother made no effort to show the slightest bit of this wretchedness.

From the first, he did not try to conceal that he was covered with filth, but he stubbornly refused to let me see that filth, much less to touch it. He was quite different from the type of customer I had had up to now. It was true that he was a strange fellow, but I could not claim to be unprejudiced. When I realized this bias, I had the feeling of being able to recall, however, dimly, that I had overlooked—no, had actually tried to overlook—something. His earnest expression, for instance, the time he asked for my opinion of his "sister as a woman." Or his thoughtfulness in details, as when he ordered a free egg from the owner of the microbus stall. If I hadn't clung so to my preconceptions, if I had kept myself at the same level with him without deciding from the first that he was a wall obstructing my view, he might have surprised me by changing from a wall into a door, through which he might have invited me in.

Of course, the wall was no more. And with it the possibility of a door had vanished too.

It was already too late.

What he didn't want to say as well as what he perhaps did want to say, as he crawled away through the dry grasses of the embankment like some broken umbrella, was now non-existent. The puzzle ring forcibly taken apart has no more relation to a puzzle.

I glanced at my wrist watch. It was 11:08, but even if I entered that in my report sheets, there was nothing to write after it. No, it was not only this moment; I had practically no hope of anything to report on, even after an hour, three hours, or ten hours. Harassed by these thoughts, I downed the remaining coffee and rose. But what should I do? Was there something to be done? Again I stood there indecisively . . . just standing, like the girl I had left behind at the foot of the library steps. Being dragged around in the dark, deprived of freedom, ignorant of one's whereabouts or objective, was vexing enough, but suddenly being picked up on the street with neither explanation nor excuse was really insulting treatment.

Behind the counter the proprietor of the shop was buried up to his neck in his newspaper. The sulky waitress, her elbow on the cash-register stand, held to her ear a small radio, the volume low, as she stared vacantly outside. As she stood there her lips were contorted in an unconscious sneer—was she laughing at the radio program, or at me standing there so indecisively, or was she laughing at something else? Following her gaze, I looked out of the window and saw something terribly unnerving. A group of three men, apparently salesmen, were passing by, discussing something among themselves. Each carried the same kind of briefcase under his arm, each had an expression filled with hostility. Beyond them, the endless flow of cars. And beyond that, the parking lot—something that stirred my memory irritatingly, like the edge of a broken molar. Digits . . . seven digits at the bottom of the parking lot sign. The telephone number!

The matchbox label . . . the Camellia coffee house . . . the classified ad in the old newspaper . . . the little piece of paper pinned to a corner of the lemon-yellow curtains—the telephone number had appeared repeatedly on all of them.

At length I recovered my sense of time and, however faintly, my memory of the map. Without removing the radio from her ear, the girl pulled the lever of the cash register. "Do you take reservations for the parking lot over there?" I inquired, raising my voice.

Instead of answering, the girl merely looked sideways at the proprietor. The newspaper sank to the counter and the man raised his eyes. When our eyes met there were sparks. He spoke in a high-pitched voice, ill-suited to his growth of beard.

"Full up, I guess. Sorry." Ignoring me, he lowered his ill-humored face to the newspaper.

"You've got a lot of free time around here."

"What's that?" snapped the girl grimly, taking the radio from her ear, overly reacting quite as if I had played some trick on her. Though I was bewildered, my imagination was unexpectedly stimulated. My resentment was washed away: it was as if I was under a hot shower, grasping my penis . . . an urge for release that made me want to laugh like an idiot, welling, pulsating within me. Perhaps I really did laugh— just a little. With my eyes fixed on the girl's face, I walked around the register and grasped the receiver. I dialed Dainen Enterprises and asked to be connected with the young clerk Tashiro.

—"Tashiro? I want to thank you for yesterday. . . ." When I identified myself, he had a moment of confusion before responding. For an instant, I suspected he might have already heard about the death, but apparently not. As soon as I recalled to him his promise to have a drink with me, his tone changed to one of friendliness and intimacy—perhaps he had little experience in sharing confidences like this with strangers. I stared at the thick line of hair behind the girl's ears. "Let's meet at S—— station . . . where you drew the map for me yesterday . . . hmm, the spot where you were supposed to meet Mr. Nemuro. . . . I'd just like to check it out. Let's say seven o'clock, all right? Then, most important, I'd like you not to forget to bring along the . . . uh . . . those special nude shots." The girl hastily brought the radio to her ear, but there was no sign that she had turned it on.

"After I've thoroughly gone over the nudes again, I'd like, if possible, to interview the model as soon as I can. . . ." Of course she could not hear the suddenly businesslike answers, so my exchange sounded quite meaningless. Then I lowered my voice and added—no, rather than an addition it was probably my real purpose: "Another thing I'd like you to think about: how would you go about blackmailing a fuel supplier? An ordinary fuel supply place . . . hmm . . . a retailer. I'd like your advice. What kind of blackmail is there? Think about it till we meet."

I had the feeling of having tweaked the girl's pug nose—as far as that goes, the proprietor's too—with my conversation. Of course, from where I stood I could not make out her nose very well, for it was hidden by the wrist holding the radio. The proprietor's face remained buried behind the newspaper and he was motionless. Immediately above his head the poster of the South American coffee plantation was comical, for one could suppose, in place of the lighting fixture discolored with dust, a sun scorching men and plants to a tawny yellow and gilding the distant mountain range. I could hear someone walking on the floor above. Slowly the sound of steps drew near, stopped directly over my head, and at the same rate withdrew again. I no longer stood motionless. When my surprise had passed, I regained my balance, like surf beating in on the shore, then returning to its original water line. His death had hurled the wave unexpectedly high, washing over my feet, sweeping away the slender line of road along the verge of the cliff, but when the water subsided there was nothing new, nothing to make much of a fuss about. In the final analysis, the burden I was charged with had simply been reduced to the limit of the first thirty thousand yen. The obligation remained for me to carry on the investigation five days more. Yet I could not even guarantee that her attitude too might not suddenly change, that she would not simply propose a cancellation, saying she would like me to drop the matter this very day. That I was somewhat reluctant to do; it would leave an unpleasant taste. But as far as business accounts were concerned, it would be by far the best way. The chief would be satisfied too, I supposed, and would probably make no objection.

It suddenly occurred to me that this might be the real reason I was putting off telephoning her. I was overcome by a strange sense of shame, as if I were looking at myself peering through the wrong end of a pair of binoculars in front of a mirror. Though I had not been asked and I myself was unaware of having done it, had I unthinkingly signed a receipt for over thirty thousand yen? Ludicrous. Among my fellow investigators nothing would be considered so ridiculous. As the chief was always saying, a client's not a person; think of him as food to stuff our craws. We're a bunch of syphilitic curs.

Actually, binoculars, if used in a certain way, give the effect of X ray. For instance, you can read more expressions and characteristics from a single photo of a given person than you can by meeting him face to face. First you set the photo up vertically and if possible remove the ears and darken the background. Adjust the source of light so there is no reflection. Then kneel at a distance about twenty or thirty times the length of the diagonal of the photo. No, you don't really have to kneel, but the picture should be at eye level. Use binoculars with a rather narrow angle of vision and a magnifying power of about fifty times. You can fill in the background any way you will by your imagination; and any trembling of your hand, rather than being detrimental, will actually help in lending mobility to the expression. At first you see only a magnified picture at a distance of about a yard. You've got to keep at it at least ten minutes. Then about the time the strain makes the eyeballs feel hottish, an ordinary photo suddenly begins to take on a three-dimensional aspect and the skin becomes flesh-colored. When that happens, you've got it. You concentrate fixedly without blinking and you strain your eyes to the point of feeling pain. It's as if your stare cannot be endured, and the eyes in the picture, or the corners of the lips, twitch spasmodically. If it's a side view, the face will seem to look askance at you; if the face is looking directly at you it will avert its glance and repeatedly blink. Next, as if nerve tendrils were stretching out and commingling in the space between the picture's eyes, its lips, and other elements of expression and your own, you begin to be able to read what lies beyond the expression as if it were your own mind. What is most important is that you see private things, things that are never exposed to others. (I had tried it once before going out, and I would never have overlooked the missing man even if I were to pass him on some escalator going in the opposite direction.) He —the husband—bit down hard on his right inner molar, projected his lower lip and half opened his eyes; his eyes moved unstably around his feet at a thirty-degree angle, and his feelings, not once ruffled, as usual carefully combed and held in place with oil, now rose up threateningly like the fur on a cat's back in the face of an enemy. For an instant it *was* the husband, with a forlorn expression he had never exposed to anyone. The method was an original technique of observation I had thought up myself, and when I saw that among my fellow investigators it was rather well thought of,

I was quite pleased with myself. The chief thought differently. He thought any enthusiasm, as such, stupid.

Of course, ideally, the time of observation should be at night. And you've got to spend at least two hours at it. Furthermore, have an imaginary meal with the subject; be his superior and issue orders; be a colleague and listen to his complaints; be a subordinate and be reprimanded. If it's a question of a woman try and sleep with her; if it's a man be a woman and try and get on friendly terms. But I had not exerted myself to this extent with the husband. Something other than procrastination hampered my zeal, and I could do nothing because the fault lay with my client herself. As for me, the real motives of my client, and not the whereabouts of the missing husband, were by far the more suspicious and offensive element. Even more, my suspicion that the request for an investigation was a feint for the purpose of concealing the husband's whereabouts had not been entirely erased.

And yet, the brother-in-law of the missing man had died, the one who had beclouded my view, who had scattered the seeds of suspicion like wind-blown pollen. The sky had for some time been rent by a strong wind, and after a long interval a frail sun was streaming through rifts in the clouds. And so, again, I attempted to look at the husband's picture upside down.

THE PHOTOGRAPH lay with its head toward me. Again I was at the window of the parking attendant's shack. "Yes, eighty yen," he said indolently. "I don't want the change," I said, throwing down a five-hundred-yen note . . . and on top of it the picture. The conspicuously uneven hair line, which he had apparently not had for long, had not yet grown sparse.

"There's something I'd like to ask you."

The old man had placed a blanket over his knees, and on it lay an open comic book; his lips moved incessantly. He pushed his preadamite glasses up on his forehead, and his reddened eyes looked suspiciously back and forth at the picture and the five-hundred-yen note.

"Say, have you got a brazier going under that blanket? It's bad for you, you know. Your eyes are so red because they're irritated by the gas."

"No, it's electricity. Sorry . . ."

"Then it's too dry."

"I've got the kettle going."

"Well, it's entirely off the fire." I laughed pleasantly, making my voice cheerful, and pushed the five-hundred-yen note closer to the old man. "I wonder if you don't remember seeing the man in this picture. Maybe quite some time ago . . ."

"Why?"

"We're looking for a stolen car," I said at random. From the upside-down picture I suddenly sensed something aggressive. My decision, which until now had been to treat the husband naturally as the victim, began, surprisingly, to waver. There was no basis for assuming that he was a victim, and there was even a fifty-fifty chance that he was an aggressor. If I let my imagination run wild, he could actually be the one pulling the strings behind the brother's killing. No, such detective-story events rarely happen. If it were a question of a game in a sealed room, the mystery man would have to sit in the chair right next to me; but in the actual world he would camouflage himself and conceal himself quietly beyond the horizon. Be that as it may, it seemed that this evening I would have to spend some length of time getting reacquainted with him through the binoculars. Even if it was too late, the leading man is the star after all.

"A stolen car, you say?"

"Not necessarily. I mean, maybe it was one that had been in an accident." I gave in at once to the old man's expression, which was like a rusted lock, and placed three more hundred-yen coins on the notes. "What's the proportion between the monthly customers and the casual ones who use the parking lot?"

He looked indecisively from the enticement, which had increased to eight hundred yen, to the window of the Camellia, thus unwittingly revealing his real concern. He replied: "We have only the five-car space in this row open to casual customers."

"Well, it's pretty uneconomical to sit here all day for five cars."

"Oh, I don't know. If you're at home all you do is sit around all day in front of TV drinking tea."

"Don't be bashful . . . Take the money."

With a hand that seemed encased in a snake-skin glove, the old man unconcernedly scooped up his liberal, if unexpected, windfall. "Besides this row, by renting the monthly tenants' eight spaces that are always empty during the day, we can take care of casual customers. It's pretty good work for an old fellow on retirement. I've got rheumatism and my legs are pretty stiff, so I can't complain. I get cigarette money out of it."

"Even so, there're a lot of cars parked. Almost the same ones as when I looked in yesterday. Are they all monthly?"

"The two rows over there are all by the month."

"Strange. There doesn't seem to be anything around here that really looks like an office, and as for the monthlies to be parking here like this during the day, well . . ."

Perhaps I had touched a delicate spot. The old man's sluggish expression stiffened like weather-beaten rubber.

"Well, uh, it's cheap . . . I guess . . . that's why," he stammered.

"Or else, could it be that there're a lot of fellows whose business it is to use the cars after dark?"

"I don't know. I've no reason to pay such close attention to things like that."

"Anyway, do you recall having seen this man?"

I picked up the picture and slipped it into my note pad, which I returned to my pocket; again the old man's face took on an expression of relief. Immediately I took him off guard.

"Say, are you that afraid of the owner of the Camellia?"

The old man's wrinkled eyelids, which exuded an oily substance, curled up and the red edges exposed to the air were brilliant. "Well, don't worry. In any case, I've been observed all along talking to you here. If you're asked just say something about being all involved with the picture of some fellow you've never seen before. Actually, maybe you know him despite what you say."

"I've been saying I *don't* know him!" He struck his knees angrily with the comic book. Seeing that he was serious, I began to feel that perhaps he was speaking the truth, though the dead brother had described the old codger as being a wily fellow. "Am I supposed to remember every single face I see?"

"There! Here's two hundred yen more. That makes exactly a thousand—a good place to stop. Shall we wind up the conversation too?" I followed the old man's rueful gaze as it avoided me, placing my elbow on the window sill; I tossed two hundred-yen coins onto the blanket over his knees. "I'm not going to tell a soul you've taken a thousand yen. You and I'll be the only ones to know. Well, be quick about it . . . speak up."

"What do you want me to say?"

"Does anyone take a thousand yen if he doesn't have anything to say?"

"You gave it of your own free will, didn't you?"

"The Camellia owner's watching us. But will he believe your story about earning a thousand yen for nothing?"

"I'll give them back. Then things'll be okay."

"Don't force yourself. What kind of people keep their cars here? From what you've said I only know they aren't people who live in this area, but . . ."

"You're just guessing. Who said that? You left your own car here, didn't you?"

"I'm talking about monthly customers, and you know it. It wouldn't be especially strange for people to leave their cars during the day if they worked in some neighborhood shop and didn't have a garage. But since you're an honest fellow, you're at a loss for an answer. And furthermore, you said you didn't remember every single face you saw. That's proof the customers—monthly or not—are not all that unchanging. When I glance around right now, it seems to me there are quite a few cars that weren't here yesterday, aren't there?"

"Say . . . ," he gasped in a voice that was hard to catch, as if he were stifling a fit of coughing, "I hope you're not from the police."

"Forget it. Do detectives pay for secret information on someone whose identity is unknowable? And furthermore, a thousand yen means serious business."

"Serious business? What are you talking about? Every now and then the Camellia owner makes it possible for me to buy a racing ticket and play the pinball machines. You won't know what it's like to be old until you're an old man yourself. Even my grandsons copy my daughter-in-law and grumble to my face about how dirty I am."

"I won't do anything to obstruct business, I promise you."

"What do you want to know?"

"I'm on the trail of the fellow whose photo I showed you."

"Somebody said the same thing yesterday. Oh, yes . . . Seems to me he was an acquaintance of yours, wasn't he. Really, there's a lot of fellows going in and out of here. A lot of them don't want their names . . . or their faces . . . known. I've already had two strokes and I'm a little feeble-minded. I've got a loose tongue. So I don't look at faces or try to remember names any more than I have to."

"If it's hard for you to talk just tell me where I can inquire ... that'll be fine."

The old man's troubled gaze, like a cornered mouse running around trying to find its hole, shifted in a triangle formed by me, the black window of the Camellia, and the burned spot in the blanket over his knees. He gave a short cough, plunged his hands under the blanket and then immediately withdrew them and rubbed them together. Resignedly, he wiped away the secretion from the corners of his eyes with the same finger he had used to wipe the dribble of his nose, and clicking his tongue, said: "Well then, please yourself. Try driving around here about seven in the morning."

"Sort of accidentally ...?"

"Yes, accidentally."

Same day: 12:06 P.M.—Visited Mr. Toyama, the man to whom the person under investigation sold the car he had been using until two days before disappearing. Toyama was not at home, but I was told that he was expected for lunch, being under treatment for a stomach disorder. I decided to ask if I might not wait for him a while. Toyama's house was not number 24, as my client had told me, but 42, and therefore it took me some time and pains to find it. Even so, I was obliged to wait. The silver lining to my cloud was that at least I reduced the waiting time.

It was a rather squalid corner of development housing. The fence was dilapidated. A '63 Corona was nosed into the narrow yard. Perhaps that was the car Toyama had purchased from the missing man. It was in excellent condition and the tires almost new. Toyama's wife is about thirty. Two children, two and four; both girls. In the yard there seemed to be something like a vegetable garden covered with vinyl—the whole complex revealed a thoroughly wholesome family atmosphere. For some time the sun had been shining and the garden was a pool of light. Since the temperature was such as to make me want to take off my coat, I declined the invitation to go in and asked if I might not sit on the verandah.

According to what Toyama's wife said . . . (at this juncture there were two short toots of a horn; Toyama himself had apparently returned).

Same day: 12:19 P.M.—Toyama's back. Since he seemed busy I took his deposition while he ate. Toyama's meal consisted of bread and a souplike mush. He complained that he had to build up his strength a lot, that he had to watch out for his stomach, and that driving a taxi was exhausting. But he seemed genuinely concerned about the circumstances of the missing man and was most cooperative in answering my questions.

The following is the dialogue that took place between us:

Q. How did you happen to buy the car from Mr. Nemuro?

A. Through a friend who had bought one previously. It had been highly recommended as being reasonable in price and the repair work was good. In fact, I considered it a good buy.

Q. Didn't you meet with Mr. Nemuro at the Camellia coffee house?

A (Somewhat surprised expression). Yes, I did. Just about the time I left my job over something quite insignificant and had been doing temporary work and fronting for some time.

Q. What is fronting?

A. Fronting is when you go directly to an office and stand in front of the door to get temporary work. As a general rule, big companies don't use the fronting system to hire drivers, but they do when they have to lay off a car because a driver's sick or absent. You can't ignore the loss. The fronters and odd jobbers are out to make money, so they don't pay any attention to the law and work a full twenty-four-hour shift. If you go round to two or three places somebody'll generally hire you.

Q. Does the Camellia have anything to do with fronting?

A (Slightly perplexed). I'm back at my old office and don't have anything to do with the Camellia any more, but—it's hard to say—some of the men are grateful to it because they don't want to do anything against their fellow drivers.

Q. I would just like to get some clue as to what happened to Mr. Nemuro. In short, was the Camellia a private employment agency for temporary drivers?

A. Yes, it was. Besides having good coffee, it opened up early in the morning, so naturally it was a place the drivers hung around. That gave the owner the idea of the employment bit, I suppose.

Q. You said the drivers wanted to make money. About what is the difference in earning power as compared to what a regular man makes?

A. To make up for severance pay, set salary, and health benefits, they used a commission system for temporary work: from forty to forty-two per cent of net income. If you work ten days a month you easily make forty to fifty thousand yen. I understand that those who specialize in temporary driving and know how to work tourist attractions, race tracks, and the big holidays make as much as a hundred thousand for three days' work.

Q. Pretty good work.

A. If you're young and unmarried and like flashy things, you don't often have it so good. If you get sick or have your license suspended, well, it's tough then, but if you can forget about tomorrow the world's yours.

Q. Were there a lot of fellows like that in and out of the Camellia?

A. No, in Tokyo alone the taxi drivers amount to about eighty thousand. That may be a lot, but out of that number only a few came, say, twenty or thirty men. And furthermore, sixty per cent of the Camellia men were temporary like myself. No matter how easy it is, a man doesn't live for ease alone, does he? Actually, those who used to work only for the money, though they looked carefree, gradually became depressed. You get in the habit of wearing first-class uniforms, the best shoes, and imported wrist watches, but in the end you get quarrelsome and irritable. After you've been a temporary driver for five years, you even look different. You can tell at a glance.

Q. Did Mr. Nemuro seem to notice the business behind the Camellia?

A. I remember having spoken to him about it.

Q. Are there other places like the Camellia?

A. Very probably there are. A little less than twenty per cent of drivers are temporary men. Just the other day, there was an article in the newspaper saying that some unlicensed agency had been raided.

Q. Are they strictly regulated?

A. They're in violation of the labor law. They're treated the same as crooks, and that's about it.

Q. Was the Camellia linked with some organization too?

A. I don't know. I didn't look that closely—and didn't want to.

Q. Can't we suppose the possibility that Mr. Nemuro was under some obligation to the Camellia or to some similar agency?

A (Surprised and thoughtfully serious). Well, Mr. Nemuro, if I remember correctly, was a division head in a legitimate business. If he was up to some shenanigans, then I could understand the obligation. Of course, there are all kinds of off-beat types among the drivers: men who used to be school-teachers, fishermen, priests, painters. It's hard work physically, but it's different from other work; the relationship between the men is not troublesome. It's a good job for someone who finds it congenial always to be his own master . . . no matter what crowd he may be in. But you can't have aspirations for the future. All year long you keep running for other people's purposes, and you get to feel pretty insecure, wondering where in the world you yourself are going to get. They used to have what they called pirate taxis, and they really were pirates. To some people on the outside they were considered regular men of the world sailing from one corner of the earth to the other, but they weren't at all. Such a queer profession . . . A street's a street whether it's a noisy main street or a quiet back one. And a customer's a customer, man, woman, rich or poor. The customer's usually a piece of baggage mouthing trivialities more than another human being. Every day you run around jostling hundreds and thousands of beings, yet you get to long for them as if you were running through some uninhabited desert. Since I'm a fellow that such a life appeals to, no matter how disgusted I get I probably wouldn't take another job if it was offered. You need that much more determination to plunge into this taxi business. If to start with you drive, say, a small private truck, you can probably get by by just shifting into another category of driver, but in Mr. Nemuro's case, it would be a little hard unless he had a real reason to do that.

Q. Supposing that he had taken the plunge. What about it, would there be a good way of locating him?

A. That's a hard question. Reputable firms do a

thorough character check at the time you take the job test, so the company wouldn't look askance at such an investigation, but if it was some place like the Camellia . . .

Q. Is it difficult?

A. Between them and the drivers there's a mutual agreement not to ask for names, to say nothing of one's past.

Q. Even if I explained the circumstances?

A. If the circumstances are known they protect their men all the more.

Q. Supposing you were still working for the Camellia, even if you were asked to give information would you refuse?

A (After a moment's thought). Why does the world take it for granted that there's a right to pursue people? Someone who hasn't committed any crime. I can't understand how you can assume, as if it were a matter of course, that there is some right that lets you seize a man who has gone off of his own free will.

Q. By the same reasoning the one left behind might insist that there was no right to go away.

A. Going off is not a right but a question of will.

Q. Maybe pursuit is a matter of will too.

A. Then, I'm neutral. I don't want to be anyone's friend or enemy.

"How BLUE it is!" exclaimed the uniformed schoolboy in an amazed voice as he looked up at the sky. Following his gaze, his companions, taking deep breaths, their mouths open, narrowed their eyes as if abashed.

"Boy! That's really blue!"

But with the deepening of the blue of the sky, the wind increased, and the boys held down their flapping coat hems with the briefcases they were carrying. With their free hand they grasped the brim of their caps and leaned into the wind, waiting for the railroad barrier gate to rise. Directly to the left of the crossing stood the interurban station. The ticket puncher's box was higher than the street by only four concrete steps. Right at the top of the stairs was a newsstand, and on a projecting shelf newspapers and weekly magazines covered with a thin sheet of vinyl were set out side by side. A middle-aged woman with a thick turban around her head was struggling with hands, arms, and even her breasts to hold down the fluttering vinyl. The sky sparkled metallically as if dusted with aluminum, and across it clouds like lightly strewn cotton floss scuttled from the northwest toward the southeast. The sun slanted to the right and all the shadows lay perpendicular to the road.

In the sky, the clouds were sailing at full speed; on the

ground the wild rush of irregular pieces of paper caught the eye. It was unbelievable that so many could be scattered over the road. Of course, one never thinks of streets as being clean. But this was the first time I had seen wastepaper up-staging the scenery. Some were white, but most of them were weathered to the color of dead leaves and, having lain in windrows for some time, were covered with dust. Now the papers came dancing over the tracks in the middle of the street. Somehow they did not rise more than two yards from the ground, weaving and frisking between people and cars, again and again repeating their complex movement. They cheated one's expectation, caught one by surprise, suggesting the swimming of certain kinds of fish. By them one was made aware that air was matter. Just as they seemed to be gliding smoothly over the surface of the ground, they suddenly changed and rose upward, flew horizontally, plastered them-selves against the side of some car, then gently slid to the ground and pinned themselves beneath it. But when the car passed, they were no longer in view; unnoticed they had crossed to the other side of the street and were following along, puppylike, after pedestrians.

Naturally, a gritty dust streamed and whirled with the pieces of paper, so that the structure of the wind was like lace. It blended with the dirt of my car, which somehow seemed unexpectedly conspicuous. Perhaps it was not dust that swirled in whirlpools, but light which assumed the form of dust. The odor and taste of February dust suggests some-thing springlike. To me, the light today was the color of cream. In order not to stand out, I had not had the car washed for more than a fortnight, leaving it to collect dirt, but perhaps it should be cleaned the next time I stopped for gas.

The alarm stopped ringing and the arrow indicating the train direction went out; the barrier gate, wide for the four-track bed used for express trains, sprang up. The human wave, like the sand in an hourglass, flowed through the constriction, while the cars, fending the surge of people, slowly began to cross over. Before the head car had finished going over, the second alarm began to ring. I was the last car to make it across.

I turned left at the second alley. Fortunately, just beyond the first telephone pole a parking place was free. It was barely enough for one car, but by backing in at an angle I squeezed in. When I got out, I noticed that in the dust on the side of my car someone had written in big letters, FOOL—when I wasn't looking. They must have been in a hurry, for the last part was blurred. There were signs of a thick glove.

I returned to the main street by the way I had just come. In a self-consciously modern display window on the right-hand corner, a mannequin decorated in tones of purple, its arms and legs detached, was suspended by wires; and various articles of clothing, each different, for hands, arms, torso, and legs, were cleverly hung onto the body. There was no other decoration, and the figure was lined up against mirrors, which stood in a complex arrangement. It all stimulated the imagination strangely, giving the effect indeed that there were more than ten mannequins.

Three years ago the street would never have accepted such a display, but now things were different. Every place has its ups and downs. Then, it was merely a typical suburban street with a pinball parlor bleating out its old records and variety stores carrying only cheap goods, all of this centered around a grimy movie theater that showed three-month-old films. It barely sustained a main-street atmosphere. Perhaps there had been a change in the up-down cycle, for the whole city was gluttonously gobbling up more and more. In this neighborhood, the structural appearance of a main street had been established without too much unnaturalness. Actually, across the way, a supermarket with an underground garage was under construction. It was useless to argue back and forth that it was because she was farsighted or that it was due to a stroke of good luck. Anyway, I had lost.

PICCOLA DRESSMAKING

From a flute-shaped arm was suspended a thick, milk-white acrylic board, inlaid with thin aluminum strips that formed a kind of massive cursive script. I could not help but recognize that it was very stylish and individual. Piccola had evidently been my wife's nickname during her school years. I did not assume that the name bore an especially pejorative meaning, but also I definitely thought it had been given her not only in a good sense. My wife interpreted it arbitrarily as being a pet name, and carrying it further, a term of endearment. Maybe that quality was itself *piccola*. I was fascinated by this aspect of her. I still maintain it implies a virtue as well as a fault.

The door next to the display window was a single black acrylic panel. Like a mirror, it reflected the board fence around the construction site across the street, and in it appeared the image of my whole body. A disreputable character much more suitable to be sought than to be seeking, with his unsteady shoulders in the mirror, as if he had risen from a sickbed, and his ruffled hair tousled by the wind. But I could not comb my hair here. From where I stood the door was a mirror, but from the other side it was quite transparent.

I pushed the door open with my shoulder and squeezed in. A pleasant, lingering warmth tickled my nose, and despite myself I sneezed. It was not the heat alone but also the peculiar air, in which sizing and new dyestuffs mingled with perfume and steam from the hot iron in the basting room at the back of the shop. On the left were display shelves for samples of goods, pattern books, and orders already made up. Besides that, there were glass cases for buttons, little pieces of fur, and costume jewelry. On the right a round table, its artificial marble top supported by slender metal legs, stood between two ivory-colored chairs; and there was a sofa. The walls and the ceiling were covered with the same material as the curtain that cut off the basting room—a gay yet tasteful rough-woven material on which dark-brown flowers lay scattered over a light-yellow background, and the balance was cleverly maintained by the simplicity of the lighting, which followed the walls of the room in the form of an extended glass rod.

My wife had placed both hands on the sides of the armchair, her back to the curtain of the basting room, and she looked up at me with a droll smile on her face. It was at times like this that I envied men who wore glasses. Glasses get foggy and you could take up time cleaning and fussing with them. Having none, I proceeded, expressionless and in silence, to seat myself on the end of the sofa nearest the door. A spring groaned; suddenly, before I knew it, I had sunk into the sofa.

"The springs are broken. I'll have to send it out to be repaired," said my wife, laughing. She seated herself in the armchair and crossed her legs. Her knees peeping out from under her short skirt seemed even better than when I had last seen them. Sensing my look, my wife tapped her legs as if she were slapping a mosquito. She spoke quickly with a velvety smoothness: "Skirts are getting shorter and shorter. It's really a help. When the price of material goes down, you can't raise the sewing charge. People have to get new clothes every time they go up or down very much."

"Don't they say that when skirts go up there's going to be a war?"

"Yes, and they say cycles exist for everything."

"Apparently, it would seem."

"What brings you here today?"

"I have a little something to ask you. Is it all right . . . now?"

The curtain behind her parted and a young assistant appeared—"Hello. Shall I bring some ordinary tea . . . or would you prefer coffee?" She was not exceptionally pretty, but her face was attractive and innocent. My wife generally wore plain, unobtrusive clothes herself, since anything would suit her small-boned frame, but for the girl she made daringly modern ones. She reckoned on the psychological effect they would have on the customers. If the woman owner of a dressmaking establishment dressed too flashily she would be resisted by her clients. Yet something overly plain would have the effect of lowering confidence in her technique and sensitivity—neither was good. The two of them together were definitely effective. However, the girl kept staring intently at me over my wife's shoulder, revealing only her face. Her open, innocent gaze was like that of a small bird waiting for a whistle. Since I was her employer's husband she could get along without being defensive. But I was the separated husband, and so her curiosity was aroused and there was no need to be particularly formal in her mistress's presence. I had the impression that the part of the girl's body hidden by the curtain was stark naked. But this coquetry was not at all the type meant for me as a man. Indeed, the first time my wife had brought the girl home with her, I had some question whether my wife didn't have lesbian tendencies. In all likelihood the girl looked at tables and walls with the same sultry gaze.

"Is what you have to talk about complicated?"

"It depends on how you look at it."

"You should have phoned in advance."

"Oh, no. I wanted a spontaneous answer. I'm fed up with prepared answers."

The girl tensed her lips, shaking her head left and right. As she withdrew behind the curtain, she glanced at me coquettishly.

"She's something of a problem for me, that girl," said my wife, lowering her voice, although speaking laughingly, like an accomplice, half conscious of being overheard. "Isn't she cute? She's a genius with her coquettish poses."

"You're ripe for that, aren't you? But just what was the real reason we had to separate?"

"Is that what you came to ask me?" she questioned in amazement, peering into my face. "Right here in the store . . . in broad daylight?"

"Don't think too much. Tell me just what occurs to you."

"I agreed to separate because I thought I knew what you were thinking, I guess. At this point, when you try to turn the blame for your mistakes back on me . . ."

"My thoughts came first, you mean?"

"Of course."

"Because I was definitely against your opening this shop."

"Are you still?"

"I admit I was the loser."

"It's not a question of who won or who lost."

"I've often been asked why I ever became an investigator for a detective agency. What do you think I answer?"

"I imagine you don't tell the truth."

"I answer like this: my wife employs a detective to check on what I do. However, this detective changes sides in the middle of the case and demands that I pay him to say nothing. I have my weaknesses, it's true, but to have my trust trifled with like that makes me feel it's nonsense to pretend being honest."

"Even when you think up your fabrications you're not satisfied unless you make me out to be the wrongdoer, are you?"

My wife's smile slowly vanished as if deflated. Then a white loneliness, like an ebb tide flowing to the distant sea, enclosed her.

"I don't say you're an evildoer, I'm only deriding the detective."

"You can't talk like that."

"Did you make out with that architect?"

"My weaknesses hurt your self-respect without my intending them to, don't they? But even you have your problems. You're abnormally jealous."

"Jealous? I've never even thought of it."

"I'm sorry. I didn't have to say that. But you're at fault too—you treat me so as to make me say such things. We're always going around in a vicious circle like this. We don't know what starts it all. But something does, and we just go on with our endless quarreling."

"We still don't have to sign the final divorce proceedings, do we?"

"Have I ever once asked that?"

"But you did, because I was absolutely against opening this shop."

"But that's all past."

"It's over because you ignored my opposition and had your own high-handed way. I'm not saying it to be unpleasant. As far as the outcome is concerned, the fact remains indisputable that you were right and I was wrong. I wonder if I am jealous . . . No, it's a little different . . . similar, yes, but different, I think. The problem is this: Why was I alone wrong while you were not?"

"You put me in a quandary when you suddenly shift like that from posing as the victim."

"But even you must recognize there's no reason for my being here, don't you?"

"Well, then if . . ." My wife uncrossed her legs and joined her two hands on them as she leaned forward. "Supposing our positions were reversed, what would you do then? I wonder. Let's suppose for the moment that you have made a big success out of some business that I was opposed to, and let's suppose that, using that as my reason, I started talking about a separation."

"Of course, I'd be at a loss to understand."

"You're impossibly self-centered."

"You should find it hard to understand too."

"I do!"

"But you said before that you understood."

"It was a bluff."

"I see. Well then, I've been going round in circles trying to explain what even I could not explain, is that it?"

Suddenly my wife sat up, clapping her two hands together. Her eyes sparkled as they peered at me.

"I've got it! You left home! You ran away."

"Ran away?"

It was obvious, wasn't it? That was my intent. I understood that without being told. Something was definitely wrong if I was surprised at this late date, as if I had made some new discovery. While I thought this, it was also a fact that I experienced a strange confusion at being reminded of the overobvious. Suddenly the indignity of it penetrated painfully into my head, as if the contents of the ashtray had been dashed over me. Why? Perhaps because I had the feeling that the husband I was investigating and I were fused. Outside the sun was shining more and more intensely, and the dark door had taken on a green color; my shadow slanted almost parallel with the sofa, my shoulder sprawling over the opposite arm. My head was severed and nowhere to be seen.

"It's true. I really think you ran away."

My wife nodded in a self-satisfied manner as she covertly watched me. She seemed to think that if she could just get me to agree everything would thus be resolved.

"From what? You?"

"Certainly not from me," she said, shaking her head vigorously. "From life, from the endless competing and dickering, the tightrope walking, the scramble for a life buoy. It's true, isn't it? In the final analysis, I was merely an excuse."

Suddenly a flaming, white pain shot through my left eye as if I had been struck with a bent nail. My broken molar, of course. I would have to have it looked after before the decay spread to the jaw.

"Isn't there competition and dickering in the life of an investigator for a detective agency?"

"The rivalry in advertising on the busiest street and a professional peeping Tom of a private detective specializing in back streets—both are competition, but the sense of the word is quite different. It's absolutely true. You left your last job and you ran away at precisely the same time. That's the crucial point. Because you could have done either one before the other, couldn't you? . . . if competition weren't the reason . . . couldn't you? You were against this shop because you thought that, even though our livelihood was assured here for the time being, it would never be a solution. Your life was such that there would never be a solution unless you won out over the competition in the office."

"Was I so ambitious?"

"Do you have a pain somewhere?"

"I've got a broken molar."

She grasped the brooch in the shape of a tiny box at her breast and opened the lid. "This is pretty good," she said, taking out three small pills. "My regular medicine. I've had terrible headaches again lately."

As if she had been waiting, the girl backed into the room, making the curtain billow. Her skin-tight tan miniskirt molded the fold of her buttocks, and her stockings with their woven design shone with a pearly light. Her collar had the rectangular cut of a military uniform, the cuffs bearing pearly buttons. Her great eyes were brimming with a teasing smile. The coffee cup that had been filled too much was about to overflow. She slowly turned around on heels the same tawny color as her skirt, glancing quickly at me, and began to advance cautiously in a sliding step. Each movement of the muscles in her buttocks I could clearly and directly feel in my palms. I could not but be charmed by the knowledge that my wife was able to cut clothes like this.

"Would you like some water?"

"No, the pain seems to have gone."

Before I had realized it the aching had let up as if it had never existed. The girl bit her lower lip, mixing smile with tenseness. When she placed the cup on the table, she let it spill over as the liquid splashed up. She seated herself, laughing, in the chair immediately in front of me. Perhaps this innocence was a technique she used in selling herself. My wife, as if wanting her approbation, said: "My husband's room is all ready, isn't it, so that he can come back any time?"

The girl looked at me boldly and murmured, evidently pleased: "I like men."

I could not, I thought, come back after all.

THE DRY pavement of the freeway seemed both black and white at the same time. I was doing nearly seventy miles an hour, about five over the limit. The motor sputtered, making a sound like a piece of wire thrust into the blades of a fan; the tires screeched like adhesive tape being torn away. I was immersed to my very core in noise, but I heard nothing; it was as if I were in a great silence. All I could see was the concrete road running straight to the sky. No, it was not a road, it was a band of flowing time. I was not seeing but only feeling time.

I could not believe that a toll gate lay ahead. I could not

and, indeed, there was no need to believe it. My taking this freeway now was itself inexplicable. The hour when I was supposed to go back to the office and see the chief had long since passed. I had quite neglected contacting my client, too. I had no need to be here; there was no necessity of getting any place, I suppose. Pure time . . . time spent to no purpose. What a luxury. I pressed down on the accelerator. The speedometer steadily mounted . . . seventy-five. The wind began to affect the steering. I was a point of tenseness. I had the sensation of suddenly awakening on a calendarless day at a place that appeared on no map. You are free to call this sufficiency flight if you wish. When a pirate becomes a pirate and sets sail for unknown seas or when a brigand becomes a brigand and conceals himself in the depths of a city or a forest or an uninhabited desert, both—surely some place, some time—feel like this. Sympathy . . . no thanks, I'm nobody. It's as absurd as a man dying of thirst in a desert shedding tears for one who is drowning.

But if this pure time was an awakening, then the sequel to the dream at once blocked the way. The toll gate. A long dream sequence after a short artificial awakening. Immediately I made a U-turn and entered the line of cars going toward the city. But for some reason my state of mind was no longer so euphoric as before. Was it because a red sports car passed me, trailing its faint humming? It was, I think, rather that my awareness of going back, of the futility of going back, which was my only choice, had let the air out of a bouncing rubber ball. Perhaps it had something to do with the sun being at my back. This time, the sky rather than the roadway stretched interminably before me. There were clouds here and there, but even so the blue was stretched taut like a sized piece of cotton cloth. Perhaps it was a trick of perspective, but in the sky before me more clouds were gathering and it was growing dark. The town lay under the dappled sky. The town that I had left behind a half hour before stretched out a great scab-covered arm, waiting for me to come back. I was a pirate who had run his ship aground, a repentant brigand. Could it be that I was merely seeing mirages? No, that was not it. There was no proof that the town I had left was the same as the one I was coming back to. There was a really very slight one-micron discrepancy between the two, and I had been able to realize the difference perhaps because it was so small. Even one micron's worth made a big difference. Just traveling on the toll road once a week away from town made a four-micron difference a month . . . forty-eight a year. If you went on for thirty years, it made 1440 microns . . . precisely one and a half millimeters. Since even Fuji was crumbling away faster, the figure was one you might as well accept without reservation.

The dirty part of the sky expanded and rose, pushing aside the blue. Again there was a slight twinge in my molar. Why should I have to be so apologetic? Was it in order to stress my own rightness vis-à-vis my wife? Or was it in order to explain to my client that I had played no role in her brother's death? Or else was it in order to demonstrate to the chief that I had no desire to go deeper into the case than was necessary? But it was indeed a part of my work. "No good hunter pursues his quarry too far. Rather he puts himself in his quarry's place as he looks for the path of flight; by pursuing himself he corners his quarry" (from *The Memoirs of a Sleuth*). Indeed, that seemed valid enough . . . yes, I wonder. Was I not, some place in my mind, intentionally competing with the missing husband? Could I be contend-

ing with *him*? That would only justify my own quandary—
in which I neither ran away nor came back, that is—vis-à-vis
the husband who had simply gone off and never returned.

Perhaps so. If I were told it was true, I should begin to
feel it was. Even if it were, I had been shaken by his brother-
in-law's death, and this was far better than my attitude up
to this point: to put the essential him out of my mind.

Perhaps the husband's silhouette had come into view. In
some corner of the superimposed town landscapes there were
empty black holes. Shadows of the nonexistent husband, he
was not alone; there was a limitless number of different hims.
Mine, hers, his. Apparently in my mind some great change
was beginning to take place.

I drove into a rest area where there was a public telephone.
No sooner had I got out of the car than the sun, as if it had
been brushed away, went behind the clouds. Nevertheless,
in the booth it was still warm and damp, and, doubtless because of its infrequent use, there was a pungent smell of
mold.

                      "Sorry. I'm late in getting in touch with
you."

"It's just as well. I'm exhausted with crying. I'm just about
out of tears."

The hoarse tone in her voice was quite the same as usual and she was unpleasantly self-contained, but the cause doubtless lay in the beer rather than in the passage of time.

"Everyone will be upset if you're late, I imagine."

"They're not concerned about me at all. Of course, the expenses all come from the association. You'd think they were closer blood relations than I am. I got these mourning clothes at a rental place."

"They suit you. I suppose it's curious to say so, but black becomes you."

A sharp slope cut across the high ground of the housing development to the south. There, a long flight of stone stairs lay between clumps of bamboo on either side. I could see the slender nape of her neck as she led the way down.

"Have you asked anyone yet about the conditions and the reason that such a thing would happen to your brother?"

"I can hardly believe it was my brother. After all, I really didn't know anything about him."

"It happened right after he left me last evening, apparently. I feel responsible in a number of ways."

"But no one has mentioned anything about your being with him."

"It's getting chilly, isn't it. Cloudy again."

The bamboo gave way to a graveyard, immediately to the right where the stairs left off. There a small old temple was situated, only the roof tiles of which had any luster. The circumstances of the town had radically changed, the parishioners had decreased, and now, probably, the only source of income was funerals. The little temple was so dilapidated that braces were attached with heavy rope to the pillars, which had been eaten away by termites. Indeed, the growth in population had meant a proportionate increase in funerals. Perhaps the desolation was the fault of irresponsible financial management on the part of the chief priest, or else a measure to avoid taxes.

When we passed through the gate we could see the black and white mottled funeral drapery suspended in front of the temple. On either side of the path that led from the information desk to the hanging, holding their cold hands over small hibachi stoves, stood youths, who gave the impression of still being children. The intervals between them were as regular as the spaces between telephone poles. Every time we approached one, he bowed his head low, one following the other like machines. Their overly formal manner, their hands on their thighs and their legs slightly apart, made an eerie impression, but one which was also comical. In our office we had people who were syndicate-oriented like that too, but one didn't expect to see such old-fashioned ritual.

Inside the curtain, it was still and hushed. The depressing fragrance of the rising incense suggested the smell of death. A lone priest kept up the soft, lazy droning of a sacred text. There were four wreaths and on each one were written the words Yamato Association. It would seem that the funeral was the second cheapest type.

In front and extending to the left and right of the main chapel was a wooden dais for those taking part in the services. Only the unoccupied cushions were conspicuous. In the right-hand seat of honor a plump, middle-aged man, who, it was clear at a glance, was from the top echelon of the syndicate, sat with his eyes closed in front of an electric heater, apparently dozing. To his left four or five swarthy men dressed in black, evidently bigwigs, were kneeling in a formal fashion.

One of them, who was sharp of eye, recognized us and

at once hurried down the side steps. His arms and legs were long and slender and he had a cleft in his pointed chin. He wore heavy dark glasses and was of sturdy build, his neck squat on his torso. He followed us with a staggering, unsure step. Either he was drunk or his foot was asleep. Somehow I remembered having seen those glasses. Yes, he resembled one of the gang of three who had been standing near the bonfire at the river bed last night. The one with the strikingly long sideburns, the ends of which curled up, the bow-legged, squashed-faced one. Moreover, the adhesive plaster on the forehead and the Mercurochrome on the nose were definitely souvenirs of the fight.

"Come in," said the pointed chin, bowing deeply in front of my companion. "I'm sorry, but the vice-president of the association and the other association presidents had to leave early on urgent business. They send you their respects." His glance fell on the dozing man in the seat of honor, and as he looked back he hurriedly scrutinized me from head to toe. "The director is taking care of everything so there's nothing to be concerned about."

My companion introduced me to the pointed chin: "I would like you to meet the man in charge of my brother's association."

Suddenly someone tapped me on the shoulder from behind. "I see you made it safely. I warned you, didn't I? It happened just as I said, didn't it."

Who was this little gray pig? I remembered the voice. Yes, indeed . . . the fellow who ran the microbus concession last night. If I had not heard the voice, I would probably not have recognized him. He wore a necktie and had trimmed his beard, and one could not imagine even the swollen and bloated face belonging to the one who had been cooking noodles in the river bed. Absently, I bent my arm and tensed my lips just to the point of a smile in response to the blandishments of the man. Just in case we should be suspected for some reason or other, an unspoken understanding was instantly forged between the two of us; as mutual witnesses we would form a united front.

The result was at once manifest in the attitude of the one with the pointed chin. His watchful attitude fell away like a fake mustache stuck on with spit.

"The man in charge should be out in front. I'll get him at once."

He hurried away, disappearing beyond the drapery as he spoke. But the one with the dark glasses, standing a step behind, his legs apart, waiting for us like baggage, made no attempt to conceal his hostility, which even the dark lenses could not screen. Maybe it was rancor at me for having torn away from him last night as I was escaping, knowing that he had come to the car to ask for help. Under his comical, Mercurochromed nose the muscles at the corners of his lips trembled unmanageably. Thinking it was time to go, I said: "Well, let's go and pay our respects."

"I already have."

She could have been talking about eating. What on earth could be the relationship in her mind between this everyday calm about her brother's death and her attachment to him, involved as she was with him, constantly bringing him up in her conversation? Of course, funerals, though not so much as weddings, were uninviting, unhappy events. The dead's memory is nailed up so that the living can be at ease—a convenient ceremony indeed. Was it that indifference to the funeral basically signified indifference to the one who was dead, or else was it a case of loving the dead one too much

. . . beyond life and death? I was seized by a sinister premonition.

I took off my shoes and put on the slippers provided at the foot of the thick slab of wood that formed the bottom step. I mounted the five stairs. In front of the altar in the main chapel was a thick, scarlet cushion run through with gold threads and an uninviting plain wooden stand for burning incense. Having reached my seat, I realized I was still wearing my gloves and hastily drew them off. I offered some incense in the prescribed way, worrying all the while about wrinkling my trousers as I knelt, and then for the first time I looked up at the photograph on display at the front of the altar. —So that was it, I muttered to myself. As if waiting for me to leave my place, the priest stopped his chanting and hurriedly withdrew. When he had gone, the group of three men in attendance gave a sigh of relief and relaxed, simultaneously lighting cigarettes. The elderly man in the seat of honor who was called director at once roused from his nap, sniffling and spreading his hands over the electric heater, turning them over and back as if he were toasting something.

Unbeknown to me the pointed chin had appeared in the corridor through which the priest had disappeared, and now he was intently beckoning to me with his hand. Below the balustrade, to the left of the dais, my companion was deep in conversation with the noodle man. No, it was exclusively the noodle man who was doing the talking, and I did not know whether she was giving him her full attention as she fussed with the unaccustomed sleeves of her mourning kimono, letting them hang down in front, rolling them up from the bottom, and flipping them behind her. The sky was again an unbroken mass of milky cloud, but the wind had almost completely died down.

I was led into a narrow cubicle beside the altar, apparently a waiting room for those taking part in the religious ceremonies. The old-fashioned gas stove sent forth a blue flame, and at once the muscles of my face began to relax. Directly beside the entrance sat a young man, his hands on his knees, waiting with bowed head. The pointed chin looked at me searchingly.

"May I . . . ?"

I nodded and he left the room, swinging his shoulders. Of course, I had not foreseen such an abrupt introduction, and I had no idea at all what I should find out from this young man on duty. Yet whether the pointed chin was here or not didn't matter one way or the other. I faced the young man from across a small black and gold tea table whose lacquer had begun to peel. Judging from his slender, youthful neck—perhaps he was the leader of the group of youths standing out in front—it would seem unsuitable to call him the man in charge. As I took my seat, he adjusted his position and looked up. The face was exactly as I had imagined it would be from the slender neck. His fine-textured young skin looked as if it had been polished with wax, and the line of the jaw was epicene, neither masculine nor feminine. Aside from the dark shadow of a beard, his features, especially his lips, were completely feminine. Even the nose was delicate. Only the eyes were strangely veiled and seemed like dangerous, flammable oil. Still, the muscles were frail. He did not seem to have at all the authority to control, to overawe young men. He was doubtless the lion in sheep's clothing. If that was true, his position had collapsed with the

death of my client's brother, and the long-cherished hatred
of the other youths would now focus on him, ideal circumstances to get something out of him perhaps. However, aside
from muscles, in handling a wild and lunatic switch blade
he probably excelled the others in violence. Sports and con-
tests of strength and killing demanded another kind of
ability. Even the lion is no match for a famished dog.

Be that as it may, what in god's name could her purpose
be? What was the point of having me meet this boy? And
the suddenness of it all; there had been opportunity enough
to let me know in advance. The badge with the lightning
design was exactly the same as the one the brother had
worn. Perhaps it was the sign of the organization they called
the Yamato Association. If this youth was the man in charge,
the ones standing along the temple walk were perhaps the
bodyguard directly responsible to the dead man. But just a
minute! This boy's badge was the same as the brother's. It
was identical with the one belonging to the fellow with the
pointed chin as far as the design was concerned, but the
color of the background was different. The dead man's badge
had been blue, and the one belonging to the pointed chin
was beige. In age, the dead man had been somewhat older.
So the difference in color probably did not mean a distinction between superior and subordinate, but a difference in
division. Then, the dead man's gang had perhaps become an
independent organization within the Yamato Association.

What was she hoping for? I wondered.

Had it been a casual idea on the spur of the moment? Or
had something occurred to make her put off bringing us
together until the very last minute? Or had she reckoned
she could use my unpreparedness to advantage by means of
this unexpected encounter?

"Do you take turns being man in charge?"

"No."

His businesslike, unfeeling tone was, of course, put on. The resulting expressionlessness had ironed smooth the creases of feeling, so that within himself he adroitly balanced absolute submission against absolute resistance. Dealing with such a fellow outside a cage was next to impossible. Once in the cage together perhaps one would have to challenge him to a dangerous gamble: bite or be bitten. But I had no time to try that here.

"I imagine you're at something of a loss . . . all of you . . . with your head man dying so suddenly."

"Right."

"Are you the only one left to take charge? Or will you get someone from outside to be head man?"

"Maybe we'll split up."

"Why?"

"The leaders of the Association had trouble with the dead boss. Because minors are easy to spot. Kids run away from home and form gangs of toughs who suck the blood of other runaways. Once they're found out the police are on their tail, and they can't do anything."

Kids who run away from home . . . something passed through my mind, leaving shock waves in its wake. Kids who left home . . . If the brother had been the head of an organization that preyed on boys who ran away from home, it would be only natural for him to have a completely different point of view from us concerning the husband's disappearance. I wondered if she knew this. Was it because she knew it that it occurred to her to have me meet this boy?

"I read the messages of condolence for the whole bunch."

He constantly shifted his body, perhaps trying to escape from the stifling atmosphere, and abruptly he became defiant. "It made me cry. The boss really had a heart. It made me cry. No matter how many times we were raided we never let anything out. Not one of us wants to go back home. The leaders of the Association never understood. Everybody liked the boss. They really loved him. Wait and see. We'll do something, one way or another; we're not going to drop things here."

"But the criminal has been arrested by the police, I heard."

"Don't be stupid. He was a scapegoat. The boss was done in with a pistol. How could workmen in temporary quarters have pistols?"

"Do you have anyone particularly in mind?"

"Well..."

"The Association head doesn't approve, does he?"

"That's why I said that maybe we'll split up."

"I wonder if the money'll keep coming in."

"Ah. Our customers are the best. The kids out front are all sexy, too."

Perhaps at long last I was able to understand just what sort of work was involved. It was somehow unbelievable that there was not a single one of the gang at the microbus stand in the river bed, but ... high-type customers ... sexy kids. A gang of boys who were in the homosexual business, and the brother pulled the strings. If this one handled things cleverly, maybe he could get by without getting entangled with the law. But not just anyone could manage it. There's got to be a marriage of taste and profit. Thinking of it in this way, I understood the meaning of the tawdry impression the funeral made. I would imagine everybody in the Association was embarrassed by this group. So the executives had quietly withdrawn, leaving only a director. From the viewpoint of profit alone, no one could shift these frenzied animals to some other pasture, unless he loved the boys and was loved by them . . .

"Do they all appear in set places?"

"Never," he said, his eyes narrowing suspiciously. "We're different. I don't think you get it . . . do you? You don't look like you were one of us. Members of our club are all first-class patrons. Say, do you think I'm cute? Do I trouble you?"

"You're a good-looking boy."

"Well then. Want me to slap you around? Want to drink my piss? What about licking the soles of my shoes?"

I shrank back from his strangely set and unmoving eyes.

"I think I'll just pass that up."

"I thought so. Dirty old men with gobs of money come around plenty . . . and every once in a while some television star, but . . ."

"I have something to ask you. You all would know, I think. Did your boss ever say anything about any fuel suppliers?"

"Fuel suppliers? You mean a customer of the club?"

"Well, don't worry about it if you don't know."

"Questions I don't like. They make me mad."

"But just one more. Can you tell me where your boss usually stayed lately?"

"The boss was a square-dealer. He never padded down in any one place."

"But I imagine he had some baggage, a briefcase or something where he kept his personal effects . . ."

"He would throw things out when he had used them, even underwear and toothbrushes. It was really something. He'd use something two or three times and sell it to us on the Q.T. for half price."

"But he must have had something, something where he'd jot down things he needed, like a diary, for instance, or something like that . . . something he wouldn't usually carry around with him."

"I never saw anything."

"I'm not questioning who has the right of possession. I had permission to borrow a diary. It's something that has no value for you boys."

"Everything we had was his, even the mattresses we slept on and the hair cream we used. We didn't need to have anything."

"Can't I get you to give me a little more time?"

"Can't do it."

"What about your family?"

"Forget it. They all ask that."

"What did the boss do if someone got homesick?"

"He was very observant. Even when he was just loafing around the square in front of the station, he noticed everything. Never made a mistake. Furthermore, he was a good teacher, so the boys soon got to like the business a lot."

"Anyway, you boys are getting older."

"Can't be helped. When you think about it, nobody can help getting old. Well, sometime I'll shake some old customers down. I'd really like to start up a snack bar or a gas station or something."

"D<small>ID</small> <small>YOU</small> know what kind of fellows those boys were from the start?"

"Yes, I did. Just let me get close and they run away terrified. I don't have a chance to say a word."

She laughed, shrugging her shoulders as if joking, furtively moistening the edges of her lips with the beer. Again I was seated in front of the lemon-yellow curtains, and as it was still light outside, the room was filled with a lemon-yellow light. In it only the black mourning clothes were at odds, seeming to have been taken from a black and white photo album.

"About the diary. I tried sounding him out about that, but it was no use. The more I tried to get something out of him the tighter he kept his mouth shut."

"Diary? What diary?"

"Your husband's, of course. Your brother was supposed to bring it over here today."

"Oh."

Disinterestedly she continued steadily licking at her beer, like some kitten: it was I indeed who was so stirred up and angry that my chest ached.

"I drove down the freeway a little while ago."

"Why? I wonder."

"As I went along I thought how wonderful it would be if I could go on like that forever. And then I felt I really could. But I shudder now when I think of my psychological state at the time. Supposing everything had come out as I wished, supposing I had gone on and on and, no matter how far I went, never, never came to the toll gate . . ."

Suddenly she raised her head from her glass.

"It's all right. You'd run out of gas in half a day."

Our eyes met in a strange look.

But she seemed to take no meaning from what I was saying or from what she herself said, and when she noticed the stiffening of my expression she was suddenly flustered. "It's strange, isn't it. My husband seemed to use the freeway a lot too. Of course, in his case it was to test the cars he had repaired. He said he used to go round and round on the freeway so much that he got tipsy. That was in the evenings when the iron roofs of the buildings still shone red in the sun, though the underparts were already darkened."

"Perhaps what I was saying was just that."

"He said that as he went up and down the freeway a hundred times, a thousand times, the exits gradually diminished in number, and that in the end he felt locked in."

"When you're driving, you never want to think of stopping. You want the moment to go on forever just as it is. But when it's over, you shudder at a state like that, with no end. There's a big difference between driving and thinking about driving."

A faint smile hovered about her lips. It differed from her usual smirk, yet it was a worrisome smile, as if she were forcing herself to be agreeable. She again lowered her eyes and I had a feeling of frustration, like some salesman turned away from the door with excessive courtesy.

The momentum of my words carried me on: "So perhaps I needn't be so concerned about the diary. The diary, after all, is imagining the driving; your husband is the one who actually drove."

"Oh. The diary . . ."

"What did you think I was talking about?"

"I thought it had to do with a man and woman," she said in an uninterested tone as if she were tossing aside an orange peel. Again she lowered her absent-minded gaze to her glass.

"Do you know anything about the contents?" At length I too was roused. "What is this business . . . your being so uninterested in your husband's diary? I don't know any more who to worry about."

"But I don't think even my brother made much of a point of the diary."

"Did you trust your brother that far? Even more than your own judgment?"

"I'm all alone now."

She closed her eyes, the upper part of her body slackened, and she seemed quite unaware of my presence. Yet I wondered whether deep in her heart a tempest was ravaging her.

"Well, have it your way. It's none of my business. However you may think of your brother. But what in heaven's name were the circumstances that got him in such a mess? Do you know, actually?"

"Oh, yes, that reminds me. I have to give you this." She picked up a large, square, white handbag that she had put next to her chair, and which was somewhat ill-matched with her mourning clothes, and lifted it into her lap. Out of it she took a package wrapped in newspaper and slid it over the table toward me. It was a strangely shaped package, poorly done up. From the sound it made on the table it seemed rather heavy.

"What's this?"

"The man who came to talk to me a while ago . . . the one with the heavy beard . . ."

"Oh. That's the owner of the noodle place. He ran a spot in the dry river bed where the fight took place."

"He said it was a memento of my brother's."

The paper tore as I was opening it, and a black metallic tube, gleaming dully, was revealed. A pistol! It at once occurred to me that I must not leave any fingerprints. I grasped it by the muzzle with an edge of the newspaper and gingerly drew it toward me across the table. A small buttonlike object, wrapped with the pistol, fell out. It was the badge.

"These things aren't very much, but . . ."

She was quite imperturbable, and it was I who was thoroughly disturbed. For god's sake, what kind of woman was she? What was her everyday world?

"Did you know this? It's a six-shooter Browning."

"Oh, it's only a toy."

"A toy?"

"Look. The barrel's blocked up."

I saw that it was indeed. The color, shape, and weight were perfect, and I could not tell it from a real revolver. Particularly the chill around the well-oiled trigger gave it an inorganic feel. For psychological effect, one needed nothing closer to the real thing.

"I heard the other man got excited when my brother pulled this out."

"Curious. The noodle fellow must have got out of there before me, so he couldn't actually have witnessed the scene."

"Once he had parked the bus in a safe place, he said, he went back again."

There was nothing I could say to that. Even I could have done something . . . rushed to the office of the temporary workmen's quarters . . . or run to the police station . . . or something. But all I did was clear out of the place. I let him die without lifting a finger, without showing him as much good faith as the noodle man.

"But I didn't go back."

"It appears his head was stomped in with a heel."

"That's questionable. According to that boy in charge I spoke with a while ago, it seems he was shot to death."

"You can't trust what those boys say. Right away imagination becomes fact. The police also said he had been clubbed to death."

"But you imagine facts yourself, don't you?"

"I guess so."

"Did the police mention anything concerning me or your husband?"

"No, not particularly."

"A thing like this revolver doesn't mean much." I was irritated at being fooled and I deliberately applied my fingerprints to the surface of the gun. "But it's something of a problem if you consider that the business your brother was running was as innocent as this gun."

"Of course. Originally, the gun was my husband's, you realize."

"What was your husband doing with it?"

"He bought it somewhere and loved to flaunt it around. My brother got all excited and took it away from him."

"That's strange too. The positions seem somewhat reversed. Your brother had no right to complain about something as innocuous as a toy pistol, when you consider what he was doing. For instance, do you know what he was up to in the dry river bottom where the fight took place last night?"

"Yes. In a general way . . ."

"He took the key money he got and had a number of shops set up for the workingmen's quarters—you know, the microbuses. That in itself would be all right, but he put women in them—prostitution right in the open. Did you know that?"

"Well, yes . . . generally . . ."

"For heaven's sake, what sort of a relationship was there between your brother and your husband? I can't believe they were individuals of the same kind. When you talk you seem so uncritical of your brother."

"I think I understand him. My brother would never permit my husband to play with such a toy."

"So that's why I wondered how he could justify complaining about the gun. I can't believe he had any justification."

"Justification? Well, I don't know . . . ," she said, thrusting her finger into her glass and then licking the beer foam from the tip. "It's a strange turn of the wheel of fortune. If my brother was killed because of this toy, it would seem my husband did it."

Perhaps her complete indifference and her tenseness, which seemed to be on the verge of tearing her apart, dwelt together in her single expression. Suddenly the pain which convulsed her breast, as she frantically stifled a cry, pierced me. It was apparently not my turn to be upset.

"You worry too much. A thing like this is a straight clue."

"Put it away right now. Please. I hate toys like that."

"I'll take it along with me. What shall I do with the badge?"

"Oh. Well . . . you might as well throw it away."

"I'll have to be leaving shortly after six."

"Would you have another beer?"

"Actually I'd prefer looking at an album or something."

"An album?"

"Yes, one with family pictures."

"We do have one, but . . . surely it'll be a bore."

Twisting around and half rising, she drew from the bookcase behind her an oversized scrapbook contained in a case, on the spine of which was printed in large letters: *The Meaning of Memories*. On closer inspection, I saw it was not printing but letters that had evidently been cut out of a magazine or something and pasted on in a line.

"*The Meaning of Memories* is a rather strange title, isn't it?"

"It's typical of him. So meticulous . . ."

So this was the meticulousness typical of him.

"No doubt the pictures inside are just as meticulously done."

"Hmm."

Turning to the first page of the album, I casually said: "What type of picture did he seem interested in lately?"

"Well, he was enthusiastic about color and he was all the time going to a rented darkroom where he could develop his own pictures. He was proud of the one that seems to be rings of colors in a puddle of water."

Colored rings . . . Apparently she didn't know anything about the nudes. But there wasn't much object in telling her at this point. The brown, faded portrait of an older woman appeared on the first page of the album. From the

way the painted ocean and cliff stretched away in the background, I supposed it dated from the twenties.

"That's my husband's mother, who lives in the country
with my sister-in-law," she commented, peering at the picture. An odor of sun-drenched hair wafted to my nose.

The pictures of the husband alone stopped with this page.
From the second page on, they abruptly shifted to the
period just after his marriage. A souvenir shot of affectedly
expressionless newlyweds.

"Aren't there any pictures of your husband before you
and he got married?"

"No. We collected them all, including the old ones, and
left them with his mother in the country."

"Did you have some reason for that?"

"We weren't particularly sentimental about the past."

The periods of the pictures kept changing as I turned the
pages. But portraits of her occupied the most space, whatever the period. Apparently his interest in photography
dated from some time ago, for they were arty shots taken
from every conceivable angle. But what was even more dis-
concerting was her disagreeably aggressive attitude that was
caught in them. One showed her face reflected in a mirror
as if she were making herself up, quite devoid of timidity.
A face clearly aware it was being looked at, a smile hover-
ing about the slightly open mouth, veiled, pensive eyes
dreamily looking into the distance. More surprising still was
that there was even a picture of her in a peignoir, through
which, the shot having been taken against the light, the
contours of her body were almost visible. A strange woman.
Had the husband taken them . . . or had she had them
done? I should have to begin by looking into that.

Mixed in with these pictures, though rarely, were others

of the family and him, souvenir photos of a time when the two of them had visited his mother. A country village . . . the front of a general store that served as a tobacconist's. It was apparently summer and a bench had been brought out. The mother was in the center, with the two of them to her right; on her left were his elder sister and her husband. They were all holding cups of shaved strawberry ice in their hands and laughing happily. At once I scrutinized the expressions of the mother and sister. Wasn't there some feature the three had in common? Some portent that hinted of his disappearance? Some genetic sign of insanity? I should have had a magnifying glass.

There was another picture in which he was fussing with a tree in the garden.

"Is this where you lived before you came here?"

"Yes. That was when he was an agent for Dainen Enterprises."

"How did he first come to do that kind of work?"

"After the first business went bankrupt, he sold magazines for a while. And then, unexpectedly, a college classmate of my brother's started a supermarket with capital he got from selling land: my husband bought his share of the store."

"What about the money?"

"My husband finished paying it in monthly installments last summer."

"So there's nothing between them any more?"

"No. My brother did the negotiating from the very beginning."

"Then I suppose your brother was also the one who received the title."

"I really don't know. Whichever it was, my husband was

the one who was promoted from branch head to section head in the main office. There's no problem there, I think."

"You're right. Of course, there was some kickback out of his earnings."

"Oh, do you think so?" She smiled wearily as she refilled both our glasses with beer. "But we . . . my brother and I . . . lost our mother and father early and always had to lead a hand-to-mouth existence—just the two of us. When one of us was picked on, the other felt it as if it were he himself. Even after I married I don't think things changed much. Actually, it was through my brother that my husband got to work in the main office. It's true. We didn't want a child of ours to go through the hardships we did, so until our insurance and retirement pay were guaranteed and our net wages were over sixty thousand yen a month we decided not to have a child. But, I would be eight months pregnant by now."

"Now?"

"Yes, if I hadn't lost it."

"Did your husband know you were pregnant?"

"Of course he did."

"What was your brother's work before he entered the organization?"

"When he was in school, he was dismissed because he was too active in some student movement . . . or, let me see, maybe he left of his own free will. He couldn't get respectable work for various reasons. For a very short time he was private secretary to some city councilman."

At length, close to the end of the album, I came to the photo I wanted to see. It was a picture of him—the client's brother. The scene was the same as the earlier one, in the garden. There was an old car with its hood up, facing the

camera at an angle. A man resembling the husband had
crawled underneath on a mat. There stood the brother with
one elbow leaning on the roof, a smile on his face, his
mouth wide open—apparently he was saying something to
his brother-in-law. But he was looking into the camera as
if embarrassed. He was wearing wooden sandals and a short-
sleeved shirt. Indeed, the photo gave off very much of a
homey feeling.

I was disappointed. Although I should have been relieved
I was thoroughly discouraged, as if my expectations had
been let down. There was clear proof, particularly in the
album. The brother and sister—as they called themselves—
had no other relatives. On the official record there was indeed a younger brother of the same family and personal
name, but for the present, there was no way of obtaining
evidence to back it up. However, from the atmosphere
which the photo revealed, almost unmistakably he was the
real brother. My persistent, sadistic daydream that perhaps
the fellow was a fake impersonating the brother and, having
a secret affair with her, had liquidated the husband, came
to naught, it would seem.

"Did your husband and your brother get along well?"

"Yes, they were like puppies, romping around and quarreling together with no inhibitions."

"At the time this picture was taken, had your brother
already entered the organization?"

"Let me see . . . I think so, but . . ."

"What was your husband's opinion about that?"

"He didn't agree, of course . . . but it wasn't his business."

"Well then—the question's rather impertinent—did your
brother think of you and your husband as one? Or did he
draw the distinction that you were a relative in fact, while

your husband was always a parenthetical relation, in the final analysis, a stranger ... or how did he think? In other words, if some antagonism arose between you and your husband, did your brother as a matter of course act as peacemaker or did he clearly act to protect your interests?"

"I've never thought about such things."

"Well, let's look at it in another way. Supposing, to the contrary, your husband and your brother came to a definite parting of the ways over something or other and claimed they had to duel, what would you have done? There was no possibility of making peace, and you had to choose one of them—which one would it be?"

"What an idea. It's nonsense."

"But you're obliged to choose."

"But my brother helped my husband the way no one else could."

"So in return your husband felt he owed him something?"

"Why should I have to answer such questions?"

"In the first place, because it's my obligation to protect my client."

"But my brother's dead!" she suddenly screamed in a low, rasping voice. I was startled. Ah, that was it! How could I have been so blind?

"I must be going soon after six." The watch on my wrist showed a little after five. "I've got an appointment to meet Tashiro. Maybe he's got some clue. Whatever you say, he's got more contacts within the company than anyone else."

But she remained silent. She had doubtless understood my meaning. Intuitively, she may indeed have realized the intent that I myself had not yet been able to formulate clearly into words—my intent in repeating these ill-natured questions, attempting to estrange the husband and the brother—at this point, the one lost and the other dead. That intent there was I could not deny. Thus I felt that I had been seen through, and I was upset at the thought. Subjects more appropriate to my role and to the play I was in were not altogether lacking after all. Even the report that I had prepared this morning was not completely worthless. The conversation with Toyama was suggestive; it had sketched for me the actual wiring chart for the connections between the husband and the Camellia. It was simpler and more reliable than any line that had come to me thus far. But something made me hesitate. As soon as I had put it into words I felt empty and uneasy, as if I had quite lost my reason for being. I could bring up the Camellia in a little more roundabout way.

"Oh, yes. I forgot to write up two or three things in my report about the Camellia. Let's see. There's a parking lot right in front of it, you know. It was there I met your brother for the first time. Accidentally. A little too accidentally, I think. But let that go. Did you know just why your brother happened to be in such a place?"

"Well . . ."

"According to his explanation, there was the possibility your husband had made the parking lot his base of operations for his second-hand car business."

"Then what happened?"

At last I had provoked real interest. But was it because the information concerned her husband or because of the mention of her brother's name? The two of us lifted our glasses of beer to our lips at the same instant, both of us feigning unconcern. Her glass was nearly half full; in mine there remained about an inch of beer.

"I really couldn't get any evidence there, but I wonder

why your brother suddenly appeared in such a place yesterday morning. He must have been investigating your husband's case over six months now. Furthermore, from the looks of it he was lying in wait for me." Her expression clouded over, and I listened to the alarm that began to sound within me. Any brakes would be useless; I should have to come to a natural stop.

"Even if our meeting was accidental, it was too much so. I suspected at once that your husband and your brother weren't accomplices. I mean, your brother knew of your husband's whereabouts, yet for some reason he attempted to conceal that from you and from everybody else."

"What do you mean 'for some reason'?"

"If we knew that, we'd have the solution. But we have to consider all possibilities. We've got to be suspicious of everyone . . . except you."

"Why am I so special?"

"Because you're the client."

"But my brother also agreed about requesting you to investigate, you know."

"That's not particularly inconsistent. You hired me. I was given charge of the investigation. But since you were able to follow all my movements, I was exactly like a cat with a bell around its neck, wasn't I."

"But why would I do that?"

"Consider a completely opposite situation. Your brother knows the whereabouts of your husband, but since they were not accomplices, he has recourse to either psychological or physical blackmail so that your husband cannot come back again. How about that? Interesting, isn't it? A given situation can be seen in different lights just by changing the point of view."

"Very interesting indeed."

"I'm not just making things up, you know." I was inexpressibly angry both with myself and with her at my gradual loss of composure. Just a little more and I would put it into words, but the depth of the crevasse separating me from that little more was too great. "It's an undeniable fact that my actions were observed by your brother, isn't it? Aside from however you would explain that, his aim was simply to observe the way I worked, I suppose. I'm not angry, really. It's very natural, psychologically, for people who deceive to be afraid of being deceived. But with such people it's also most natural, psychologically, to think that we don't know how deceptive they are with everybody else."

"My husband and my brother got along very well."

"Yes, of course. To the point of being purple with rage about a toy gun."

I came to the last page of the album . . . a light sepia cardboard with nothing on it. It was the one I kept looking at longest of all. Slowly I closed the album, and again there appeared the words: *The Meaning of Memories.*

"My brother of course knew of my pregnancy."

"If I were a police detective, as a matter of course I would have been suspicious even of your aborted child, you know."

She raised her eyes from the foam in her glass. For an instant the thin, translucent ice shone blue between her eyebrows; with the next sparkle it had already melted. It would take considerable courage not to protect this woman. That was the only point I could understand about the missing husband. Anyway, the husband had had that courage. Even if one didn't question whether that courage was one of life or death . . . She continued to stare directly at me. The line of her cheek became like moistened sand on a beach, the softness and hardness delicately mingled as she sat against the lemon-yellow curtains that had gradually begun to fade. The color of her skin was that of a mellowed piece of unpainted furniture in which age and freshness smoothly fused. As we sat there the color of evening deepened, and the freckles on her face blended into her skin. She said nothing. The hem of her mourning kimono formed a link with the dark floor; it was as if she had become some plant. From window to window a street peddler was crying his wares through a portable microphone. "The second time I met your brother . . . ," I began, lowering my voice slightly, following the progress of her eight fingers (the two thumbs were invisible) creeping like some optical illusion along the edge of the table. I continued: "No, I'm not talking about the place where the fight occurred. It was a little before that. It was right there in town, at the M Fuel Supplier's about a mile from where the fight happened . . . the place I mentioned last in my report last night. Again it was a repeat of the same fishy accidental meeting. I had gone there to make inquiries, because I had the feeling that the documents your husband had arranged to give Tashiro on the day he disappeared were very probably destined for M Fuel Supplier's. And then there he was again . . . it gave me a very funny feeling. We could wrap the case up pretty quickly if we could say that the fellow I was pursuing was the brother and not the husband. Do you have any idea what your brother was doing there?"

"Yes, if it concerns M, I do."

"Oh, did you know M?"

"I've told you a hundred times," she replied tonelessly. Was she stifling her feelings or was it something not worth expressing her feelings about? "The fact is that my brother was very cooperative with my husband in his work."

"Do you mean that it was your brother who started the business with M Fuel Supplier?"

"He said it was really big business."

"Yes, of course. But it looks like the business last evening wasn't so above-board. It comes to the same thing, I suppose. In the end, it's for the two of you. Yes, perhaps so. If you don't know the means he used it doesn't make any difference."

"I wonder what the business was."

"Blackmail."

"Blackmail?"

Her faint voice and pursed lips gave the impression she was sucking on some ripe fruit. For her even blackmail was preserved in sweet syrup. When I thought about it, the very sound of "blackmail" conjured up in my mind the small fruit of some tree.

"Do you plan on my going on with the investigation after this week?"

"Yes, if I can."

"In that case I suppose you had arranged with your brother about the expenses, hadn't you?"

"Yes."

Suddenly she had trouble breathing, as if she were choking on the beer. But the glass was on the table, softly reflecting the last faint rays of light. She was gagging on reality. No matter how much she hoped to float like a foetus in the lemon-yellow liquid, talking to herself, alone with her beer, the death of her protector, who had checked the encroachment of reality, was itself this very reality. She was gasping like a fish in a dry pond. "But there's still the savings, and my husband's retirement pay hasn't been touched. And then, there's the joint life insurance I have with my brother, though it's not very much."

"Ah. There!" I was badgering her in a way that surprised even me. My words poured out in a torrent. "That's just what I was saying. I've been knocking myself out, trying to get you to give me information. Well, now look here, supposing for the moment that I had ferreted out the business about the life insurance and not heard it from you. I couldn't have helped but suspect that your husband's disappearance was a fake one, set up between you, the objective being the perfect crime: your brother's death."

It was already too dark for me to see her expression. I could only guess at it from the tense silence. One, two, three seconds, four seconds . . . the meaning and depth of the silence evolved with the passage of time. Suddenly her cheerful surprise lightly turned my aggressiveness aside.

"Oh. How dark it's become!"

She turned on the lights and stood by the wall that cut off the kitchen. Bookshelves, lemon-yellow curtains, telephone, Formula I cutaway view, Picasso reproduction, stereo set, artificial lace throw . . . She raised her arm slightly, and pushing through the draped curtain, passed into the kitchen. Apparently she had raised her arm excusing her departure, or else it had been merely to look at the sleeve of her mourning kimono. As I filled my glass with beer and drained it in a draught, I felt the same eddying deep within me come slowly and quietly to the surface. Before I knew it we had finished off the third bottle of beer. I alone had surely emptied two. A good excuse for leaving my car where it was. A good excuse for being able to come back again when I wished. Unworried and composed, she had let a faint smile hover around her lips. Perhaps it was because she had left her seat . . . perhaps it was the fault of the beer . . . or again possibly it was because of the electric lights, symbols of security. No, more than anything, it was likely the mourning clothes. The offensive odor of death, like a light mist. It was the fault of the mourning clothes that had gone away, that were impregnated to their innermost fibers with death as with some volatile gas. Clothes for hire that had wandered among deaths too numerous to count. If that were true, my feeling of liberation would not last long. When she returned with her clothes of death, the air in the room would be thick, as it had been before, with that oppressive gelatinous liquid.

The telephone began to ring, breaking the impression that the lemon-yellow room was some solitary island; the outside world bored in through a black hole. I felt uneasy, for the spell had been broken. I was chilled and ill at ease as if the muzzle of a gun pointed at me from the hole.

Since, on the third ring, there was no sign that she was coming, I automatically called behind the curtain:

"Shall I answer it?"

An unexpected voice came from an unexpected direction.

"Oh, yes. Would you mind?"

I had expected the kitchen, but she was in the next room. Most of all, I was intrigued that she could so simply entrust the telephone to me. I was not all that suspicious, and I certainly harbored no disgraceful thought that the husband's disappearance was faked and that they remained in secret contact by telephone. More generally, the degree of transparency in her situation was greatly increased by the fact that no secret telephone call was expected. Apparently she

was quite willing that I act as her official representative.
Scarcely able to control my hard breathing and my tensed
muscles, I rushed for the receiver, trying to get there before
the telephone rang a fifth time.

However, my expectations were disappointed. A rude in-
terruption of the role I was deliberately playing. It was the
chief. Another tedious lecture. Why did he always have to
start all over again from lesson one? Because an investigator
was no more than a drain cleaner, that was why. He crawls
around in the midst of filth, unexposed to light. —"I want
you detectives to be far more careful about cleanliness and
pay attention to your health." I realized, without being told,
the chief's perplexity when without contacting him I broke
my promise to put in an appearance at the office after noon.
Although he was most considerate and thoughtful of others
he demanded the strictness of an ascetic in matters of self-
defense and the cash register, but only in these areas. My
thoughts about a chief like this were never unhappy ones.
I rather admired his professional conscientiousness when I
reflected that many people put up a pretense of evil and
hypocrisy as temporary painkillers. —"You had better watch
out. As far as your client's brother's concerned, it's a case of
murder. It's preposterous. May I remind you again, if you
get involved in a police case without consulting first with me,
from that instant on you're going to have nothing more to
do with this office. It sounds unfeeling, but I can't do anything about it. It's company policy. You get in trouble if
you force a man to stay here who doesn't really fit in." I did
not usually find this tone unpleasant. On the contrary, it
usually made a favorable impression on me. But today for
some reason it was without effect. My client came back at
just the right point in the conversation. Moreover, she had,

in the meantime, changed from her mourning clothes into an ordinary dress—extremely rapidly, I thought. Apparently I no longer had to fear being plagued by the stench of death. It was a dress of black crepe that loosely molded her body. I wondered if she remembered that I had said black became her. She tilted her head to one side. I shook my own from left to right, indicating with my free hand that the call was for me. She circled the table and sat down immediately in front of me. At the closest point we were about eight inches apart. Her hair was long, the peculiar waves equally divided between shallow and full ones. The curve of her shoulders would fit in the hollow of my hand, were I to place it on them. Without realizing it, I laughed, interrupting the chief's words. —"Thanks for the enjoyable scolding. These days I've been doing nothing but walking around and looking for someone. It's not at all unpleasant to have someone looking for me." No, it was not a lie. But after saying that, I realized rather sentimentally that my words were those I might have used to my own wife rather than to my chief. Any number of times I had visited my wife and had got in touch with her, but when I thought about it she had not once contacted me. Perhaps it wasn't right. The fact that I didn't have the courage to wait in silence until she sought me out may have eroded our relationship.

I returned to my seat, appropriately leaving on the other end of the line the ceaselessly scolding chief. Her beer and her pathetic smile were not the slightest bit unnatural now. I too put my fingers on the corner of the table in the same way she had done and resumed the rather irritable conversation we had been having. I had that lazy Sunday-afternoon feeling that comes after the pleasure of an unaccustomed late morning in bed.

"But let's forget about the business of expenses. There are still about four days to go. I'll do the best I can in that time. We can think about expenses when the time comes."

"When it comes to that point, I'll try and get a job somewhere. My brother's not here to scold any longer. I realize the world isn't all he claimed."

"Things are discouraging now, but the investigation has made some progress."

"You said before you had to be suspicious about the child I aborted. What did you mean by that?"

The tone was casual, quite as if she were discussing the weather, but her innocent expression was not to be trusted. I had had enough of this strain.

"Did I ever say anything like that?"

"I suppose you meant it was my brother's child, didn't you?"

"How can you say such a terrible thing with a straight face? I was only trying to say that one can pose all kinds of hypotheses. But I understood your brother's tastes, and you did show me the album."

"It's curious, I felt that myself. And I talked about it with my brother. He was disgusted. He abhorred women and evidently he disliked children too."

"You're an amazing woman. I didn't mean anything so far out as that by what I said. I meant something a lot simpler . . . a conventional *ménage à trois* or something like that. He might have pretended to be a brother so you could hide the relationship. That's a possibility, isn't it?"

"What do you mean, 'pretended to be a brother'?"

"Frankly speaking, it was an equivocal situation."

"I wish you had said that to my brother."

"Of course, I'm not suspicious any more." I quickly leafed

through the album, trying not to look at her expression. I showed her the page with the picture of the brother and the car. "Look at this picture. It's written here that you were the one who took it. Your husband has crawled underneath. Your brother's standing to the side, looking rather absently at what your husband is doing. No, he is pretending to look, smiling like some accomplice in the direction of the person who's taking the shot—that is, toward you. Naturally your husband can't see his expression."

"I wonder if he wasn't beginning to be suspicious."

"No. This is a record. It has been left specifically as such. That's precisely the sense of *The Meaning of Memories.* Both the one who's taking the picture and the one who's having his picture taken must be very much aware of that. If the two of you had had anything to be ashamed of, you would have consciously avoided such a scene."

"You're a clever fellow, I knew it." Suddenly her voice became animated, and she laughed as she filled up my glass, which for some time had been empty. I did not demur. There were only about two inches of beer left in the bottle. "I like this kind of talk. I want more of it."

"What do you mean, 'this kind of talk'?"

"Talk that reverses itself, where top becomes bottom, as you're listening to it. Maybe I can do it too with one subject: my brother. Shall I try?"

"I've just about a quarter of an hour."

"Some years ago my brother had a real lover. I mean a girl, of course . . . someone he had met in a student movement, he said. That was winter. He seemed terribly happy on through the spring. But one day in the summer the girl said he smelled like cat piddle and couldn't he have some operation or treatment."

"I suppose it was an underarm odor."

"Anyway, my brother meekly began going to the hospital. But when the treatments were half over he decided to have nothing more to do with her. Instead his old dislike of women came back. I began to be more and more important to him. I was the only woman in the world who, for him, was not a woman. We loved each other . . . really. It was funny we didn't have a child. But then my husband came on the scene. And I became a real woman."

"Well then, they must have vied with each other."

"On the contrary, they didn't. Right away my brother got along perfectly with my husband. It was much better than if I had made friends with other women."

"But he could have wanted exclusive possession of you, couldn't he?"

"Well, he did have exclusive possession . . . of a boy."

"Oh, I see."

"I really liked everything about my brother."

"Can't you talk about your husband that way?"

"But my husband didn't have such a double life."

"Yet he was the one to run away."

"Yes, and that's why it's so horrible."

Terror flashed in her eyes, a pathetic fright like frost-covered wires moaning in the wind.

"You're frightened because you're thinking of your husband who's not here. Try instead to imagine him being somewhere. You may suffer but your fear will go away."

"It's the same thing."

"Even if you imagined he was living with some other woman?"

"If I don't understand why he isn't here, it's the same thing."

"I wonder if the news about your brother is in this evening's paper. If it is, your husband may see it and get in touch with you quite normally."

"Do you mean that my brother was the motive behind my husband's disappearance?"

"That's a silly idea, forget it. Anyway, it's not good to have made up your mind to something. I myself was obsessed until just a while ago with the idea that the matchbox I had in my possession was material evidence definitely unfavorable to you. It contained both black and white sticks. Someone who valued the matchbox but who rarely frequented the shop had, in the course of events, replenished the matches. If he had gone to the shop regularly he could have got new matches any time. Now, what kind of situation can you assume? One, it was a man who went out but rarely. Two, he was someone interested in the telephone number printed on the label. Three, he was a man who needed a secret telephone contact."

"Can't you jot a telephone number down in a notebook?"

"If anything happened, an address book would be checked first thing, but no one's going to pay any attention to a matchbox from a coffee house. But that album a little while ago quite removed any basis for suspicion. I was relieved. It was a real dilemma for me. The matchbox was a very troublesome item because we investigators can't go around suspecting clients. A good example of having made up my mind in advance. Shouldn't you try being more tolerant toward the relationship between your husband and your brother?"

"You're the one who's prejudiced against my brother."

"Well, let's drop your brother then. It's time for me to be going. It'll take me about ten minutes to S—— station by subway."

She dropped her eyes and nervously bit twice at her thumbnail.

"SAY, THIS article was in the newspaper last year." Young Tashiro peered through thick glasses as he presented me with a tattered newspaper clipping, barely waiting until I had sat down.

"I must say, your map was pretty hard to follow."

"It says there were over eighty thousand missing persons. I was amazed. Mr. Nemuro's case wasn't particularly exceptional."

"Were you the one who decided on this place?"

"Yes. The view's rather interesting, don't you think? You can see both the people going up and the ones going down the stairs when you look over there. You have the feeling of viewing the world absolutely privately, unnoticed by anyone, as if from some nonexistent hole in space. I really like this spot. It's interesting, people walking around without even knowing they're being watched."

"Be that as it may, your map is wrong. I missed the corner four times. I'm nearly twenty minutes late."

"It's all right. It's not so much the map . . . the underground passages are hard to follow."

"It's not all right." I ordered coffee from a white-jacketed waiter who came to take the order. "With a map like this, it's conceivable Mr. Nemuro might not have been able to get here."

"You're exaggerating. I waited exactly one hour and ten minutes. It may be complicated, but it's not impossible. And he knew the name of the shop perfectly."

"Was there about this much of a crowd that morning?"

"The morning rush hour's not like this. You can't see the floor for the people."

"But there's a considerable crowd now."

I was seized by the hallucination that I had retrogressed three or four hours in time when I thought of the calm of her room. One had no idea of the direction governing these walking people, where they came from, where they were going. Perhaps it was because, with the tiled floors and the tiled pillars, all the lines of the passageways and stairs converged here, and anyone could follow the line of his choice.

"The people around now are most interesting . . . each one has his own way of walking . . . his own expression."

"Well, let's take a look at the pictures, shall we?"

"Do you think it's all right? Here, I mean? They're pretty hot."

"We're not going to pass them around, after all."

"No, I suppose not, but . . ."

He passed a square envelope over to me with an air of secrecy. Opening it, I found a paper wrapping held by a rubber band. Inside that, six card-sized photos lay in a pile between two slightly larger pieces of cardboard.

"They're all color shots," he said, lowering his voice and leaning toward me. "See there, the poses are different. They're a lot hotter than the professional ones in magazines. The model might not be so good though. The legs seem too small for the body . . . sort of like an insect's, aren't they. But you certainly get the idea. You can just see a bit of hair there at the buttocks. Hair's absolutely out for the magazines, they say."

"Every picture's taken from the back. Did you pick out only this kind?"

"I guess it was Mr. Nemuro's taste. For some reason they're all back views."

"The model seems to be the same in them all."

"Boy! That hair's something. Looks like a horse's tail."

Indeed, the pictures had no narrative quality, that indirect suggestiveness of a professional's work, and no penetrating analysis of the subject. As a whole they seemed flat—perhaps it had to do with the lighting or the shooting technique. And then the model always filled the picture to the same extent and the surrounding space was not made the most of. It was pointless to criticize such things, for the husband's interest was doubtless more in the subject than in the composition. Nevertheless, there was *some* purpose to the six photos, a will to find something. It was not just some naked girl who had been snapped, but a model. Then, every photo was from the back, and though the various poses were different the chief point of interest was the back down to the hips, the buttocks to the thighs. The face, of course, never appeared. The back of the head with the hair falling down was half out of the picture, the face being completely hidden by the back as she squatted over. Tashiro's criticism that the legs were short for the body and that they were like an insect's was not, on close inspection, because of the model, but, I felt, a conscious distortion produced by the lens. Take, for example, the one that Tashiro said was like a horse's tail. The buttocks were turned toward the camera in a posture as if for an enema, and the white backs of the two heels occupying the two corners of the photo were magnified in the greatest detail as if there alone a magnifying glass had been applied. The focus was not quite perfect, but even the pores could be seen. The single hand that was grasping the flesh of one buttock was so heavy-boned and ill-matching that it gave the illusion of being someone else's—from the perspective, a man's. It quickly narrowed and faded into nothing as one's gaze followed it from wrist to elbow. Surely the effect of a wide-angle lens. Once he had decided on the purpose of the picture, being technically minded as he was, then this kind of effect would be relatively simple. But the purpose was the problem. I could interpret the picture as a desire to dissect the woman right out of existence. If it had been the brother's work, I could have understood; but as it was the husband's, I was at a loss. My client, at least, was not one to inspire such vengefulness. She was rather an enigmatic type, the opposite of physical, and a man would get pretty irritated in his effort to understand her. What in heaven's name ever made the husband so enthusiastic about such work?

"What did you say the model's name was?"

"Saeko. She says she's twenty-one, but I'd make it twenty-five or six." Pushing up his glasses, he spoke sharply: "Watch out! The waiter's coming."

I turned the stack of photos face down and raised my eyes. Directly across the open space outside, in the shadow of a pillar, a middle-aged man was squatting on his heels, absent-mindedly looking around him. The hem of his overcoat touched the tile floor and was folded back: judging from the folds, the material did not seem cheap. The briefcase put down at his side suggested that he was a very ordinary office worker. The coffee was placed on our glass-covered table and the bill slipped under the cream pitcher. The man in the shadow of the pillar followed the randomly and constantly moving crowd around him with an unfocused gaze quite as if he were looking at scenery. It was not as though he were watching for some specific person, nor did he look as if he were waiting to be found. From his position and attitude it was not likely that he was some vagabond at a loss for a place to go. Where he was now was an area only for walking, a space where people passed by and vanished, each step taking them closer to their destination. It was, as it were, a nonexistent world of emptiness for people other than photographers, detectives, and pickpockets. His sitting there was an unnatural act, which the more one saw of it the harder it was to understand. But the passers-by appeared to be little concerned with the strange man, perhaps because he was a part of the space there, vanishing among the legs like the tile design of the floor.

It suddenly occurred to me that the man might be dying. Was he not appealing, with difficulty, entrusting to his eyes the agony of his final hour, unable to call for help, his throat constricted by his swollen tongue? But his call was fruitless. The space here was only for walking. No matter how he might appeal, no one would turn and look at something that didn't exist.

But suddenly he arose as if nothing were wrong and quietly moved off into the crowd of pedestrians.

"By the way, that last picture . . . that's too much. Not only is the photography strange, but the girl's a little funny too, isn't she?"

The expression "too much" didn't exactly fit the case. In terms of indecency, I had seen worse. The background was completely black. Against it a girl with knees spread was half squatting, the weight of her body on her left leg. She was bent far over toward the front, and coiled behind her buttocks was her hair, which passed under her crotch. She was grasping it with her right hand, which she had extended around her side. Her position, for all its unnaturalness, was quite unexciting. The picture itself simply made one feel a psychological resistance to the continuing physical discomfort of the model. Only the expanse of flat, white hip, unrelated to the model's twisted limbs, was as expressionless as the carapace of a crab. Beneath her shell the girl was forced into an almost impossible position. It was an incomprehensible picture. There was no obscenity, no sadistic stimulus, only unnaturalness, only a feeling of strangeness, like flowers arranged with their cut ends up. If I had to find something positive about the picture, it would be the strange cooperation of the model. I could understand it to some extent, I felt, if I interpreted it as showing his power to dominate her, but...

"Tashiro, do you think there's any hope in following up this model?"

"I really couldn't say. But this is a side of Mr. Nemuro that wasn't known, I guess. I felt obliged to tell you about it."

"But since he went so far as to entrust the safekeeping of such pictures to you, you had his confidence, didn't you?"

"Yes. Mr. Nemuro was, how shall I put it, on the difficult side when it came to personal relations. He was nice on the outside, but inside he didn't trust others very much."

"I think you're going to have to let me have a look at your room one of these days. Perhaps there's some other unexpected clue of importance among the things Nemuro entrusted to you, something I would recognize if I saw it but that would appear insignificant to you, if you noticed it at all."

"Ah. To tell the truth . . ." His eyes grew smaller behind his glasses; he was flustered. "These pictures weren't in my

room. Look, you remember the rented darkroom I told you
about the other day? Mr. Nemuro had a locker there for his
own exclusive use."

"If it's a locker, it has a key, I suppose."

"Sure. Lockers do ..."

"How did you open it?"

"Well, there's a master key and ... uh ... this chum of
mine runs the place."

"You mean you opened it without permission?"

"Actually, I found the newspaper clipping in the locker.
Don't you think it's quite important? It's dated the end of
July or the beginning of August. Just about the time Mr.
Nemuro disappeared. Maybe he was put up to it by reading
the article. It probably occurred to him that with eighty
thousand missing persons, another to swell the ranks
wouldn't make much difference."

"One way or another, you did open it without permission,
didn't you?"

"But it was for Mr. Nemuro's own good. When someone's
on the verge of committing suicide, I don't think it constitutes a crime to break down the door to get in."

"I'm not blaming you particularly. I'm just asking for the
facts."

"What for?"

"Why didn't you tell me from the first that the shop in
F—— Town was a fuel supplier? Don't tell me you didn't
know. You haven't been frank with me. Is there anything
else you've been hiding?"

A blush spread over his face. Defiantly he stuck out his
lips. His breathing was heavy. "You really do say things that
destroy a person's good intentions. I showed you those pictures of my own accord ... without any thought of reward.

If I hadn't said anything you would never have known about them. What a fool I was to tell you."

"It's strange of you to say that. Weren't you particularly trusted by Mr. Nemuro? Isn't it natural for you to cooperate spontaneously with me?"

"I don't think it can be put that simply," he said sulkily, biting his lip. "You'd like to put it that way because it's your business, but . . . there's more to life than just pursuing. Sometimes it's more important to shield."

"But Mr. Nemuro's disappearance doesn't necessarily depend only on his own will. Perhaps he's been killed, or maybe he's being held by force somewhere."

"Don't be ridiculous!"

"Does that mean you're shielding him?"

"How would you expect me to have such power? Personally, I hope Mr. Nemuro will come back. But I don't think I'm entitled to say so. Supposing, for the moment, I saw him somewhere. I don't know whether I'd go up to him or not. I don't know whether I could do that even if I wanted to. If I had the chance, I would like to talk to him with the understanding that I would say absolutely nothing to anyone. It's natural, because I'm very interested in the case. He's great! I could never do what he did."

"He didn't do anything so great."

"Well, could you do what he did?"

"Unfortunately, I've never yet been the head of a section."

"I couldn't. That stupid business. I'd like to put the torch to it when I think how they prostitute valuable human lives for a business like that. But I suppose it's the same no matter where you go. As long as you work there, somehow or other you've got to try and rise to head clerk, then section head, then department head. At least it's just too miserable if you don't do something. You get ahead of your fellow workers and dance attendance on your superiors. Even fellows who don't have any hope for advancement try to pull the others down. They're all mixed up together like so much fluff."

"Then, unexpectedly, a fellow who has sought shelter by disappearing from another world slips in among them."

My companion looked at me in surprise. Since he was trying to see me through glasses that had slipped down his nose, his face was somewhat elevated, and some hairs left by the razor stood out like thorns above his pointed Adam's apple.

"Yes, indeed," he said, lowering his voice somewhat, as if relieved and expectant. "Look. So many people all the time walking somewhere. Each one has some goal. A fantastic number of goals. That's why I like to sit here and watch. If you cling to trifles, you're left behind. They all keep on walking like that without resting. Whatever would they do if they lost their goals and were put in the position of just watching others walk? Just thinking about it paralyzes my feet. Somehow it makes me feel lonely and miserable. I really know how lucky they are to be able to be walking, no matter how insignificant their goals may be."

Suddenly, quite out of context, I was skeptical as to why my client had not tried to go to the crematorium after her brother's funeral. Even though the syndicate had taken charge of everything, she was the only blood relative, and it would have been natural for her to insist on going along. Or did she wish to avoid facing her brother's death? I wondered. I could understand how she felt, though it was unnatural. Under the circumstances I felt not the slightest suspicion about that unnaturalness precisely because she had acted so naturally. Or wasn't it probably that she had come to think of her beloved brother as dead, as nonexistent, even while he was alive? It made sense, if you assumed that her almost unconditional way of trusting him was a kind of mourning for the dead one. I also felt that I understood the reason why she had not shed a tear as she so agitatedly talked about her brother at the foot of the hill when they were carrying out the coffin. In the living room filled with whispers and idle thoughts, there was no need to be formal even if a dead man had joined the company. The same went for the missing husband as well . . .

"It's already a long time ago, but I once had a terrible experience that still makes me shudder," continued Tashiro, his gaze flitting regularly between me and the outside. I had the feeling he was quite off his guard. "At the time, I was relaxing on a bench in some park. On the bench right next to mine a beggar was stretched out asleep. He was over three yards away. Since the day was terribly hot, I was obliged to put up with him for a little. Meanwhile, it occurred to me that things had got pretty noisy around me, and then a huge demonstration came along from somewhere with a lot of red flags and blue flags. Groups singing songs, groups shouting threateningly through loudspeakers, groups imitating double time, their arms linked, streamed endlessly by. Before I realized it, the beggar had arisen and was looking at them. Suddenly he burst out crying. His lips were all contorted, and he was shedding great tears as he clutched the front of his torn shirt, his shoulders heaving. Never before or since have I witnessed such mournful sobbing. He was weeping for the demonstration, of course. Since the day was hot and he was covered with dust, beggar that he was, the teardrops falling from his chin were pitch black, like dirty water wrung from a mop. You're pretty far gone if you get sad and lonely just watching people walking by."

"Let's go someplace else and have a drink, shall we? It's on me."

"You don't have to do that . . . really . . ."

"That's all right. Besides, I have two or three more things I'd like to ask about."

"Ah. You mean blackmailing retailers and that sort of thing?"

"Where's a good spot? Some place not very expensive . . . one that's interesting."

"Then let's go to the bar next door to the studio where Saeko is. The models on call spend their time drinking there while they wait. It's not exactly regular, but the management's in on it and they give a discount to customers waiting to be called. In any case, you'd like to meet Saeko, wouldn't you?"

"Are you a regular customer?"

"Absolutely not. How much do you think my salary is?"

From evening on, the cold was not so biting, perhaps because it had become cloudy. But the wind had ceased and apparently the fog was coming in; it was like looking through wet glass. The neon lights and the street lights fused, clinging together like cheap water-soaked gumdrops. The commercial main street was making preparations for closing, but the minute we turned into a side street we found ourselves in a section where the most animated hours of the day were just beginning. Coffee houses large and small, arcades with pinball machines, drinking stalls, eating stalls ... and mixed in among them all, second-hand camera shops and book shops, shops with materials for Western clothes, and somewhat more elegant record shops. Last of all there was a whole block of nothing but bars and coffee houses and one pharmacy. We crossed another main street and there was a block of bars, small drinking stalls, and night-clubs. Buildings were sharply etched against the evening sky colored by the light of the neon tunnel behind us, but the sky where we were was strangely black, and men loitering in groups filled the street; gradually their contours began to fade. Beyond lay another block of brilliant neon, lighting a concentration of Turkish baths and ambiguous hotels. Just before them we turned left and entered a quiet alley behind a dilapidated movie theater. "When you think about it, the men walking around here so feverishly are like temporary missing persons. The difference being a few hours or a lifetime."

"It's quite true. I was going to say exactly the same thing a moment ago in front of the pinball arcade. The mental attitude of someone playing pinball is the same as that of a person who disappears. God, that music's annoying. Look. See that place over there just before the telephone pole, with the entrance at an angle and a little set in from the street? You can't get in unaccompanied. I suppose people feel guilty because they're playing the game of missing persons."

There was a door made of narrow strips of wood with a knocker and creaking hinges. The old-fashioned lighting made the shadows stand out. Besides the bar with high stools there were three tables—a very utilitarian atmosphere. But the unfriendly attitude of the bartender, shaking his leg as he stood behind the bar, went somewhat beyond the bounds of the practical. Leaving me seated on an uncomfortable bar stool, Tashiro went out the rear door to open negotiations with Saeko. He was strangely sure of himself for someone who wasn't a regular customer. —"A double rye-and-water." The bartender continued to jiggle his leg without answering, but his movements as he mixed the drink were agile and skilled. There were only two other customers, their heads close together, at the table near the entrance, and judging from the animated tone of the conversation, one of them was not a customer but a shopman involved in business negotiations. The drink was placed before me. The bartender, looking back over his shoulder, turned the knob of the jukebox. At once ear-splitting, frenetic music began, shutting the rest of the bar off from me.

"We're in luck. They say she'll be here right away. I'll have a rye-and-water too," Tashiro said, rubbing his hands with glee and laughing broadly. He took off his coat and clambered up on the stool next to mine.

"While we're waiting I'd like you to tell me something. About blackmail . . . Supposing for the moment some small fuel supplier was being shaken down . . . what could be the circumstances for blackmail?"

"You have some actual case in mind? For instance, could Mr. Nemuro be involved in it, maybe?"

"No. I swear it has absolutley nothing to do with Mr.

Nemuro. It's only a question based on an assumption. But any world has its underside, invisible to outsiders. Like the door you just passed through. If you didn't know what it led to, you wouldn't have any idea of what was inside. At this point, I have to know something about the circumstances. Maybe the blackmailers are swarming like cockroaches at the back door. What are the possibilities of blackmail? If we attack a case theoretically, we can frequently find its real nature in no time at all; it's a method we use a lot."

"I've been thinking of a lot of things since I received your call. But they're all specifics and not generalities. There are possibilities, but ..."

"Well, fine. Tell me."

"In the business world there are brokers who buy and sell rights to chain-store orders and blenders who water down gasoline. There's a big difference in tax rates depending on the type of oil. It's a thieves' business where they make money on the difference in mixture. So even retailers, if they're big enough and if they're favored geographically, privately go in for blending. Or they actually overorder lamp and spindle oil for diluting and then sell the watered sales slips to the blenders. I wonder if it's not something like that."

"We're getting off the subject. Do you know Mr. Nemuro's wife's brother?"

"Her brother? Well, I've met *her* two or three times, but ..."

"Somehow he gives you the impression of being a good-for-nothing. A broad-shouldered, lanky fellow. Did he ever visit Mr. Nemuro in the office?"

"Well, that doesn't give me much ..."

"Actually, he was killed last night."

"Killed?"

"Moreover, barely a mile or two from the fuel supplier in F—— Town."

"Why would such a man . . . we all lead different kinds of lives. I wonder if I'm the only one who knows nothing."

His suspicious, probing eyes, filled with amazement, opened wide behind his glasses; he seemed like an unsteady pot. He looked as though he would fall over with the slightest push. Apparently I could believe him. As for the brother's blackmail, perhaps the objective was purely and simply to make money. If he had even the slightest connection with Dainen Enterprises this timid, suspicious office clerk would not have spoken, even inadvertently, of the possibility of black-market dealings.

Suddenly a rather dry, businesslike voice broke in: "Sorry to keep you waiting." It was a girl with a bad complexion and a prominent chin. She had on a long, loose, purplish-red gown with a dark blue border. Except for her long hair, there was nothing to suggest the girl in the photos. Bits and pieces of a girl have no connection at all with a complete woman. Except for the slightly upturned nose, the thick, stubborn lips, the traces of faded pimples on both cheeks, and the puffy eyelids that looked as if one could squeeze pus from them were rather too vulgar for commercial pictures. One would have to explain away the face by saying the photographer was interested in her back. All her various parts would do if you just took the face away. And as far as the face was concerned it might have been possible to turn her into another person by adding another expression and getting her to assume that cooperative pose.

"It's all right if you want to come back to my room."

"Let's have a drink. It's on me." I drew a stool aside, opening a space between Tashiro and myself. "Would you like a beer . . . or something stronger?"

"It won't be any cheaper . . . time-wise. Is that all right?"

"Don't worry about it."

Giving a derisive, nasal laugh, she climbed onto the bar stool; the front of her gown gaped open and her leg was bared to the fleshy part of her thigh. A beautiful leg, quite unexpected after the face and from the photos which had been distorted by the lens. It was a shapely, well-developed leg, which would have made one think of an athlete's if it had not been so white. One could only say that his bias for backs, which had made him exclude even such legs, bordered on eccentricity. Doubtless a professional, she left her long naked leg uncovered, tapping in time to the music against the bar with the sandal hanging suspended from her toes.

"Well then, bartender, watch the time. I guess I'll have a gin fizz. I'll restrain myself."

"You were especially recommended by a man named Nemuro."

"Oh? Who's that?"

"I think you know him. He showed me some pictures of you a while back. They covered you inch by inch."

"Someone who took pictures . . . that must be a customer on the outside. You probably know that we don't let customers take pictures in the studio."

"Well, what do you do in the studio?"

"Isn't it obvious? They like to see me naked . . . but they only look."

"But the poses in those pictures were something. Terrific. They really got you."

"I'm different from the beginners. But recently I haven't been going out. I am going to be married soon. If I go out all sorts of things happen . . . it's bad for my fiancé."

"Congratulations. But if it's true, there'll be a lot of disappointed customers, won't there?"

The bartender, his face perfectly expressionless, placed the gin fizz in front of the girl. The surface of the drink, with the bursting bubbles, seemed like a deep lake spewing forth a white mist. Tashiro's rye was already gone and he had popped the huge ice cube into his mouth. Perhaps he was listening to our conversation, perhaps not; he stared absently at nothing. It was as if he was gazing at a crowd of unfeeling pedestrians who passed him by and ignored him. I gulped down what remained in my glass and ordered another round. Nervously bracing himself, Tashiro looked at me.

"Mr. Nemuro particularly will be one of those who are going to be disappointed," he said, raising his voice above the record, but judging from the manner of his answer—he had not got the point at all—the music had made a wall unexpectedly thick, and apparently he had heard almost nothing of our conversation.

"Shall I turn down the sound further?"

"No. It's fine. It's best this way."

The girl smiled sarcastically. Placing both hands on the counter, she drew herself back and, raising her naked leg, crossed it in a large arc. Her thick gleaming thigh completely filled the space between the counter and the bar stool. Putting her weight on the arm that held the glass, she turned the upper part of her body toward me, reducing the distance separating us by half. "Is the customer you were talking about the man next to me?"

"No. He's not the one. But it doesn't seem to be the first time here for him either. Do you remember him?"

"I can't remember the face of every single customer. The light's right in my eyes and the customers are as black as crows at midnight."

"But Mr. Nemuro's pictures were terrific," I said, gently caressing the girl's leg with my fingers. Seeing she put up no resistance, I boldly placed my palm on the curve of her large white thigh, while over her shoulder I could see Tashiro averting his gaze in confusion, clamping his lips on his second drink, which had just been brought, as if he could bite the glass. "Letting someone go so far in taking pictures of you is proof you were rather intimate, isn't it?"

"What sort of work does he do?"

"He's a section head."

"Office workers run out of money. My fee for working outside is high. In return, I do what the client wants." Suddenly she finished off her gin fizz, which she had been sipping slowly and, holding up her glass, ordered a second without requesting permission. "But I'm going to be married in a little while. I want a big ceremony. My bridal gown is definitely not going to be a rented one. I'm going to put up all my friends at the most expensive hotel and have a party where everyone can drink as much as he wants, all night long, free."

"By 'friends,' you mean model friends? In that case, your fiancé must know about your work, doesn't he?"

"None of your business." I seemed to have touched a sensitive spot; she peevishly brushed my hand away. "I don't do this work for the fun of it or to show off. Of course, I've had my dreams too. But I wasn't lucky. I'll never take second place to anyone. If the others think they do better than I, let's just compare bankbooks. Your purse is empty if you play the lady and do bathing-suit ads for discount houses. For my kind of work twenty-five or twenty-six is the peak, and after that the only thing left is what's in your bankbook."

"Then you can look your fiancé in the face."

"It's true. Nobody has to spend money on me. I'm the one who provides all the expenses for the ceremony and the down payment on an apartment. I'm not going to buy anyone to marry me."

"If that's so, then those pictures are pretty valuable articles."

"What pictures, for heaven's sake? You're so secretive."

"The ones of only your back and buttocks. Don't you remember? The fellow who specialized in backs and buttocks. The charming dimples about the cleavage in your buttocks. Look. This one."

Grasping a photo I had ready in my pocket, I held it in front of her eyes. Suddenly her expression changed and even her voice took on an uncompromising severity.

"How can you know it's me?"

"Because I do." Again I placed my hand on her thigh, absorbing her through my palm. "First of all, your hair, for instance."

"What do you mean?" Suddenly she laughed nervously, at the same time frowning suspiciously. "That's silly. Not everybody, but most of us wear any wig the customer demands. Right now I'm wearing long black hair on order."

Abruptly she turned and looked at Tashiro over her shoulder, swinging her long tresses and lashing out the ends, which she grasped in her hands. I could not tell the meaning of her high-pitched woman's voice. The expression on Tashiro's face was hidden by the girl's head before I could see it. Hmm. Had it been a wig? Then I could not state positively by the hair alone that this girl and the model in the pictures were one and the same person. I could not arbitrarily claim that a wig was impossible, even in the strange pose where she had passed the hair between her thighs. If, for instance, she had held firmly between her teeth the part of the wig that attaches to the head she could have assumed approximately a similar position.

"Look. I'm sorry," she said, comparing her thigh—the network of shallow bluish veins lent a unique feeling of transparency against the whiteness—with her hand resting on it like some great red spider. Her angry voice spat at me as I basked in a feeling of security that came through my hand. "I want you to stop these false accusations. You said pictures of me—which I find strange. I wouldn't do that. Do you think we let pictures be taken that can be used as evidence later? I'm not an amateur. Look at this and you'll see what I mean."

Abruptly she raised both hands to the base of her scalp and stripped off her hair as easily as if she were peeling a ripe peach. With the long tresses of the wig, which was transformed into a separate creature, she struck my arm sharply, and laying the wig on her thigh, she roughly scratched her short-clipped hair. The bartender, who was looking down at the sink, slightly changed the angle of his head, and in profile he seemed surprisingly broad and muscular. Perhaps because of the light, the area below his sideburns was shaded as if scooped out, maybe the scar from some cut. Was his gloomy expressionlessness only on the surface of his face or did it penetrate beneath . . . to his very heart . . . or was it some incurable disease . . . ? Whichever,

there was no call to waste any more time here in disregard
of its warning. When I withdrew my hand from the girl's
thigh she seemed to notice it for the first time and jerked her
leg and glared at me as if she were looking at an enemy.

"I suppose I can't expect to be invited to your wedding."

"What're you going to do? If you're coming back to the
studio it'd better be quick. Time's about run out."

The music changed. The moment of silence pierced my
ears, and the girl's last words cast a shadow over the whole
bar like the wings of some enormous bird. The two men
at the table by the entrance turned in surprise to look in
our direction. The next record began with a guitar solo. It
merely turned the atmosphere around us a pale white and
did nothing to shut off the rest of the bar. I finished the
remainder of my rye-and-water as I got down from the stool.

"I'll be leaving now. I suddenly thought of something I
have to do." As a tip besides the amount I owed, I placed
a pile of hundred-yen pieces on the two thousand-yen notes
that I had ready. "It's too bad . . . since you're all ready now.
But since there seems to be a bit of time left, if it's all right
with you, I'll let Tashiro here have it. You don't have anything particular to do, do you?"

The alcoholic blush had spread from Tashiro's face to his
neck; only his nose and his chin, as if separated from the rest
of his features by a glass shield, remained whitish. His strange
behavior, neither refusing nor accepting, was after all a kind
of acceptance.

"You're a bachelor, I see . . ." Looking over her shoulder
at Tashiro, the girl didn't even attempt to dissimulate her
frankly scornful laugh. "People wouldn't make fun of you
if you'd use the same color of thread to sew the buttons on
your shirt."

But Tashiro remained standing as he was, bolt upright, saying nothing, rubbing the inside of his glasses with the tip of his finger. The bartender, silent as usual, gently dropped before me the paid bill for the drinks, which settled like a huge snowflake, and handed me the change. I passed by the two men at the table, as profoundly engrossed as before in their discussion, but just as I arrived at the door, the girl, noiselessly, had already caught up with me. The dusty smell of cheap cosmetics made me think of her comfortless bed.

"I'll send you a special invitation to the wedding soon," she murmured, as if nothing had happened. She opened her gown for a bare instant. She was stark naked. Her flesh was solid, but the belly was slack and gave one the feeling of being full of water. The faint frizzled shadow at her crotch was definitely not the same as the model's in the photo.

"It's on the house," she said, affecting a smile. "I'm unexpectedly conscientious, I guess. But I don't want my fiancé coming to a place like this, not if I'm going to have a family. Drop in again . . . before the marriage . . . won't you?"

Tashiro stood rooted to the same spot as if he were some cleverly made doll. I lightly touched the girl's fingers and pushed open the door. It screeched like a startled bird, and a chill wind struck at my collar and the openings of my sleeves. With each step the music receded and changed into the formless gray cacophony of the city, into a stammering like some auditory hallucination. My own senses, fusing with the darkness, continued to scatter. I hastened my steps in the direction of the area beneath the neon-lit sky. I strove to copy the gait of the pedestrians who were walking toward their own goals.

BUT THE faster I walked the more I realized that still another step was pursuing me, undauntedly seeking its goal. The passers-by were not frequent, but in the main street in front of the movie theater, the flow of taxis was unbroken. I continued walking, perhaps because there was none free, but I also wanted to be quickly overtaken by those pursuing steps.

At length a rapid breathing fell into step with me at my side. Without breaking my pace or looking around, I pretended to ignore it, as if it were my own shadow. A soft, pleading tone began to coil around my cold ear like a hungry snake.

"What happened? Don't you like that kind of woman? I think she has marvelous legs. Even in summer she gives the impression of being a soft, cool cushion. Really, I suppose tastes are different. Why don't you say something? Ah, of course, you're dumbfounded, aren't you. Well, it can't be helped. I didn't mean any harm. Somehow I tried too hard to satisfy you. I wonder if I'm shy. I've come to hate myself. It's always like this. I know very well I'll regret it later . . . to the point of wanting to kill myself. Why was I born with a character like this? I hate myself. Do me the favor of forgetting the stuff about the blenders and waterers, if you can.

I was talking out of turn. To tell the truth the average retailer is an honest fellow. They wouldn't dare risk such
dangerous acrobatics. As for shady dealing, they go about
as far as keeping double accounts for getting around taxes.
And even if they do water down bills, they're so incredibly
inept at it they get themselves caught. It's true. Generally
they set up a ghost business with only a name, and so even if
they're discovered they've taken precautions so that the main
store's never dishonored. So it's useless, absolutely useless,
no matter how you snoop around."

I made no answer. I neither concurred nor disagreed, but
continued walking at exactly the same pace, urgently, like
some night insect toward a man-made light; the pedestrians
began to be more conspicuous. Tashiro had fallen silent but,
at length out of patience, he resumed hurriedly: "There are
two reasons why I have to make up stories like I did. I was
afraid . . . you know what I mean . . . when I considered
that Mr. Nemuro had disappeared for no reason, I realized
I had been completely abandoned. No, I suppose that's not
quite right. Maybe I should call it an inferiority complex . . .
or jealousy. The best things in life are kept from me, only
me; I'm the only one who's left out. So I explained the disappearance by any old reason . . . and I was satisfied. People
react that way, don't they. Then, one more thing . . . it's hard
to say . . . I've been worrying about this but haven't mentioned anything to anybody until now. Before I do, I've got
to be more honest. I'm going to get it off my chest—I'd best
confess everything now. To tell the truth, those pictures
were fakes too. I'm sorry. Everything was a lie. I just happened to pick up the pictures in the street, as a matter of
fact. They were interesting, and I looked at them a lot.
Gradually they got all mixed up with my imagination. May-

be it was because of Mr. Nemuro's wife. Say, what do you think about the wife? Seems to me she's playing innocent, or taking people in, or some way looking down on you. Maybe it's because she thinks of me only as Mr. Nemuro's subordinate. I may be a subordinate, but why does she take such a supercilious attitude? One way or another it's not my business, and I shouldn't get so serious about it, I guess. But I'm involved with her some way. I wonder why?"

I remained silent. Breaking in during his confession would only project my companion into another easy lie. I should profit from the momentum of his fall as long as it lasted. I kept walking. Before I was aware of it the streets were filled with a secretion of light—a wedge of artificial day was inserted into the night—the lunatic rhythm of time stimulated the passers-by, spellbinding them.

"Come on!" Tashiro's throat was painfully tensed, his breathing labored. "Have you found out? I told another lie. Lies come out of my mouth naturally, in spite of me. It's a sickness, I guess. Maybe I'm a compulsive liar. Even those pictures—to tell the truth, I took them myself. At this point there's no use in trying to keep up appearances. The model's not the same as the girl back there, of course. I took only back views because the feminine element is most obvious from the back. But I swear that's the last lie. You probably won't believe me even if I say so. Please, please do. I'm really ashamed. I have a terrible secret. I'm very upset. I go so far as to tell lies I don't have to, trying to get away from the pressure of it. If I can just get someone to believe them, I feel they would become the truth. But I'm tired. I want to confess everything, I really do. I'd like you to give me back those pictures. They have nothing to do with Mr. Nemuro; they're just things that add to my shame."

I made no answer. The whirlpools of people were urged on by unseen goals under the night sky, where the neon was already sighing; a festival of darkness for fake runaways who, no matter how they regulated their speed, never pulled away more than three yards from strangers they did not know; imitation exercises for the eternal festival repeated every evening. I stepped to the edge of the sidewalk to hail a taxi. Tashiro made as if to turn in front of me, and as he spat a yellow spittle sprayed my earlobe.

"Please . . . listen to me. It's a terrible secret. I saw him. I saw Mr. Nemuro. It's not a lie. Why won't you listen? It's your business to find him, isn't it? Don't you believe me? Even if you don't, can't you at least listen? I saw him walking along with my own eyes."

I paid no attention to Tashiro. Spotting the red For Hire sign on a cab, I raised my arm. The driver slammed on his brakes and cut his front wheels sharply, bringing the taxi to a clanking, tinny halt and opening the door with a thrust as if to cut me down. I neither invited nor repulsed Tashiro, who, clinging to the door, pushed in with me.

THE DRIVER was very excitable. Even when I told him my destination he did not so much as nod, much less answer, but violently jammed at his screaming gears, making the ancient motor cough and wheeze without any indication of sympathy for it. If the husband had ducked out the back way at the Camellia and escaped to a different world, was he spending his days like this driver, his nerves raw as slivers of glass? Was this world so unbearable that one had to go on eternally escaping until one could put up with such a life?

"I saw him."

Tashiro's glasses, as he peered at me from the side with an anxious expression, began to steam up as I looked at him; the heater made the car too hot. I felt suddenly light-headed as the tenseness left my cold-benumbed cheeks. Evidently the two and a half bottles of beer that I had downed were beginning to enter my blood under the stimulus of the rye.

"That's what I wanted from the start. Why haven't you given me such important information until now?"

"But am I qualified to do that?"

"Qualified?"

"The section head I saw in town seemed like a different man. Not a thing withdrawn or pitiful about him. His step made you think he felt life was worth living."

"I take it you mean he was walking?"

"I was so surprised I almost stopped breathing. I was just on the point of speaking to him, but seeing his expression, I somehow felt timid. I wondered if I really had the right to interfere."

"Was the street wide ... or narrow?"

"An ordinary one ... about like this sidewalk."

"Did he give you the feeling of brooding or nervousness? He might have seemed vigorous at first glance ..."

"Absolutely not. I made no mistake. He was just the

opposite of nervous. He was carefree and seemed to be fully enjoying his walk."

"Then I wonder why he didn't notice you. You had plenty of time to study his expression. Funny, don't you think?"

"But it was terrifically crowded. The offices were just letting out."

"Well then, I suppose you were in the position of following after him, weren't you?"

With two fingers, Tashiro jammed onto his face the glasses he had finished wiping with a wrinkled handkerchief, grinning broadly at me.

"Ha! You think I'm going to be taken in by that? You wanted me to say yes, and then you would ask how I had made out his expression walking behind him. Unfortunately I am telling the truth. You can't catch me like that."

"All right. But even so, you mean you let him go right by you?"

"Well... I guess so..."

"Is it as important as all that?"

"It's a question of being qualified. We've decided that people have established residences and that we should put a chain or something around runaways' necks and bring them home. But just how valid is such a concept? Who has the right to interfere with another's living and against his wishes?"

"You leave one place and you're bound to settle in another. It's not a matter of will, is it? Rather you've got to consider your obligations and responsibilities to the first place you lived."

"Perhaps even the abandonment of those obligations is itself an act of will."

"When did you see him ... and where?"

"The newspaper clipping I showed you a while ago claimed that missing persons run at the rate of one per thousand. One out of a thousand ... and that includes people who can't move of their own free will, like invalids and children. I think it's serious. If you take into account the people who expect to run away but who have not yet done so, the figure's astronomical. Those who don't run away, rather than those who do, are the exception."

"Was it in the summer ... or after it got cold?"

"Before going into that, you've got to clear up the question of qualification."

"Doesn't the worry of the one left behind make any difference? You remember, I think, the story about Mrs. Nemuro's brother being killed."

"Does that have anything to do with the worry of someone left behind?"

"What was the color of the suit he was wearing at the time?"

"You know, I'm scared to death when I'm squeezed like a sardine in the streetcar in the morning. Just by being on friendly terms with a number of people—a hundred, a thousand—whom you know by sight, you feel you have your own place in the world. But the people who hem you in so tightly, so close to you, are all strangers; they're by far the bigger number. No, I suppose what I'm really afraid of is that the streetcar will finally get to the end of the line."

"Just tell me the color of his suit. If you go on like this, saying whatever comes into your head, I've come on a fool's errand."

"Oh, I'm sorry." Suddenly he shrank back, ashamed, gulping again and again. "The color of his suit . . . if I remember right . . . ah, yes, I think it was a raincoat, not a suit."

"Are you certain?"

"It didn't rain that day, but maybe it looked like rain. Anyway, Mr. Nemuro was always prudent. All of us used to laugh at his mania for licenses: license for driving, license for radio operator, license for stenography . . ."

"I know all about that."

"I think all those things are related. Even if you're alone among utter strangers you can manage not to be nervous . . . whether you're in a crowded streetcar or lost in an unfamiliar town . . ."

"What was the color of the raincoat?"

"Very ordinary . . . let's see, a yellowish-brown or beige, I guess . . . the color of any raincoat."

"Was it new or did it look as if it had been worn a long time?"

"No, it wasn't new. It was quite worn. It seems to me there were grease spots on the cuffs and the collar. Yes, I remember. It was one Mr. Nemuro had been wearing a long time. He was strong on repairing cars, and often instead of overalls he would wear the raincoat when he crawled under the car."

I abruptly ordered the driver to stop. A darkened town, where only the streets were broad, bespeckled with street lights. A sign about night work on a water main was lit by a spotlight and shone red, while a number of helmets painted with a phosphorescent paint repeated again and again the same tedious motion.

"Let's get out of here and cool off. You know the reason without asking."

"How can I know?" he said, shrinking back defiantly. "I was just about to tell you everything."

"Think it over until you do know. Come on . . . out you go."

"You'll be sorry."

"That's enough. Unfortunately, the raincoat I have right at hand in safe keeping. Start all over again after you've thought up a cleverer lie you can't see through. Take an aspirin. Have a good night's sleep."

I jabbed him roughly in the neighborhood of his fifth rib with my index and middle fingers locked together. Tashiro gave a little grunt, twisting his body as the upper half fell forward. He sprang up on one leg, barely avoiding falling over, and, facing the closing door, shouted hoarsely: "I followed him! I followed him! I did!"

I LEFT the car at the top of the slope on the plateau where the housing development was situated. Besides the money I had spent for coffee with Tashiro, there was the unintentionally large tip I had given the taxi driver because I was drunk and the unexpected expense at the bar of the nude studio. What could I claim as justifiable expenses? I wondered. A claim had to fit with the contents of my report. Of course, I could not say that there was nothing worthwhile at all to report on. Even killing time has some value. I thought that I should get a really first-rate eraser for the purpose of erasing the equivocal and useless lines which for over two hours had connected me with a potential pseudo-runaway.

But it was close to impossible to put together in an objective report that would be meaningful to others such vague results. Writing that a liar confessed he had lied was the same as writing nothing at all. Even in thinking it over the only thing that stood out clearly was the naked white thigh beneath the counter, only the feeling in the palm of my hand that seemed to adhere to it. As for the dissected parts of the girl, supposing I could fit them into the jigsaw picture without going any further than I had, then it would seem I could only seek the remaining parts behind the lemon-yellow curtains. Like some insect lured to a light trap, I again walked the street of the housing development in the direction of her window. I didn't even particularly wonder at the fact that I had no reason, none worth the name, at least . . .

No, that was not quite true. My car, abandoned there near the steps that led up to her place, just beyond the second street light from here (I had left it on the pretext of being drunk and now I was even more so) became flimsier and flimsier as a reason. I walked over the trampled path in the dead grass, shortening the distance between me and the lemon-yellow window. At length, some thirty-two normal paces from the corner of Building 3, I raised my head, and the line of street lights, glass eyes that no longer knew how to blink, stood in a row like charms, summoning a festival procession that would never come; the faint rectangular light that burned in the window had long since given up such things as festivals. I was struck on the side of my face by a wind like a wet mop, and as I stood there motionless I raised the collar of my coat. It was about here that the missing husband was said to have last been observed.

Supposing he were standing here now and not I . . . supposing he had come stealthily, concealed under the cover of darkness, looking up at the house he had abandoned, what would he be thinking? I tried as best I could to put myself in his position, but it would not work. I didn't know why, but the silhouette of the driver of the taxi I had just taken forced itself before my eyes. That slimy, malicious runt, from whose entire body rose an animal stench, breathing dissatisfaction instead of air, circulating in his veins venom instead of blood. Such a man would not stand around here. He would have no time to compare stealthily his own fate with the lemon-yellow window. But it didn't mean that all drivers were always like that. For instance, there were also family men like Toyama, who had bought the car. Of course, the husband had to be himself. He couldn't let himself be replaced with someone else. The husband . . . he had tried to run from the filing cabinets of life, turning his back squarely on whatever hopes he had for festivals. Had he not wanted to set out for some eternal festival that could never be realized?

One day, unexpectedly, he had come upon a poster pasted on some wall or telephone pole . . . a broadside telling of a great festival, inconspicuous with its faded colors, and blanched by the wind and the rain. The time and place were blank, but that only served to stimulate his hopes. Without looking behind, he set out in search of the festival that was announced . . . he went toward an eternal festival, one that would end only with death, one that was different from the pseudo-fêtes each night that only the darkness and neon lights could cover up. If darkness were indispensable for the festival ceremonies, it would be a world of perpetual night. He joined the unending, circling waltz, unrelated to the pieces of paper dancing in the wind, the sadness and fatigue that come after a festival.

Now he is standing here, balancing the weight of unfulfilled dreams with what he has lost. What will he do? I search and fumble for him . . . but in vain. This blackness I am seeking is after all merely my own self . . . my own map, revealed by my brain. I am the one standing here, not he. Properly speaking, the place where I should be standing is not here but in front of the board fence around the construction site from which the window of my wife's room is visible. I stand trembling, seeking the window of a stranger who has only the accidental relationship with me of being my client. Perhaps the husband is standing under some unexpected window too, one that does not even appear on his own map. Is he sleeping now in that place, that place nobody else can ever reach? Or is he awake, is he laughing or crying . . . is he angry or bored . . . does he despair or is he in good spirits . . . is he helplessly drunk, does his tooth ache, is he frightened, is he fuming like a burning pot, is he all upset or is he relieved, has he lost his way, is he falling down with a crash, is he concentrating on counting out his pocket money, is he addicted to memories, is he gathering together his appointments for tomorrow, is he alone with his nightmares, is he tearing out his hair with remorse, or with faint breath does he keep forcing the blood from a deep wound?

But I was the one standing here now. There was no mistake, I was the one. I thought I was following the husband's map, but I was following my own; I wanted to follow in his steps and I followed my own. Suddenly I was frozen still. But it was not only because of the cold . . . nor was it the fault of the liquor alone, nor of my shame. My perplexity gave way to uneasiness, and that changed to fear. My gaze traveled along the corner of Building 3, running up and down; looking back, I counted the buildings from the end. Again, a second time, a third time I counted. My eyes continued like a madman's up and down, down and up along the corner of the same building. It wasn't there! The lemon-yellow window was gone! Curtains of white and brown vertical stripes, completely different, were hanging in the place where the lemon-yellow window should have been. What in the name of God had happened? If I wanted to know I had only to advance thirty-two paces, go up the stairs, and ring the bell at the left of the door on the second floor. But I could not. Since the curtains had changed so radically, the person who would come to greet me would doubtless have turned from lemon to zebra. Was not this striped curtain a flag indicating the husband's return? There was one possibility in a thousand that, having seen the article in the evening edition, he had returned half out of dislike for the brother . . . that his one chance in a thousand had materialized. What a boring conclusion . . . a splendid disappointment. A very easy map to understand. A dialogue indistinguishable from talking to oneself. All right. Everything was perfectly resolved—not a thing was left in doubt. I could completely withdraw from the case with no unpleasant thoughts, although I should never be able to brag of my success.

Yet, there was not a single reason to be unhappy. Subconsciously, I may have wanted the case to go on forever, but the source of funds had been severed by the brother's death, and no matter how much savings she might have there was no reason for her to let an almost hopeless investigation go on any further. In the three and a half days left till the term of our contract expired, no matter how active I might be, it would not amount to much. There was no reason to be disappointed. Musing that I had just wanted my briefcase from the car, that I had made a detour for it, I withdrew with a heavy heart by the same path I had come. A dark path . . . too dark. Just one more time I turned to look at the altogether inappropriate, unsightly striped pattern and then went down the slope in the direction of the subway station. I passed a middle-aged couple going in the opposite direction, their necks sunk into their coat collars against the cold, their shoulders hunched timorously; between them a schoolboy dressed in a uniform was volubly discussing something or other. A number of small pieces of paper, each striving to be first, were being sucked into the entrance to the subway, scooped out by the brilliant illumination. For dinner I made do with curried rice with an egg and stew at a cheap restaurant just before the entrance. Although it was dead winter a huge green bottlefly, slipping and sliding, was buzzing as it tried to crawl up the shade over the electric light; it kept circling around but there was no need to worry: flies know the seasons better than humans, and their wisdom is great.

REPORT

14 February: 6:30 A.M.—I went on a secret reconnoitering expedition on the basis of the tip that from half past six to seven in the morning the Camellia coffee house engaged in unlicensed placement of temporary taxi drivers. If this unlicensed placement was a fact, then the Camellia matchbox that the missing man had left, with its black and white matchsticks and the way it was scratched, would be profoundly significant. I suppose I shall have to look again into the ad for recruiting drivers that appeared in the sports paper. The Camellia owner's ad for private drivers could naturally be considered a ploy to fool people, and it is quite possible that it was a special private code understandable only to temporary drivers. (F.Y.I. a couple of examples: they could be giving notice of reopening after a raid by the size or arrangement of the letters; or they could be suggesting a change in the contact place; or it was not at all impossible that there was some special meaning over and above the words.) And so it doesn't necessarily follow that I will be able to find traces here of the missing man at once. Since drivers in the metropolitan area alone number roughly 80,000 and out of them

15,000, or about twenty per cent, are migratory, similar unlicensed employment agencies can be supposed to exist in quite large numbers. However, there's doubtless nothing to stop me considering it a reliable fact that the Camellia constitutes a meaningful clue. The above are the reasons I went on secret reconnaissance of the Camellia. Fortunately the driver Toyama is a good-natured fellow and since he has a satisfactory history as an employee of the Camellia for the time being, and though I do not have a proper letter of introduction, his name will be very helpful to me in getting information.

BUT THAT was all fake. It was still twelve minutes until the fourteenth of February. There was still one fourth of the day's time left until dawn. The preparations seemed too perfect, but there was no call to act like a heady schoolboy on a picnic nor to devise Tashiro's kind of vicious, irresponsible talk. The contents of my report would not change were I to wait six hours . . . ten hours. Furthermore, I did not need to fear meeting death within six hours, and tomorrow, if after my search of the Camellia I wanted to visit her place as quickly as possible, there was no better excuse than this report. Whatever the meaning of the un-

sightly striped curtains, I must be able to pass the barrier
openly. In any event the harvest in terms of information
would probably fill several lines of my report and I had absolutely no need to feel ashamed. It is self-evident that every
night has its morning.

In the little apartment room that I used only as sleeping
quarters and where I lived my unaccustomed solitary life,
the night was as slow in falling as the day was in rising. I
set the hands of my alarm clock at a few minutes before five
o'clock, wound it up, and placed it just out of reach on the
window ledge; I turned on the radio to drown out the sounds
from the mah-jong players on the second floor and crawled
into my cool bed, which because of the whisky I had spilled
began to stink more than I did myself. From among the
nude photos I had taken from Tashiro, I chose one which,
though not characteristic, best showed the woman's female-
ness and placed it side by side with the picture of the husband on the table by the bed. As I sipped my whisky straight
from a small bottle I concentrated intensely on the relationship between the two photos. The somewhat elongated face
of the man, suggestive of an enthusiastic type, was slightly
asymmetrical. The surface of the face seemed rough, perhaps
due to the splotches of color and not to the roughness of the
skin . . . evidently a type given to allergies. The right eye was
strong and gave a feeling of willfulness, but the left one
drooped at the corner, and had a conspicuous sag in the lid,
giving a kind of sorrowful, doglike expression. The long, thin
nose was bent slightly to the left. The lips joined in an
almost straight line, as if drawn by a ruler. The upper lip
was thin and nervous, but the lower was heavy and calm.
To the left of the mouth were some hairs skipped by the
razor. The main impression I had had up to now was of a
businessman's temperament, but tonight—perhaps it was my

own fancy—the face had taken on the cast of a visionary. I felt no hostility or resistance, but I could not believe that a real man would materialize and speak to me. The face was one that was best suited to the present pose, as if he had been born as an image on a piece of negative paper. A blurred line of light ran diagonally across the background, perhaps a part of a building gleaming in soft beams of sunlight, or an elevated toll road.

In the other picture, a woman's hips, naked, flesh-colored, and broad, were set against a background of solid black. Broad they were, but although they filled the whole picture the hips themselves gave the feeling of being rather small-boned. The form made me think of something. Yes, a loquat . . . a weak-looking, deformed loquat . . . a cross between a loquat and a pear . . . a pellucid hemisphere slightly tinged with green below, perhaps because the color of the carpeting on the floor was not a pure black. A cleft underneath ended in the swelling at the tip of the lumbar vertebra. The inside was boldly colored a dark brown and resembled the dampness of mucous membranes. The upper half was an opaque white faintly tinged with a soft pink. The opacity was perhaps due to the downy hair and maybe the white too was a diffused reflection caused by the down. Because the subject was bent far over toward the front, from my viewpoint only the planes of the protuberances of the spinal column, in rows like clusters of old tombs buried in the sand, were the color of scorched flour, polished in texture. The color disturbed me strangely.

Downy hair like expensive velvet, so soft and fine as to be almost invisible. The fine-textured skin of a young boy with a touch of brown. Of course, even though one might have the highest technical competence, color film was incapable of reproducing exactly the actual tones. At this point I had no intention of rejecting Tashiro's confession, but if I was again suspicious of a lie based on another lie, it was not at all imposible that the first lie had become true. Moreover, it was true that she herself recognized that her husband was crazy about color photography. The possibility that this nude picture had actually been taken by the husband could really not be ruled out. Since I was suspicious of the way Tashiro had got excited and took back what he had said before, there was probably some question as to how he had come by the photos. When I thought about it—I do not know whether such analysis is possible—on the husband's face creases characteristic of a peeping Tom seemed to have been etched. The inhabitant of an upside-down world, who could not believe in the existence of something until he had all alone completely absorbed the object into himself.

Thus, I still had reservations. In the first place, I wondered whether Tashiro had the know-how to use a wide-angle lens. Furthermore, there was the album—*The Meaning of Memories*. In it she had been composedly aware of being photographed and had even put on a performance: the picture of her, dressed in her peignoir, through which the contours of her body were visible. (Was it out of disinterest or absent-mindedness, was she fully aware of what she was doing, or was it out of natural coquetry that she had calmly permitted herself to be exposed to my eyes as she did?) Yes, it was quite possible. The model in this picture was his wife, my client herself.

I had grown stiff. Leaving only the picture of the woman, I put the husband's photo aside. Although I would have to be up early in the morning tomorrow, I had without being aware of it finished off a small bottle of whisky. The radio continued ceaselessly playing American folk songs. Under the blankets my body at last had gotten warm, and less and less was I able to take my eyes from the loquat. In my fancies she had almost become a young girl. The crevice in the loquat was glistening and moist, like the membrane between the toes of a frog. Certainly a very short, crimson dress would suit her well. She overlapped and was inextricably involved —precisely like the Picasso reproduction in her room—with my impression of the eccentric girl who helped in my wife's shop. I was an acrobat indefatigably repeating my dangerous act, almost falling, on an absolutely safe rope stretched over level ground. How would it be if I took her with me to my wife's shop to order a dress? Actually, I seemed to recall her saying she wanted to find a job. If I could get them to take her at my wife's place, the membrane between the frog's toes would be even more beautiful—like purple rubber. What was broken? What was left? Again the usual face appeared in the veneer ceiling printed with the straight-grain cypress wood . . . a laughing moon . . . why was the dream I had a couple of times every year, where I was pursued by a laughing full moon, so frightening? It was still a puzzle I could not understand no matter how I racked my brains.

4:56 A.M. Thinly, like emery paper, the ringing of the alarm clock impinged on my senses. My mouth was dry, and a thick phlegm stuck in my throat, making it impossible to smoke. Rather than a hangover, I seemed still to have last night's inebriation; no matter how much cold water I dashed over my face, my eyes felt as hot as after a number of headstands, and no matter how I blew my nose it simply would not stop running.

However, I had already entered my arrangements for to-day in the report. I could only act as if they were accomplished. The smallish room with almost no furniture gave me the feeling of being embarrassingly large. Perhaps it was due to the cold. Turning on the gas, I placed my two hands on the kettle to gather up its warmth. I would set out immediately after I had had a cup of strong coffee. If I left the apartment at 5:30, I would get to the housing development on the hill by 6:10. If I got my car back and made a couple of passes in front of the Camellia to check the lay of the land and then went in, it would be about 6:30, just as I had written in the report.

I shaved and changed my clothes. Just as I was looking over last night's evening edition as I sipped my coffee, a bell again began to ring. It could not be the alarm clock this time . . . the telephone, of course . . . the only valuable fixture in my room. Though uneconomical, I had had it installed, thinking it would be of some use for my business. I was almost never at home, but on the rare occasions I overslept I could call in at the office. There had not been a single incoming call in over a fortnight. I wondered, indeed, whether I should not get rid of it. The bell rang a third time. It was unbelievable. Maybe a wrong number. No, maybe it was her. Some unforeseen happening that had made the curtain turn a lemon-yellow again. Or was it my wife? If it was my wife . . . at half past five in the morning . . . it must be something like an attack of appendicitis or maybe acute pneumonia. Without waiting for the fourth ring, I picked up the receiver.

"Yes?"

"Were you asleep?" came a murky, effeminate voice. Good God, Tashiro!

"For Christ's sake," I blurted out angrily, "what time do you think it is?"

"If you hadn't got up after one more ring, I was going to hang up. But really, I want to talk to you."

"Listen, it's still dark outside. Quit behaving like a spoiled child."

"It's not true. The sky's beginning to change color . . . such a sad color. And where I am the milk's been delivered and I can hear the paper boy. A dog's barking, too. The first streetcar has already left the barns."

"Stop it. I'm hanging up."

"No! You'll be sorry later if you treat a man's parting words like that. You will . . . because I'm just about to kill myself. I've spent a sleepless night thinking, and I'm fed up. Hey, there's the paper boy running. Oh, yes, the newspaper. Tonight's edition'll have an article on my death, you can bet. The reason . . . what is the reason? I wonder. A breakdown, I suppose."

"I'm absolutely impressed by your big scene. But I'm busy, sorry. Let's let the rest go till tomorrow, shall we?"

"You don't believe me. You're stupid. You absolutely can't tell the lie from the truth in what I've said. As long as it's expressed in words, any lie has some meaning. But I'm going to make you believe me this time. I'll make you regret it your whole life long. It's a good feeling. I'll show you what it is to be insensitive."

"Where are you calling from?"

"Someplace . . . any place. Looks as if you're beginning to get worried."

"Do you really think I'd worry about you?"

"You wouldn't?"

"Well . . . I'm hanging up."

"Wait! I won't take up your time. I'll be dying pretty soon. I'd like you to hear what my voice sounds like when I do. Since you treat me like a worm, I wonder if it'll have no effect on you to witness my death. Anyway, I'm sure you think I'm just faking again. That's good enough. With that in mind, listen while you drink your tea."

"I'm drinking coffee."

"That's even better. It becomes you. Are you listening? I'm up on the scaffold . . . it's a suitcase . . . I'll put the rope around my neck . . . no, I'll stick my head in the noose."

"Have you left a note?"

"No, I haven't. I thought about it, but if I really started to write, I'd never stop. If I wrote a short note, it'd only be: Goodbye."

"Don't you have anything else to tell me about Mr. Nemuro?"

"You unfeeling bastard. You're a pig, not a man. How can you say such a thing to somebody who's on the brink of death? You're ridiculous. I don't give a damn about his disappearance. It's pretty sneaky . . . something a coward'd do. What's the point of putting up such a great fuss about somebody like him? I'd never do that. There . . . I've put the rope around my neck. The position is right, it'll bite right in. Pretty soon I'm going to feel the blood coming out of my nose. I'll be gone further than anyone who's disappeared . . . much, much further."

"Suicides and missing persons are pretty much alike, aren't they? And a corpse is dirty. But a missing person's as transparent as air, cleaner than glass."

"Damn, somebody's coming. Well, then, this is it. I'm

going to kick away the suitcase I'm standing on . . . now. Tell Mr. Nemuro's wife . . . it's too much, hiring a detective for a missing person."

"What's too much? For whom?"

But there was no answer. I thought I heard a sound like someone stamping on a rubber bag filled with water, but even that was canceled out by a terrible noise of something violently hitting the receiver . . . that was all . . . I could hear nothing more. There was a soft sound like that of a puppy scratching itself in a box. Perhaps I only fancied it. It was unbelievable that he would commit suicide. What should I do? If by any chance he had actually done it, as the last person present at the time I would be raked over the coals unmercifully by the police. Aside from being gone over by the police, whatever explanation should I give? It was absurd. Should I say that I had been piggishly insensitive? As far as the police were concerned, a satisfactory explanation would be that I had kept badgering the poor fellow to the point of driving him to suicide. It was inevitable, since for them that would be the only convincing, logical one. He had taken fine revenge on me. Revenge for what? It was so beautifully done that I had no idea why he had acted as he had. Of course, it could not be suicide. He was a sort of madman. It was his nature, he had to get people's attention by doing something especially spectacular. Like someone who likes to wear a breastful of decorations. In a minute, would his voice come snickering or sobbing over the receiver? There! A sound . . . the squeaking of a door hinge. But a man's sonorous cry struck my ear . . . a hoarse, panic-stricken, screaming voice.

It was true! I replaced the receiver, confirming the truth around me.

AND AGAIN the dark street. The dark, dark street. The women out shopping for the evening meal of course, and the baby carriage and the silver bicycle were already painted out by the darkness; most of the commuters too were already in place in their filing-drawer houses. A half-forsaken chasm of time where it was still too early for some laggards, playing at being truants, to return home. I stood still . . . precisely where he had vanished. The brown-and-white striped design hung in her window as it had the night before. There was a lot I should have to report . . . starting with Tashiro's suicide, but somehow I hesitated. At least, when I pulled into shape the report on the Camellia, that would definitely touch on the husband's movements. For instance, even if it were against the facts, by claiming I had made some progress, the outcome would be good, one I need not be ashamed of. But thanks to Tashiro my plans had gone completely awry. There was nothing for it but to go around to the Camellia tomorrow morning after all.

The wind whistled through the spaces between the buildings. The stream of cold air striking the corners set up a low, almost inaudible howl. Before I was aware of it, my pores froze over and my icy blood reached my heart where it became a red, heart-shaped ice bag. The ravaged asphalt sidewalk . . . and as usual the abandoned white rubber ball on the lawn . . . and my dust-covered shoes that shone as if they were gilded, under the street lights . . . and the crack-filled corpse of the street . . . and the manhole under the dry grass quite as forsaken as I.

Today I handed in my written resignation. If by chance Tashiro had left any evidence, any place, that I was the one who had spoken to him last over the telephone, I should not be able to escape being found by the police, and my position would be all the more disadvantageous for not having reported at once to them. It was an extremely touchy situation, which the chief wanted to avoid at all costs. The chief had not particularly urged my resignation, but neither did he refuse it when I handed it in. He repressed any expression, and only his eyes were more than usually kind when he suggested that I might indeed work independently but that fellows like me would run wild if not held in by somebody like him, and that judging from past experience independent men ended in failure. "You seem rather well controlled," he had said, "but imagine committing such a blunder. In this business the future's full of pitfalls. Don't take it amiss, but you might have the courage to change professions now. The world's a big place; there are all kinds of livelihoods. Next time you'll come here as a first-rate paying client. Out of our long friendship I'll do you a big favor and assign you a top-flight man."

I waited in the apartment a half day. Good news or bad news, it would be worst of all for me to be suspected of running away. The police hadn't appeared after all. Apparently, I had escaped the worst. The danger was not entirely gone, but the only ones who knew of my discussions with Tashiro were my client, the chief, and, of course, Tashiro himself.

Waiting was a bore. With work one understands one's own effort is everything, but in waiting one can't use one's own strength. Furthermore, my hangover had got worse and my stomach was in knots. But perhaps beyond the window she too was waiting. Evidently the striped curtains were not necessarily a sign that the husband had come back. If he had, she would have called the office and I would have had a report from the chief. They must have some other, some different meaning. I suppose she was waiting, too. Yet I did not have the courage to ring her bell. Like the transformation of the curtains, some change had definitely taken place inside, even if not the husband's return. A big change had occurred for me too. I had already resigned from the office where she had filed her request for the investigation. I was no longer an investigator working there; and she too had stopped being a client. As my last job, I had been ordered by the chief to check directly with the client herself as to whether she had the intention of proceeding further with the investigation, even though the investigator was changed. That too, if possible, I wanted to do *after* exploring the Camellia tomorrow morning. Perhaps I was reluctant to give up the case, but there was nothing left for me to do, there was no goal to walk toward.

The husband had disappeared, the wife's brother had been killed, the clerk Tashiro had committed suicide, and I had not even had a call from my wife. The only thing left before me was my waiting client. Everyone had vanished. From the standpoint of my colleagues at work, I too was one of those who had disappeared. But I was not the only one; what really proved the existence of my client, talking to herself, living on her beer, was that she was on the government tax lists.

A comical game of hide-and-seek where nonexistent players hunted and searched for each other.

Despite the glare of the street lights I could see nothing but the darkness. Now and then a bus would pull up, and there would be the thin sound of someone walking, but not a soul was visible. The black, vacant perspective in which I wearily waited was all there was. But I kept waiting, walking slowly in one direction, stopping, turning round, and walking back again. I would wait forever. As long as she went on waiting I too would wait with her. In the distance an iron grill was violently slammed shut, sounding through ramifications of pipes, finally striking my ears as a sigh from the earth. The faint howling of a dog came rushing through space. How could everyone have ceased to exist?

I COULD only assume someone was watching me. Outside it was all white, and although colors had not yet returned to objects, it was already light enough to distinguish clearly the shapes of things, and drivers were beginning to turn off their headlights. Yet the inside of the shop was still lighter, and through the loose weave of the Camellia's black curtains I could clearly make out the interior. The shop, which had always been so deserted and

forlorn that it made me ill at ease, was now a confusion of
closely packed black figures. Just by changing the fourteenth
to the fifteenth in my report I could let it stand as it was,
apparently. People on the inside could not yet see out very
well, and as a matter of fact everyone was facing the counter,
his attention focused on something or other. There was absolutely no indication they were keeping watch outside or
being particularly vigilant. It was conceivable that the attendant in the parking lot somehow or other could secretly
contact them.

Furthermore, even I took no precautions. My goal was
simply to glean some clue concerning the husband by seeing
a familiar face, but they were close-mouthed fellows and I
had no intention of forcing anyone to talk. Out of work I
was, but I hadn't yet thought of trying a shakedown by exposing the unlicensed operation. My eye was caught by the
rewritten help-wanted ad, Female Clerk Wanted, and I
calmly pushed open the accustomed door and shouldered
into the heated atmosphere and commotion.

It was impossible to discern exactly what was going on.
Two or three men standing at the front turned and looked
at me with hostile eyes; the next instant I was seized by the
collar by hands extended from the corner near the door,
while an arm violently beat on my head, which unexpectedly
began to reel. No, it was not an arm, but a blackjack perhaps . . . something soft and limp like a rubber truncheon.
The heavy dizziness in my chest was an inverted cone. I
could taste the bitter gastric juices dripping from its point.
My face was struck or I was kicked, but I felt no particular
pain. That came when I was carried unconscious outside.
Beside my car, parked immediately in front, I was kicked
about the neck and hips. A sharp pain exploded with a flash

like shooting fireworks, piercing my heart. Perhaps it was that that brought me back to consciousness. Someone opened the car door and two others, supporting me on both sides, thrust me in. My legs were folded in under the dashboard and the door was violently closed. They were experts. Unfortunately I was unable after all to see the faces of the men who had manhandled me.

The pain brought back my energy. I tried moving my shoulders; fortunately the ache had nothing to do with them. My two hands were covered with blood. Looking into the rear-view mirror, I could see splotches of blood on my face, as if someone had been playing tricks with paint. My nose was blocked, and it was difficult to breathe. I took out from under the seat the old towel I used for cleaning off the windshield and wiped away the blood. But I couldn't do much against the slimy red that clung to my face. My nose hadn't stopped bleeding yet. I pinched my nose with two fingers and, leaning my head against the back rest, I waited for some time with my face upward. But I could not spend a long time like this. There were almost no passers-by yet, but the window of the Camellia had already become a black mirror, and the surroundings had taken on color with the onset of morning. Then the quiet and deserted street was suddenly swarming with people. I could not let a face like mine be seen. I rolled up a Kleenex and plugged my nose. Aware of the eyes that were surely peering at me from the window of the Camellia, I started the car and slowly pulled away. The booth at the parking lot was still dark, and fortunately the figure of the old man was not to be seen.

AND AGAIN the white sky . . . to which
the white road seemed directly connected. The street lights
had already closed their eyes; the street had broadened to
about ten yards at a rough estimate. Only in the open mouths
of the various buildings and in the entrances to stairways did
a remembrance of the night still linger; a boy on a bicycle
had just made the last milk delivery and now passed the car
on his way down the slope amid the clicking of empty bottles
in his sack.

Fortunately there was still no one else around. I rushed
up the stairs, two at a time, and rang the white bell in the
white iron door, bordered with its dark green frame. Although it had only been a day since I had been here, I felt
like someone who has been on a ship and touches land for
the first time in a month. Whatever the meaning of the
curtains that had changed to stripes, this blood-spattered
face of mine should afford me free admission.

At the second ring the cloth over the peephole was rolled
up. It was not surprising she had taken so long, considering
the hour. I heard the chain being hurriedly unfastened. The
handle turned, the door opened wide.

"What has happened to you? It's so early in the morning
. . ." she gasped in the amazement I had anticipated.

"It was the Camellia. Will you let me wash up my face?" At least there were no men's shoes in the entryway. She wore a net over her hair and had on a strange pajamalike quilted garment that made her look like a young girl. I still couldn't make her fit in with the impressions I had gleaned from the photo that I had spent two successive evenings intently studying.

"When you say 'Camellia,' you mean that coffee house?"

I took off my topcoat and my jacket; my sleeves and my collar were blood-soaked. As I carefully wiped away the stains with absorbent cotton, which I dipped into the basin of lukewarm water she had brought me, I briefly explained the situation to her. With exaggeratedly painful breathing I told her about the worrisome information I had got out of the parking lot attendant . . . and the driver Toyama's story which supported it . . . and the unlicensed employment agency for temporary drivers that was forbidden by law.

"You'd best not touch the cuts too much. Shall I change the water?"

"A nose bleed, I guess. The cuts don't amount to much. They sting, but they're no more than bruises."

"Why did they have to be so violent, I wonder."

"I guess they had to be."

"Anyone who takes refuge there must be desperate not to be found out."

"Did you know that Tashiro committed suicide?"

"Suicide?"

"Why does everybody want to run away?"

"What was his motive? I suppose he had some reason."

"Motives . . . I have some things to tell you about when I get the time, but . . . To make a long story short, he got lost . . . where was he? . . . did he really exist the way he thought he did? It was others who proved both his existence and his whereabouts, but since not a single one took any notice of him . . ."

"If that were the case, I'd have to be the first to die," she said, her tone of voice suddenly normal again as she tossed back her remark. "Do you want to try on my husband's shirt? I hope it fits you."

"But I've lost my job on account of him. The chief's got an extreme case of police phobia. If there's any possibility at all of getting involved in complications, it means dismissal. What about it . . . will you let me go on with the investigation for the remaining two days plus, even though I've lost my status?"

"Maybe it's my fault."

"You changed the front curtains, didn't you?"

"I've put on some coffee. Yes, let me think, it must have been the day before yesterday . . . the day of my brother's funeral. That's right, it was right after your visit. The coffee stain just wouldn't come out. Then I sent them to the cleaners. I was talking to someone who absolutely had to have a cup of coffee. I prepared it all right, but as I was carrying it out, he suddenly tickled me from behind . . ."

Suddenly I felt a rising nausea. A violent pain radiated from my eyes, reverberating against the back of my skull, focusing at the back of my neck, knotting my throat.

"Was this fellow another dream about your husband?"

"Yes, I guess so. I guess it was, when I think about the tickling."

"I liked the others . . . the lemon-yellow ones better, you know."

"They'll be back in two or three days."

"I have fifty-eight hours to go. A whole two days and ten

hours . . . until the investigation contract expires . . . it said a week, but with Sunday out, it comes to six days."

"I'll go out to work. I'm worrying about expenses."

The nausea was growing worse. My stomach was as heavy as lead and I was chilled.

"There are apparently some eighty thousand taxi drivers in Tokyo alone. There are about four hundred companies, but if you include the independents, there may be more than a thousand. Even if I want to visit taxi companies every day, at the rate of five per day, you can see how long it would take to cover them all."

"Do you feel bad?"

"A little, yes."

"Then you'd better lie down . . ."

The pain in my head and the nausea had reduced my vision, and all my senses concentrated shamelessly on her small hand that lay on my arm, as if that were the cosmic axis. I leaned forward, desperately fighting down the vomiting that threatened to erupt at any moment. For the first time I passed through the door to her room. I saw the white bed still rumpled from her sleeping . . . and the depression she had left in the sheet. I could clearly catch her scent despite my stuffy nose. The depression she had left lay away from the center, slightly toward the wall . . . a vessel for my sleep . . . the purple membrane between a frog's spread toes.

"Sorry. Anyway, the map I drew was too simple compared to the actual town."

"It's not good to be talking when you're nauseous. There are still thirty-four hours to go."

She sat down at the foot of the bed, staring at me intently from some place I could not see. Was she really looking at me? I wondered. Or, like the guest she had had to coffee,

was I being made to join the phantoms who played the foil
to her monologues with herself?

For whom does it beat . . . this enormous heart of the
city that goes on pulsating, not knowing for whom? I
changed my position and looked for her, but she was no
place to be seen. If that were the case, where in heaven's
name was I, looked at by that nonexistent her?

"What time is it now?"

"After five."

Suddenly the floor lamp at the bedside was lit and she was
standing in front of me. The quilted pajamas had changed
into a soft yellow kimono; the hair net had vanished and
long tresses cascaded across her shoulders.

"Five after what?"

"Just about five minutes ago the contract expired."

"What?" Taken by surprise, I rose up in bed. "What does
that mean?"

"Don't get upset." She glanced over her shoulder, and
taking three or four steps, stopped in the middle of the
room. "I go to work from tomorrow on."

Her faint freckles spilled from her face just before she
looked around, leaving a delicate taste on my lips. An un-
recognized recollection pressed hard on my chest. How did
I know so well that she had been doing something before
she had turned on the light? Now her gaze followed the wall
beside my bed to the waist-high window immediately beside
the mirror stand . . . the chestnut-colored curtains with a
white-dotted crystal pattern.

"What were you looking at?"

"A window."

"No, no. I mean what were you looking at through the
window?"

"Windows . . . lots of windows. One by one the lights are going off. That's the only instant you really know somebody's there."

"Well then, it must be evening already."

"Five after."

"Has it been as long as that?"

"No. I'm going to bed now."

She shook her head, exposing the nape of her neck, and slowly swung her long hair in great arcs, to the right and to the left. Through the kimono the flesh of her hips and the two supporting columns could be distinctly seen twisting and turning. I quietly slipped my body to the edge of the bed and placed my left foot on the floor. Leaning my whole weight upon it, I left the bed. I took a step forward, and stretching out both hands, I thrust them under her arms and suddenly tickled her hard. Giving a short cry, she wrenched free of me and made as if to escape. But she went neither for the door nor for the window—she came directly at me. We crashed together and fell onto the bed. In my eyes faint brown freckles smiled . . . and the beautiful purple membrane was stretched taut. The depression she had left in the bed . . . the vessel for my sleep.

A wardrobe stood on the other side of the bed. It had large, burnished, light metal fixtures; the surface was painted a smooth dark-brown teak color, and it reflected like a mirror anything within two yards. Somewhere—perhaps in the kitchen—she was humming in a low voice. Since I could hear only the higher tones, I could not tell what the song was. I put on my coat and began walking . . . and she too began to walk . . . when she crossed in front of the lemon-yellow curtains, her face became black, her hair white, and her lips white too, the irises of her eyes became white and the whites

black, her freckles became white spots, white like dust that
has gathered on the cheekbones of a stone image. I began
to walk too . . . Muffling my footsteps, I began to walk in
the direction of the door.

I SLOWLY came to a halt there. I stopped
as if pushed back by the spring of the air. The weight which
I had shifted from the ball of my left foot to the heel of my
right flowed back again and came down heavily on my left
leg. The slope of the road was steep.

The surface of the street was not asphalt but a rough-
textured concrete with narrow grooves about five inches
apart, apparently to prevent slipping. But they did not look
as though they would be much help to pedestrians. The purposely rough concrete surface was covered with dust and tire
shavings, and on rainy days, even if one wore old rubber-
soled shoes, it would surely make for difficult walking. No
doubt the pavement was made in this way for cars. If so, the
grooves every five inches would be very effective. When the
drainage of the street was obstructed by melting snow and
sleet, they looked as though they would be useful in channeling the water into the gutters.

Yet there were few cars, despite the care taken to build

such a road. Since there were no sidewalks, four or five women carrying shopping baskets had spread out over the width of the street and were walking along completely absorbed in their chattering. A young boy perched on a roller skate and imitating a horn came sliding down the middle of the slope. Hastily I gave way to him, for I too had naturally been walking down the middle of the street.

I slowly came to a halt there. I stopped as if pushed back by the spring of the air. The weight which I had shifted from the ball of my left foot to the heel of my right flowed back again and came down heavily on my left leg.

On the left-hand side was a high protective wall where rocks were piled up on a slight incline. To the right, beyond a little ditch, rose an almost perpendicular cliff. Its surface was screened by a similar protective wall, but from there the road made a wide curve to the left and soon came to the plateau at the top of the slope. If one advanced five or six more paces, the view would suddenly open up and the town on the plateau would be visible. There was no room for doubt. It was a road I was so used to taking that I passed by quite oblivious to its very existence as long as nothing drew my attention. The road had become completely familiar after how many hundreds of times I had been over it. Now I was going over it as usual . . . and I was returning to my own house.

Unexpectedly I came to a halt. I paused as if forced back by the spring of the air. I halted, in spite of myself recoiling at the strangely clear impression I had of the sloping road that I usually took no notice of. The reason for my stopping was clear, of course, to me alone, but it was hard to believe. Why, no matter how I tried, could I not remember the scene

that must lie beyond the curve just ahead, the scene which
I must know by sight as well as I did this stretch of road now
before my eyes?

It was not yet anything to make me feel uneasy, though.
When I thought about it, I had the feeling that I had many
times before experienced similar lapses of memory. I would
wait a minute. I had had the experience of having my eyes
go out of focus and of losing my sense of distance as I gazed
at a wall covered with small square tiles. Nor was it especially
strange for me suddenly to forget, for no reason at all, the
name of an acquaintance. I put my left heel on the ground,
steadying myself; it should not take too long and I would
wait until the focus was right. For I was certain that beyond
the curve lay the plateau with its town, and in it my house.
Although I could not remember it, its existence was an indisputable fact.

The sky was covered over with a thin smooth blanket of
blue-gray cloud, typical of the season, making the time—
4:28 by my watch—an ambiguous early evening. The street
was light enough for me to be able to make out the five-inch-
spaced grooves, yet not light enough to cast shadows. On the
protective wall to the left—doubtless due to its material—
the moss, mottled with dampness, was rapidly absorbing the
darkness, changing the surface into a mass of shadow. At the
top of the wall a vague, weathered line diagonally blocked
my view; only there was the sky suddenly bright. It was, of
course, impossible for me to see what lay beyond, but, if I
remembered rightly, there were only three small wooden
houses and a building surrounded by clumps of trees that
seemed to be an inn or a lodging house, forming a cluster
half way up the slope. Another road led away from the foot
of the slope, and as I had seldom been there it was not

surprising that my memories of it were somewhat hazy. I wanted to pin my hopes on the fact that such contours of memory, vague as they might be, had been preserved. If the scene before my eyes was not opening up some avenue to the past, such memories would never have arisen. Actually, if I was imagining I recognized a completely unknown place, shouldn't all the worlds outside my vision completely disappear? But it was only the town on the plateau beyond the curve that had vanished.

The low ground at the foot of the cliff on the north side —ha! I could even give the direction, though I couldn't ascertain the position of the sun—was already well known to me. At this point a row of houses lay below, and I could see only a labyrinth of vegetable plots formed by the roofs of thatch and tile, a forest of antennae absorbing electric waves, and the chimney of a public bath, standing almost as high as the stone wall in front of me. But I was confident that I could faithfully follow in my memory the entire stretch of road that led to the public bath at the end, in the middle of the labyrinth. The street that the old men, smoking their cigarettes, sitting in front of the bath, waiting to be first in, used to like to walk down . . . the street where after three o'clock, women would hurry along, wash basins in hand. And the roundabout way by the edge of the cliff where the little trucks carrying fuel came and went. I seem to recall that once the broken handles and frames of placards had grown to a large pile by the side of the road.

Shifting my weight, I tried to reduce my breathing little by little. As I reduced it an uneasiness gradually welled up within me. Or was it perhaps that my breathing slowed down because the uneasiness had come welling up? Far from coming into focus, the town on the plateau beyond the curve became more and more of a blank as if continually erased by some supereraser. The color vanished . . . the contours, the forms vanished, and ultimately its very existence seemed to be negated. A sound of someone walking up the slope drew closer. An office-worker type passed me, carrying a document case under his left arm and an umbrella in his right. He was leaning forward, walking on the balls of his feet, and with each step he swung the handle of his umbrella forward. Apparently the snap was broken, for the folds of the umbrella opened and closed quite as if it were breathing. Of course, I did not have the courage to address him, but for an instant I felt inclined to follow him. Perhaps it was best to forge ahead unfalteringly like that. In any event, I should be able to see beyond the curve in five or six more steps. If I could make certain the reality of the scene with my own eyes, I felt that things would resolve themselves quite simply, as easily as flushing down with water a pill that has stuck in one's throat. Now the man was just rounding the curve. His figure disappeared, but I could hear no scream. Perhaps the town on the plateau existed, as the man was convinced it did. What he could do should not be impossible for me. Anyway, it was a question of a bare five or six steps, and a loss of scarcely ten seconds of time. It was not worth considering that it might come to nothing.

But was it really not worth considering? If I went ahead without waiting for my memory to return, and if by chance the scene turned out to be one I didn't know, how would I bring things under control? Even this scenery on the slope, which I thought I knew so thoroughly, might suddenly be transposed into an unknown world for me. There was the possibility. Perhaps the row of houses midway up the slope was merely an imaginative collage, and even the memory of the labyrinth at the foot of the cliff could be called a very ordinary association of ideas coming from the chimney of the public bath. I suppose I could easily infer from the way the slightly dirty moss was growing, extending its oozing domain from the protective wall to the concrete pavement, that this was the northern side of the slope.

In the final analysis, supposing this sensation of familiarity was actually not really memory, supposing it was merely the false sense of *déjà-vu* disguised as memory, then even my conclusion that I was now on my way home became similarly merely a pretext for rationalizing this feeling of *déjà-vu*. If that were true, my very self would be open to doubt, something I could not call me.

Unable to hold my breath longer, I let it out. Passing by the man with the umbrella who had overtaken me, a young girl in a long green jacket went hurrying down the slope with a springy step, jingling the coins in the purse which she clutched in her hand. As if by sleight of hand, someone was constantly vanishing beyond the town that was out of sight, and appearing from it. Using the fact that I had come to a halt as an excuse, I took out a cigarette and put it between my lips, fussing purposelessly and interminably over striking my match. I would have been glad if some acquaintance had chanced by. But supposing, as with the town on the plateau, even faces which I should know by sight were to change into unknown strangers, what then?

Nausea rose in my gorge. Perhaps it was because I had strained my eyes, trying to force myself to see something invisible. In addition to the nausea, I was dizzy. Whatever, I had been hesitating much too long. If I did not have the courage to round the curve, I would have to resolve to act differently. The instant I began to change directions, a comical blast on a horn sounded behind me. A dented three-wheeled truck loaded with vegetables was coming up the hill, sending up a cloud of white exhaust. But was it an illusion? I wondered. I tried to avoid it by moving toward the protective wall, and from one instant to the next the three-wheeler was nowhere to be seen. But that was not the only thing to vanish. The forms of people instantly were suspended and the surroundings were completely depopulated. I was overcome by an unbearable sense of loneliness. I was wretched, as if I had had ink eradicator poured over me, and I rushed full speed down the road I had just come along. However, the abrupt slope was much harder to go down than to climb up. The smooth concrete paving gave poor footing and the antislip grooves were almost useless for pedestrians. I had to keep my balance by knee action. The protective wall, which had shifted now to my right, gradually grew higher, and the street lights were lit at the point where the slope leveled off. A sign with the name of the town, white letters on a blue ground, was nailed to a lamp pole. I felt it was the name I had expected, but the self-confidence I had experienced before was gone.

SUDDENLY the road broadened out and led into a main thoroughfare with sidewalks. The lights at the foot of the slope were on, but scarcely ten yards from there the streets were still light. Yet in whatever direction I looked, it was deserted, and I was overcome by an unspeakable terror. It was as if I were trapped in a landscape where the painter had forgotten to put in the people. And since there were no people, naturally no cars were to be seen. All the same, there were signs of living beings right over there. For instance, the smoking butt of a cigarette lay by the edge of the sidewalk. From the length of the ash, it gave the impression of having been tossed away a few seconds before.

First I began running to the right. I could see the entrance to a subway and felt that the main part of town lay in that direction. Surely the intersection with its traffic light would seem to be the center; there were also an insurance building, a bookstore, and some small food shops. In every one the door was open and the goods spread out in apparent expectancy of customers, but neither customers nor clerks were to be seen. The traffic signal changed from green to yellow, from yellow to red, and from red back again to green, but there were neither moving cars nor stopped cars. However, the smell of exhaust gas in the air was almost the same as usual. Apparently people and cars had vanished but an instant before.

I looked into the subway entrance. The deadly silence had returned. Even the stirring of the air reverberating in the long tunnel was inaudible. There was a snack bar close by and I looked in through the half-open door. No one was there, but some uneaten curry stew on the table was still giving off steam. I began to run. I ran back toward the foot of the slope. Stopping, I looked up at the top, and when I had made sure that my memory of what lay beyond the curve would not return I called out, first in a quite weak voice and then somewhat louder. The sound melted into the deserted, blank scene and was absorbed by it; not even a deadened echo came back.

Again I passed by the foot of the slope and ran back into

the town. I passed through the passage beneath the elevated tracks and turned left at the corner, beyond which one after the other stood a tobacconist's, a plumbing store, and a cleaner's. When, at the next intersection from the gas station, I saw a parking lot I thought I had reached the place that somehow fitted in with my own feelings of how things should be. Perhaps that was not my destination. But I had the feeling it was some kind of starting point. I stood in front of the entrance to the parking lot, looking in; the tall chimney of a public bath rose up at an angle beyond the street and before it stood a coffee house. It was a scene that had remained tucked in my memory, clear as a picture postcard. My heart beating in anticipation, I cut obliquely across the street and thrust open the door to the coffee house. Then, exactly as I had expected, I was at last able to come face to face with a living human being. Seated high on a stool at the front of the shop was a woman with a girlishly slender neck, her legs crossed. Apparently she had just turned on the radio as I was coming in, for suddenly a cacophonous sound welled up. When I looked back over my shoulder, I could see, through the black mesh curtain, people coming and going in the street and a solid stream of cars. The relief made me forget for a moment the lost town at the top of the slope. It was, of course, only a fraction of an instant. I had been unaware that outside the evening dusk was gathering; the sky was still lighter than the skyline of buildings, but the cars had already turned on their lights. I had no idea where time was going. When I thought about it, it seemed strange that my breathing was almost unaffected, although I had been running for so long.

I NOW took up my position by a window in the backmost seat in the shop. I scrutinized the woman on the stool as I grasped with two fingers of my right hand the wallet in my inside pocket. The stool was near the door, and the woman on it was sitting with her legs crossed.

Though I was seated in a window corner, there was only a single row of seats, and from the back of the shop, where I was, to the door there were only five tables with four seats each, lined up in a row. The woman on the stool was the only employee, being both cashier and waitress. Behind the counter there was a window like the opening in a dovecote, through which orders were passed out. The window was about the size of a sheet of newspaper; the wall was of a different color. I could see the hand that passed out the orders, but I did not once set eyes on the face. The hand was soft and white, but both age and sex were unascertainable. If it was a man it would be an effeminate one, and if a woman a masculine one. But in my fancy, the owner of the hand must surely be a man, perhaps the woman's husband or someone she lived with. Perhaps consumed with jealousy he had shut himself off behind the wall. Imagining the eyes of the customers creeping over his wife's body, he was surely agonizing behind the wall. Perhaps there was a peephole somewhere in the wall through which he secretly observed the customers. Otherwise, there was no need for her to be perched like a bird, her legs exaggeratedly crossed, on the high, round stool which had been installed in front of the counter. When she had languidly finished taking an order from a customer, she would return at once to the stool, flicking her shoulder-length hair. The hair in front fell becomingly across her forehead. The freckles under her eyes suited her languid expression. Then she remained motionless in that strange pose, her legs crossed as if she were advertising stockings. When she sat thus, her small body, which seemed as delicate as a girl's, suddenly became a woman's, and yet one had the feeling she was absolutely defenseless. She was worth being jealous of. Even I, who had no relationship with her at all, could only be jealous— in spite of myself.

Of course, if I could remove the wall, things would be resolved at once. They say that people are much happier in coffee houses and restaurants if the customers can see the work procedures. Without the wall the girl's performance would at once appear rather artificial, and depending on the man's attitude, quite comical. Of course, the price would be high. Her worth would be reduced by half at least. On consideration, her being worth jealousy was a part of her value, and it would be a severe loss. Regardless of who was responsible for the performance on the stool the man would never give up his own place. He is compensated in his own way by locking jealousy behind the wall with its agonizing thoughts. Indeed, I would do the same thing and would continue to patronize the shop. Providing, of course, I recognized beyond any doubt that I really was a regular customer here.

The two people near the door, engaged in what appeared to be a business discussion with much gesticulating, arose. The woman, uncrossing her legs and arranging her skirt, got down from the stool. The outline of her shin seemed to be shaded with a faint light. The down on it gave the impression of shining, but she couldn't possibly be barefoot. Yet for all of that, the hair style and the short skirt were ill-matched. Taking advantage of being the only customer, I boldly took the wallet from my inside pocket. It was square-shaped and made out of black converted cowhide; the corners were nappy and gave evidence of having seen considerable use. First I wanted to take out all the contents and line them up, but they would be much too conspicuous on the light-pink tabletop. I decided to take them one by one, starting with the money. I loosened the clasp almost noiselessly. The flap turned into a key holder with two keys, one large and one small. One was for a regular cylinder lock, but the other was of a very simple form. Each was stamped with a number, but there was no other indication on them. Unfortunately I had no recollection of their use.

The middle flap was a commutation-ticket holder with transparent vinyl on both faces. As soon as I had opened the outer flap it was clear that it was empty, but it was common sense to have the purse separate from the commutation ticket. Unconcerned I decided to go ahead. I opened the fastener and counted what was inside: three absolutely new ten-thousand-yen notes and two thousand-yen notes. There were also 640 yen in small change—32,640 yen. Even though I couldn't see my house, it looked as though I could somehow get by for the time being. Yet I needed some explanation for the amount of money. I thought that the sum was considerably in excess of which an average salaried man would carry around for a day's expenses. Surely some special use for it had been expected. A thirty-thousand-yen purchase in cash would be no little matter. The point where the explanation that I was suffering a lapse of memory would hold good had long since passed. Of course, the use of the money was not restricted to buying something. It might have been collected at work and entrusted to me for the bereaved family of some colleague who had died. But if the explanation that it was only a temporary lapse of memory didn't hold good, there was not much to choose between the two. I would take things easy and not overtax myself. When I considered things, there was absolutely no basis for me to think of myself as being an office worker. It was merely a far-fetched self-portrait. It did not necessarily mean that by deceiving myself, the truth was any different. Was I still incapable of getting a clue about my own name?

Suddenly a numbing pain shot from the nape of my neck to my forehead. The nausea, which I had fortunately forgotten about since I came here, again rose from deep within me. There was no doubt that I had quite forgotten even my name. The only thing left was the consciousness that I was myself.

Suddenly the cup on the table sprang off its saucer with a clatter. Fortunately it was empty and the cup itself was unbroken. I could only assume I had made it jump with my knee; and if that were true, I myself had jumped up. When I put my elbows on it, the table made a clattering sound, and I rose in confusion. I hurriedly began searching my pockets with both hands. If only I could find a commutation ticket I could somehow get my footing again. I felt some reluctance about learning my name and my address before I knew who I was, but at this point I simply had to go on.

I began spreading the contents of my pockets haphazardly on the table.

A handkerchief . . . matches . . . cigarettes . . . a button that had come off the sleeve of my suit jacket . . . sunglasses . . . a small three-cornered badge . . . and then a scrap of notepaper on which a sort of diagram was drawn.

The window glass emitted fire. The headlights of a bus licked at the pane. In their light the slender branches of the trees along the street appeared like a ragged net. At once I riveted my attention on the bus. Immediately I began to be able to feel it vividly as if it were all an extension of my body —the feel of the worn steps, the place and mounting of the stainless-steel rail, the whole inside, the strained search for an empty seat, the hanging advertisement behind the driver's seat, the special smell blended of people and gasoline, the vibration of the motor, which differed according to the year of its make. Carried along by these impressions, I began to move with the bus. Numerous important stops, views with special features and well-known buildings, swam into view as a single structure in which they were all squeezed together. Must I still be suspicious of the intimate link between the bus and me? I wondered. If I really wanted to I could somehow explain even the business of the commutation ticket. Maybe I had dropped it, or it was picked from my pocket. No, better still, it had just expired and was being renewed. Yes, it could be that in part the thirty thousand yen were intended for that.

Putting forth such speculations served no purpose at all. Moreover, my bus went every place except, in the final analysis, to my destination.

The real bus accelerated and moved away. Again the window became a dark mirror. The woman's figure was reflected just where the headlights had been. Since a part of the street light covered the reflection of her face I could not be sure, but somehow she seemed to be observing me. When I thought about it, it was not unreasonable. It was natural that she should want to observe me. An awkward scatterbrain emptying his pockets on the table. Of course, it was another question as to how much she was aware of the gravity of the situation. Surely it was some lost article, she would think; never in her wildest dreams would she believe I had lost myself. No, perhaps I was not the one who had lost himself but the one who had been lost. I had experienced a moment's pain as if I had been thrown off the bus when it had started off a while ago. If that were true, the I here was not the lost I but the I that had suffered the loss. In other words, rather than saying that the town on the plateau beyond the curve had disappeared from my path, the other world had disappeared, leaving only me between the point just before the curve and this coffee house. Actually, when I thought back on it, I felt more strongly that midway up the slope my memory had begun rather than having been taken away. Surprisingly, the missing town was not the problem, but this very portion that remained and had not disappeared might well be. For me, this coffee house might indeed have more significance than I imagined. The woman who had summoned back to the streets the pedestrians and inhabitants who had vanished . . .

Not to be outdone, I returned the woman's gaze. As the mirror of the window was too dark and the headlights of the constantly passing cars hindered my view, I looked directly at her. Indeed, she was quite aware of my gaze. But she merely continued her observation in the glass, not at all perturbed, a strangely self-possessed figure. Perhaps she was the one who held the key. Perhaps she was a far more important clue than the things on the table that I had taken from my pockets.

New customers entered, a young boy and girl. I had the feeling that the boy was a clerk in a nearby store. The girl was his friend, a younger sister, or maybe a cousin from the country. They sat down at the second table from mine and the boy, holding up two fingers, ordered coffee in a loud voice. At once they were absorbed in a muted conversation, their expressions tragic, as if they were discussing the medical expenses of a dying parent. Since the woman had left her stool, I too ordered another cup of coffee for myself. I hardly thought that that gave me a real excuse for still being here, but it had been almost forty or fifty minutes and I was beginning to feel uneasy about the man behind the wall. Of course, the man behind the wall was merely my imagination. But it would seem that this imaginary person shared the same fate as I. Since he was imaginary I must not make fun of him. If I assumed that there was a law and logic about loss of memory, then this imaginary person was also, naturally, a crucial element and it was fitting that he be assigned a place equal to the woman's.

I stared at the woman. I kept on staring. I persisted, trying by sheer force to draw her gaze through the part in the hair which fell over her face. I secretly adjusted my breathing to the hollows that formed behind her knees, extending and contracting smoothly in harmony with the movement of her legs under the very short skirt. At the same time I kept my ears pricked to the wall. I was in a dither at the thought that, deranged by jealousy, he would drop a kettle of boiling water. But wait as I did, I could hear not a single click of the tongue, to say nothing of the sound of breaking china.

Instead the same white hand reached out. I could not see any trembling of the glass on the tray. Rather, I was the one who was trembling. The thumb I placed on the edge of the table to steady myself continued to tremble like the wrist of a drummer concentratedly thinning his strokes, trying to leave a melancholy afterbeat. Unbelievable! Explosive power is proportionate to the power of compression. Well then, I would really try seducing her. Even if I left the shop my world would come to a dead end just before that curve. For the present, the only place I could feel at home was here. The relationship between me and this shop had become more than that of a regular customer linked to it by several cups of coffee. It was not at all impossible that the hidden meaning of the ordeal which had visited me really lay in the task of seducing the woman. Peering into the mirror of the window, I smoothed down a recalcitrant wisp of hair above my ears. I stuck out my chin and adjusted the knot in my tie. It was not a very expensive one, but it had a fashionable design that had just come out. Of course, I didn't pride myself on being a qualified seducer. But my position was definitely strong. It was like a simple chemical equation, for I would be snatching from a man who knew only jealousy a woman who knew only of being loved. Anyway, it would be sufficient, my just being a seducer. She would finally begin to show the required reaction. At the right point I would give her money and ask her to close early and take me home with her. Her reactions would gather speed according to rule, and then at length reach their climax. The man would explode through the wall, I supposed. Naturally, I too would be liberated from my role. I felt some reluctance to leave, but on the other hand I was regaining the world beyond the curve.

Again the hand was extended through the little window, apparently this time with my coffee. Carrying the tray in one hand, the woman approached through the narrow space between the tables and the wall, pushing back the chairs that stood in her way as she came. I too quickly cleared the table, returning to my pocket those items I clearly realized were superfluous.

The handkerchief (no initials were embroidered on it) . . . matches (from this shop) . . . cigarettes (four left) . . . the coat button . . . sunglasses . . .

Sunglasses? Perhaps my eyes were weak. As long as I looked into the window I had the impression that the self-portrait I had painted as an office worker was not far off. My business suit was of average quality, plain with matching pants, and could not suggest someone out of the ordinary parading as a salesman with sunglasses. Yes, indeed, it was not particularly strange for salesmen and public relations men, who went from place to place, to wear sunglasses most of the time—except when they were meeting clients. Furthermore, that would explain why somebody like a consignment buyer for a company located in some remote locality, who had his office in his own house, wouldn't be carrying a commutation ticket. Yet, considering that, weren't my personal effects a little skimpy? I could not understand why I didn't happen to have a single calling card. Or maybe I was in the habit of keeping them in my briefcase, which I had checked in some station for a while.

When the woman arrived at the table, I had purposely left out two items: the scrap of note paper and the badge. Somehow it seemed a tale hung thereby, and these articles alone would not interfere with serving the coffee. Furthermore, I wanted to check the woman's reaction. Certain articles are significant and might conceivably afford me the opportunity of unraveling the threads of my memory. The woman placed the coffee on the table, arranged the creamer and sugar bowl, and filled my glass with water—during which time she glanced at least twice at the two objects. But I could perceive no real reaction. Would it have been the same with the cigarettes, matches, and button? I wondered. In my disappointment I failed to get out even the two or three innocuous questions I had prepared; I was fascinated at the strange expression with its freckles that grew darker toward the corners of her eyes. One of the questions, for instance, was to ask what day it was—meaningless in itself. Her reply would furnish a clue that would tell me how I affected her, and it would be instructive as to whether to ask her further and more probing questions. One way or another, at this point she was the only one I recognized; how much help would she be if she would lend me her aid? I wanted, if possible, to get her to tell me everything she knew about me. All the more because I would need to proceed with caution, trying to avoid any mistakes.

The woman again returned to her stool and crossed her legs. The heel of the shoe on the upper foot was half off and the roundness of her ankle was more provocative. I lowered my eyes. Well, I would attempt some final challenge with these two clues. The badge with its slightly raised center was an equilateral triangle with rounded corners, and a border of silver lay on a blue cloisonné ground. In the center, in high relief, was an S, similarly of silver. It was a deformed character made up of straight lines, and at first glance seemed to be a flash of lightning. Or perhaps it was not an S, but had been lightning to start with. If it were a lightning flash I assumed it must have something to do with electricity, but for the present I had no clue. Yet I couldn't go through the telephone book from the beginning for the name of a company that began with S, and I was quite at a loss what to do. But from the way it was made, it didn't seem to be a child's plaything, and I imagined it had a meaning of its own. As I looked at it intently, I began to have the feeling that it was the badge of some dangerous secret society. But except for the anxiety it produced in me, I had no idea what it might be. After all, it was only something that made me aware that I could not carry it in my hand.

The scrap of note paper was mystifying to me, and the result was the same as for the badge. It bore something like a map, and there were what seemed to be designs for water or gas conduits, and something like the cross section of a pump—they could be almost anything, according to how you looked at them. In the corner were seven finely written numerals . . . perhaps a telephone number. Naturally I had no memory of having written them myself, nor any recollection of having been given them by anybody. These figures were impossibly vexing as if one were presented with an unanswerable question. But what about actually trying to get the number on the telephone? Using it as an avenue to my past, I might be able to call back my memory.

The phone was in the corner next to the cash register. The woman's stool was right behind. Even when I passed in front of her, she scarcely changed her position. The knee that was sticking out was about to graze my arm, but she gave no indication of trying to avoid me. She pursed her lips, compressing the air in her mouth, and when she released them made a faint sound like a kiss. It was like a greeting, but if so, it was a very dangerous one. If not, I had no idea what it could be.

But when I picked up the receiver, an uneasiness welled up within me. I had the impression I was undertaking to disassemble a bomb, the technique of which I was unfamiliar with. Perhaps I was jumping right into a waiting trap. Slowly, checking the number, I dialed. How should I start talking if there was an answer? The most important thing was not to let the other person become suspicious. Somehow I would have to prolong the conversation and find out the person's identity and address. No good . . . I was getting the busy signal. I tried redialing, but the line was really busy. I let a little time go by as I smoked a cigarette and continued dialing, about seven times in all over a period of close to twenty minutes, but each time the same sharp busy signal sounded again.

Absently I shifted my gaze; the woman was intently biting on her thumbnail. The red-lacquered nail was like a peach stone. Her lips moved mincingly. The end of the nail was inserted between her two lips and was being gnawed by the upper and lower teeth. She had completely lost herself in the act of gnawing. Since it meant she had forgotten herself, she had surely forgotten about me too. I was suddenly uneasy. If she had completely forgotten, would not the street then return to its deserted state? I must make her stop at once. In order to bring her back from her absent-minded state, I placed my bill on the counter. As if surprised, the woman ceased biting her nail, concealing in her fist the ragged and scratched tip of her thumb.

Saying nothing, I gave her the thousand-yen note, and she returned my change in silence. She did not speak, but three times she made the sound with her lips she had made before. I had no idea whether there was any meaning to it or not. Yet for an instant I waited, expecting her to speak.

She smiled as if in apology, and I was embarrassed. The freckles on her cheeks suited the smile. Even if she smiled at me again, I could do nothing about it. There must be words before the smile. I was made aware that I was the one who had confused the order, like it or not. Furthermore, I had already received my change and there was no reason for me to stay here any longer.

I HAILED a taxi. It was a dark-blue one with only the top painted yellow. The automatic door closed, screeching as if it were on the point of disintegrating. In the ashtray that had been left open the preceding customer's cigarette was still smoking. I was some time in telling the young driver my destination, and he furiously tore off his regulation cap and slammed it down on the seat beside him. I gave him five hundred yen and asked him to take the direction I indicated, since it really was quite close. At once his attitude changed, but he did not put his hat on again.

"Say, just what's the name of the place at the top of the slope?"

"You mean High Town?"

"Yes. I suppose they call it that because it's up on a plateau."

The street was choked with light. It seethed up in the final

animation of the day. But for some reason I did not feel
it to be essentially different from the deserted scene of a
while ago. I now no longer understood why I had been so
frightened by that deserted view. If the same situation by
chance happened again, I would not be upset. Supposing
that, in place of people and cars, crowds of emus and giant
anteaters began walking around, I would accept that as
factual and simply try and understand.

At length, the slope . . . but the taxi neither slowed down
nor stopped. Suddenly the sound of the motor changed,
making my blood run cold, but the driver had just shifted
into a lower gear without losing speed and now was circling
in the direction of the curve. I pressed my feet on the floor
and my body against the back of the seat. I held my breath,
waiting to see the actual form of the town that had run away.

I was not thrown into a vacuum. Far from a vacuum, it
was an immense housing development as far as I could see
that stretched away before me. The groups of four-storied
residences, although they were on high ground, had sunk to
the bottom of a dark ravine, unfolding an orderly fretwork
of light. I had not dreamt that such a view would appear.
The very fact that I had not posed a problem. Spatially there
was no doubt that the town existed, but temporally it was
the same as a vacuum. Although it did exist, how frightening
it was to say that it did not. The four wheels of the car were
certainly turning on the ground and there was no doubt that
I was experiencing vibrations. Nevertheless, my town had
vanished. I should perhaps never have gone beyond the
curve. Now it would forever be impossible for me to go
beyond it. White perspective of street lights. Crowds of
people hurrying home, becoming transparent with every
step. I screamed at the driver who had begun to slow down

as if to make some inquiry: Turn back, quick! Get out of this development as quick as you can! I had to get to a place where freedom of space was secure. If it had anything to do with a place like this, I would lose even space, to say nothing of time. I would be plastered into the wall of reality, exactly like the white hand in the restaurant.

Fortunately the other world was safe. It was perhaps well that I had chosen this taxi, a vehicle for anyone's use. We came out on a main street and I got out of the car in front of the first public telephone. I had only one clue left now: the telephone number underneath the map. If I were not careful I might well have an experience like the treatment I had received beyond the curve a while ago. I picked up the receiver and inserted a ten-yen piece. I dialed, and this time the line was free and I could hear the bell ringing. I was flustered. Evidently I had been off my guard, assuming the line would be busy. Maybe I'd best put the receiver back. Even if there was an answer, in my present psychological state I could not possibly go through with it. I began counting the cracks in the booth window, which had begun to deteriorate. If there were an even number I would hold on, if an odd number I would hang up. But before I had finished counting, the ten-yen piece fell through and a voice answered.

It was a woman's voice, strangely clear, as if she were around the corner. At once a glib lie came mechanically to my lips.

"Excuse me, but I've found a purse. There was a piece of paper in it with this number on it. I called, thinking it might by chance be yours . . ."

The response was more than I expected. Suddenly the woman broke out laughing.

"What? It's you, isn't it?" she said guilelessly and smoothly in a low, throaty voice. "What were you saying?"

"Do you know me . . . who I am . . .? Someone . . ."

"Don't go on with that ridiculous joke."

"I want you to help me," I pleaded, concentrating all my thoughts. "I'm in the telephone booth at the foot of the slope that leads to High Town. Please. Come and get me here."

"You're terrible . . . at this hour! Are you tight?"

"Please! I'm sick. Please. Won't you do something?"

"You're impossible. Well . . . wait there where you are. Don't move. I'll be right down."

Replacing the receiver, I squatted down right there where I was in the telephone booth. A rolled-up newspaper lay in the corner; the dried black tip of a turd of human excrement peeped out from underneath. The tip was tapered, and there were ropelike depressions in it. In the depressions some vegetable fibers, like the tufts of a rough painter's brush, stood out. There was no particular smell, but without thinking I rose. The cracks, like those on the shell of a broken boiled egg, which covered the tapering head end, frightened me. This was excrement that had stood for a long time. The man must have held it back until he had had to go in the telephone booth . . . it was probably a man . . . it might have been a woman . . . but it was probably a man. Some lonely man denied the use even of one of the innumerable toilets in the limitless labyrinth of the city. When I imagined the figure of the man crouching over in the telephone booth, I was stricken with a feeling of dread.

Of course, it didn't necessarily mean that the man was someone who, like me, had lost a place to go. Perhaps he was a simple vagrant who did not even realize he had lost anything. But there wasn't much difference between the two. A doctor would be inclined to insist that I had lost my memory, not something beyond the curve. Who would believe such a statement? There was no reason why any normal man would know about a place other than the one he was acquainted with. It was the same with anyone, enclosed like me, in his small, familiar world. Yes, the triangle formed by the place just before the curve, the entrance to the subway, and the coffee shop was a small one. It was too small. But when you expanded the triangle ten times, what then? What would the difference be if you blew the triangle up into a decagon?

Supposing I were to realize that this decagon was not a map to endless infinity. Suppose the savior who would come in response to my urgent call was a messenger from outside the map, who would make me realize that my chart was nothing more than an abbreviated map, full of omissions . . . then that person would again look beyond the curve which although existing was nonexistent. The telephone cord could also be a noose for hanging oneself.

I slammed the booth door, but just before it closed the force of the spring failed and a crack about one inch wide was left. There were many passers-by, but no one to whom I could speak. Apparently my rescuer had not yet arrived. People hurrying along the street, smiling to themselves. One, a young pregnant woman, was twisting her body, pushing her way through the waves of people, concerned about the drops of water from the frozen fish in her shopping basket. The only person who glanced at me was a seventeen- or eighteen-year-old with a bad complexion. He stepped half

way into the booth and with an experienced movement
threw something in; then he disappeared into the crowd.
Perhaps it was a call-girl's card or something like that.

A slight opening appeared in the stream of cars. I at once
made a dash for the other side of the street. Directly opposite
the telephone booth were some plane trees along the street.
The rough bark made one think they were quite old, but
they were not big enough to hide behind. About five or six
paces from the subway was a black opening like some de-
cayed tooth . . . a narrow alleyway between a small shoe store
and a liquor store that doubled as a tobacconist's. I casually
walked over and nonchalantly concealed myself in the alley.
Turning eagerly toward my objective, I intently fixed my
eyes on the booth, looking through the ceaseless flow of
cars. At last a woman appeared. I at once realized it was she,
for no one else had passed in that fashion. She stood there
looking into the booth and around it. She was the one . . .
the woman from the coffee house who had sat with her knees
crossed on the stool, her long hair falling over her shoulders.
I was half disappointed, but I also felt it was right. She went
down the street as far as the red fire alarm box and again
returned to the booth and looked in. She looked uneasily
around and went and stood by the fire hydrant. Once she
glanced over toward me, but she could probably make out
nothing in this narrow, dark crevice. I continued to conceal
myself as I watched her. She looked up worriedly at the
sky, searching. I continued to wait intently, choking back
my screams behind clenched teeth. Nothing would be served
by being found. What I needed now was a world I myself
had chosen. It had to be my own world, which I had chosen
by my own free will. She searched; I hid. At length she began
walking slowly away as if she had given up; suddenly she

was cut off from view by a car and was already gone. I too left my crevice in the darkness and began walking in the opposite direction. I began walking, relying on a map I did not comprehend. I began walking in the opposite direction from her ... perhaps in order to reach her.

I would forget looking for a way to the past. I had had enough of calling telephone numbers on hand-written memos. There was a strange eddy in the stream of cars. I saw that even the passing heavy trucks were trying to avoid the body of a cat that had been run over and crushed as thin as a sheet of paper. And when, unconsciously, I tried to give a name to the flattened cat, for the first time in a long time an extravagant smile melted my cheeks and spread over my face.

ABOUT THE TRANSLATOR

E. DALE SAUNDERS, translator of Kobo Abe's *The Woman in the Dunes*, *The Face of Another*, and *The Ruined Map*, received his A.B. from Western Reserve University (1941), his M.A. from Harvard (1948), and his Ph.D. from the University of Paris (1952). He is a retired Professor of Japanese Studies at the University of Pennsylvania, having previously taught at International Christian University, Tokyo, and at Harvard University. Among his publications are *Mudrā: A Study of Symbolic Gestures in Japanese Buddhist Sculpture* and *Buddhism in Japan.*

ABOUT THE AUTHOR

KOBO ABE was born in Tokyo but grew up in Manchuria, where his father worked as a doctor. He received a medical degree from Tokyo Imperial University in 1948, the same year in which he published his first novel, *The Road Sign at the End of the Street*, and has been writing ever since. (He never practiced medicine.) In 1951 he received the Akutagawa Prize for his novel *The Crime of S. Karma*, and in 1962 his novel *The Woman in the Dunes* was awarded the Yomiuri Prize for Literature. A year later the film version received the Jury Prize at the Cannes Film Festival. His other novels include *The Face of Another*, *The Ruined Map*, *Inter Ice Age 4*, *Secret Rendezvous*, *The Box Man*, and *The Ark Sakura*, and his most recent book is the short story collection *Beyond the Curve*.